Janet Tronstad
and her novels

"Janet Tronstad presents a warm, touching story."
—*Romantic Times BOOKreviews* on
At Home in Dry Creek

"Janet Tronstad's quirky small town and witty
characters will add warmth and joy to your holiday
season."
—*Romantic Times BOOKreviews* on
A Dry Creek Christmas

"This sweet romance is both suspenseful and
entertaining."
—*Romantic Times BOOKreviews* on
A Baby for Dry Creek

Going to the Chapel

Janet Tronstad

Steeple
Hill
Café

Published by Steeple Hill Books™

STEEPLE HILL BOOKS

ISBN-13: 978-0-373-78579-7
ISBN-10:   0-373-78579-8

GOING TO THE CHAPEL

This book is dedicated to my cousin, Elaine Svec, who blindly agreed to be any character at all if I used her name. She's a good sport. It goes without saying that she is much nicer than the Elaine you'll meet in these pages.

Chapter One

I'm a toppler. You know, down the stairs in my mother's high heels. Head over heels off my first bike. You get the picture. I've always been right there taking the next step without looking to see if there's a place for me to land. Of course, I don't intentionally topple down stairs or fall into trouble. Sometimes things just happen.

Like now. Here I am in the middle of a typical Julie White moment. If you could see me, you would think everything is fine. There are enough men in tuxedos walking around this hotel ballroom to make Cousin Elaine's engagement party look like the Academy Awards. And I fit right in. This rented gown sweeps low across my back and, I must say, it looks good, especially with the black-tie man on my arm.

It might be Elaine's party, but I know people—aka the aunts—will be looking at me, too. The aunts have measured me against Elaine all my life and I am tired of coming up second-best. That's why I wanted to make a good showing tonight at her engagement party. Since I wasn't sure until a few days ago that I had either the dress or the man to make any kind of a showing, I should be feeling pretty good.

Instead, I'm standing here with my mouth half-open and my fingers locked in a death grip on the handle of my crystal punch cup.

I've got a problem.

Here's the deal. My date—the black-tie guy—has followed orders and has been holding his elbow out to me like a gentleman for the past two hours. The reason I asked him to do this was because my aunts notice those kinds of things in the same way they notice if a collar needs starching or a cuticle needs fixing. The elbow was my extra insurance for tonight.

Of course, all of that elbow holding looks rather odd now that my date is standing here in front of Aunt Ruth giving me The Speech. You know the one—how he's not ready for commitment and…it's not me, it's him.

Of course, it's him.

I try clearing my throat to bring Doug back to reality, but he doesn't pause in his recitation. He's so into his role, he's forgotten something important. He's a pretend date; he's not the real thing. When we walk out the door, we both fly free. He goes back to the coffee shop where my best friend, Cassie, met him and I go back to my no-date, but okay life. There is no commitment to be feared. We're not a couple on the verge of anything. We're barely past the name tag stage.

Unfortunately, I can't say any of that to Doug because Aunt Ruth is right here listening.

You may have figured out by now that most of the people here tonight might be under the impression that Doug is quite taken with me, or at least knows me much better than he really does. As I said, Doug and his elbow were my extra little bit of insurance for tonight and we sort of got carried away putting on a show for everyone.

Even Aunt Ruth, who has been distracted since the party started, has apparently surfaced from her worries long enough to make the assumption that Doug is very interested in me. Which was what I wanted, except that I never thought Aunt Ruth would come over and ask me when I was getting engaged like her dear daughter, my cousin, Elaine, the perfect one. The fact that Aunt Ruth then turned to Doug and said he looked like a fine young man shouldn't have set his teeth to rattling, but it did.

Right now, Doug has his eyes firmly focused on Aunt Ruth and is telling her all of the reasons why he isn't ready for a commitment like that.

Aunt Ruth has clearly scared away any common sense Doug has. I know she does that to people so he's not completely to blame. I look at him closer. She might have upset his breathing, too. He hasn't inhaled once since he started explaining himself to her.

It's a Sunday evening and all Doug was supposed to do was smile at people, do the elbow thing and occasionally look down at me adoringly. It didn't seem that hard when we first talked about it on Friday. He wasn't even going to say very much to people.

Now, however, Doug has an earnest expression on his face and there's no way to stop his flow of words. I take a deep breath and try to relax so Aunt Ruth doesn't think I'm having a problem listening to Doug say he's not ready for a committed relationship. Maybe if I stay calm she won't realize that he is dumping me right here in the middle of Elaine's engagement party, even though that is what he is clearly doing or would be doing if there were anything between us to dump.

Aunt Ruth has a distracted look on her face and I'm hoping she's still thinking about the lead in the punch cups. You heard that right. At the last minute, Aunt Ruth demanded the hotel replace the punch cups because they were not made of twenty-four percent lead crystal. Aunt Ruth knows her crystal and mere glass wasn't good enough for Elaine, the princess. Of course, it wasn't good enough for Elaine's fiancé, either, but that's another story.

I wave my cup at Aunt Ruth just in case it catches her eye and reminds her that there might be something else the hotel is doing wrong that she needs to correct. There's got to be something in a place this size that should make her want to go talk to the manager one more time tonight. If Aunt Ruth will just step away from Doug, I can whisper a few basic truths in his ear that will stop all of this madness.

I keep my smile stretched across my teeth and try to relax. Aunt Ruth's gaze is firmly settled on Doug so the cup distraction did not work. I remind myself, however, that Aunt Ruth is confused enough about the way people date today that she just might think that this no-commitment talk is actually a prelude to something involving an engagement ring instead of a postlude to almost everything else.

Wouldn't that be nice?

And it might work. After all, Aunt Ruth did think Elaine was playing hard to get when she broke up with her fiancé last month. As for me, I thought Elaine was finally seeing the light, or at least seeing that this fiancé of hers was in serious need of a little more personality to go with his very proper, buttoned-up East Coast ways.

Gary—that's Elaine's fiancé—is from some Connecticut family that Elaine says has tons of *old* money. She always says it that way, too, with the emphasis on the *old* instead of just the money, the way anyone else would say it.

Money is money in my book, but Aunt Ruth and Elaine are both impressed by a family that has been rich for generations. I've already seen Gary's parents at the party tonight and they look like old money, too. They don't have any glitter to them, but they have a faded, pressed look that says they should be in some mansion somewhere with a butler who offers them a tissue on a silver tray every time either one of them happens to blink a little too hard. I'm sure that's why Aunt Ruth ordered so many waiters in tuxedos for the party tonight. She wants Gary and his parents to think that our family is in the same social class as they are.

Good luck with that.

The fact that all of the males in our family had to rent their tuxedos for tonight should speak for itself. The fact that they had to drive two hundred miles to Palm Springs to pick them up should speak even louder. Aunt Ruth is very particular about which tuxedos are rented for all of Elaine's wedding events.

Nothing in the small town of Blythe is good enough

for Aunt Ruth any longer. Of course, she still lives there, as do all the aunts and cousins except for me. But she no longer claims it as her hometown. If anyone asks her where she lives, she says she lives adjacent to Palm Springs. There's nothing Palm Springs adjacent about Blythe. She might as well say she lives adjacent to Beverly Hills. Or the moon.

Not that I blame Aunt Ruth for wishing she lived someplace else. There are entire months in the heat of the summer when the whole population of the town wishes they were living someplace else. The deal is, however, that I've never believed it does a body any good to pretend to be something they're not. If you live in Blythe, you're a Blythite not a Palm Springer and no amount of tuxedos will change that fact.

Of course, I may be biased, because disaster always follows any futile attempt on my part to be something I'm not. You might have noticed that from what is happening right now. The only good thing I can say about now is that the huge disco ball spinning over our heads is distracting so many people that not everyone here is staring at me. I think the hotel is charging extra for the disco ball and, right about now, it's worth every penny Aunt Ruth is paying.

Aunt Ruth is very proud that she is hosting this party in the Petite Ballroom of the Grand Carlton Hotel, one of Palm Springs' finest hotels—she even included "finest hotel" on the embossed invitations she sent out. I suspect she only sent out invitations to what is mostly a family party because she wants the aunts to put those invitations in their scrapbooks so that everyone in the family will remember until the absolute end of time that Elaine's party was held in one of Palm Springs' finest hotels, a hotel that was so busy the party took months to schedule.

You can see why I needed a date. Without one, every time the story of Elaine's engagement party is told—and, believe me, once it's in the scrapbooks, it will be told—someone would say "and poor Julie didn't even have a date." Of course, unless I work fast, it will be worse than that now. The story will end with "and wasn't that the night when poor Julie's date dumped her right there in front of Aunt Ruth?" And won't I, poor Julie, sound pathetic if I try to explain that he wasn't really a date to begin with?

By now Aunt Ruth is listening to Doug as if he's making sense.

This has got to be one of my most embarrassing topples ever. Aunt Ruth's eyes are darting back and forth between me and Doug and her mouth is forming a little "O." She's finally getting it.

Even if I had to get engaged right now or die, Doug Brenner wouldn't have to worry. He wasn't even my original choice as a fake date for Elaine's engagement party. He wouldn't be here if my first choice—a third-year med student from Modesto who looks like Brad Pitt and is Cassie's cousin—hadn't surprised everyone two weeks ago by running off to Lake Tahoe and marrying a woman he met a few months ago. I've got to say, true love has never done me any favors in the past so I shouldn't be surprised it let me down now.

Cassie was the one who arranged the date and, when her cousin canceled, she felt responsible. Dates with medical students aren't that easy to find and I had set my mind on having one. Elaine might be impressed by the Brad Pitt types, but Aunt Ruth swears doctors are the only men worth marrying.

That's where Doug came in. He's not a doctor, but he's an X-ray technician and he generally wears his white lab coat when he goes to the coffee shop that's next to where Cassie works. She's seen him there, drinking coffee, for months. Cassie figured the white coat was close enough to a doctor's coat to count in an emergency situation so she promised Doug all the fancy hotel appetizers he could eat if he came as my date.

I know it's pretty lame to need your best friend to set you up on a blind date for your cousin's engagement party, but I was desperate. No secret there. However, I wasn't delusional. I can't believe Doug thinks I'm going Girlfriend on him when I'm the one who planned the whole elbow business in the first place.

How crazy does he think I am?

It's not even as though I was trying to prolong our time together. We would have already said our goodbyes if Doug hadn't run into my cousin Jerry in the men's room and heard that Aunt Ruth had complained enough about the buffet appetizers that the chef agreed to send out some premium crab-stuffed mushrooms before the party ended. Doug wanted to stay and sample them.

I look over at the buffet table hoping those mushrooms will already be there. No luck.

I sure hate having Doug give me The Speech.

Well, I suppose he *is* giving The Speech to Aunt Ruth more than to me at the moment. Doug has moved on from the fact that he's not financially ready to get married to the fact that he's never been to Europe and a man should see something of the world before he settles down.

The only part of Doug's face I see right now is the left side. He doesn't look at all like Brad Pitt. He's more a Donald Trump kind of a guy. Okay, so he has a little more hair than Donald. But that's it. Of course, Donald Trump has certainly seen the world. I wonder if Doug would look any different if he'd seen Paris or Rome. He's talking about Sweden now.

Apparently, Doug's always wanted to do one of those Swedish ice plunges. Even if he's not my real date, it is a little hard on a girl's self-esteem to be given up so a man can experience a severe drop in bodily temperature.

I should have known Doug had something to prove in his life. When Cassie invited me over to the coffee shop to meet him, he was talking about having gone to this huge Billy Graham kind of rally just to please his aunt. He said it was worse than the time he was sent to the principal's office in the sixth grade, but that he was glad he'd gone to the rally because it was morally bracing to do his duty.

Now, I've gone to church with my aunt Inga lots of times, but I've never found it morally bracing. I know about duty because I feel obligated to go when Aunt Inga asks me. She's the aunt who stepped in and raised me after my father died and my mother left, so I owe her and, if me going to church makes her happy, I'm there. I wouldn't go if she didn't ask, of course, but I don't complain about going, either.

Still, I could tell right away that Doug is not as familiar with religious things as I am and he's having a hard time figuring it all out. If you know how to dodge in church, you don't need to worry about being morally braced and I'm an expert at dodging. Unlike Doug. He was still fretting about that rally on the drive out here today.

About now Doug is so pale I'm starting to get a picture of what he'll look like if he ever does take a Swedish ice plunge.

I want you to know that I don't usually care much about a guy's looks. It's just that I wanted some extra reinforcement today when I listened to the official wedding announcement. I thought if Elaine saw me with a Brad-Pitt-doctor date she wouldn't be quite so, well, Elaine. I can see her looking over at me right now giving me The Look, the one that says she is, of course, better than me. She's always felt better than me, so being engaged must make her feel even better yet. I hate seeing her give me The Look.

I don't need an ice plunge to make my heart run cold when I have Elaine. I was half hoping that, if anyone gave The Look tonight, it would be me looking at her that way for a change. And it could have been that way if I had a date who looked like Brad Pitt.

Unfortunately, here I am stuck with a date who is looking less like Donald Trump and more like Donald Duck every minute. Right now, Doug's so pale I think he might be going to hyperventilate. At least, he's stopped talking. Maybe he's thinking about how cold it would actually be in one of those ice plunges.

Anyway, I'm not going to waste the silence. I smile

and tell Aunt Ruth that Doug and I need a private moment to work things out. Aunt Ruth looks relieved. She's okay with men and women arguing as long as they have the decency to Get Back Together Again. Aunt Ruth is big on keeping couples stuck together. You don't find her giving my uncle Howard any wiggle room. He might walk around with that tight, pinched look on his face, but he knows right where he belongs.

I give Aunt Ruth another reassuring smile before I take Doug by the elbow and walk him over to the ferns that spread out on one side of the ballroom. Someone has put a few metal folding chairs halfway behind some of the ferns. There is one of those little tables where waiters collect the used appetizer plates and punch cups. This is obviously the kitchen side of the room. Doug should feel at home. At least, he can keep an eye out for those stuffed mushrooms.

"Relax," I finally say to him as I put my punch cup on the tray sitting there. "Your freedom is safe with me. You have no reason *whatsoever* to worry about any commitment expectations—*whatsoever.*"

I add that second "whatsoever" for emphasis. I add the third one under my breath for the sake of my pride.

Doug looks at the ferns as if he's suspicious of what's behind them. "You're not going to be mad at me, are you?"

I'm beginning to wonder if he really is going to pass out. "You should sit down and put your head between your knees."

If it's possible for a man to go even paler, Doug does. "Is that when you're going to hit me? Your cousin Jerry told me you hit people."

I swear, don't any of my cousins ever let anything go? "I was eight years old. I tripped and hit him by mistake when I was falling. He knows that—I've told him it was a mistake a thousand times."

"He says there was nothing around for you to trip over."

"We were in the middle of what was left of Aunt Inga's garden. There were dead tomato vines everywhere. All over the ground. Lots and lots of vines."

"He said he couldn't open his eye for a week."

"He just said that so he wouldn't have to go to school. We were studying the Romans in history and he didn't like them. Something about Caesar and how you couldn't trust a guy who had a salad named after him. Jerry hated salad—except for the croutons. And those he only liked because he liked to throw them at people."

I wish I had a crouton myself right now.

Even more I'm beginning to wish we'd had a big storm in California two weeks ago. I know it's only the end of October, but early storms happen. That's when Cassie's cousin impulsively drove to the Nevada side of Lake Tahoe and got married. Just think about how weather can affect your life. If the snow had been falling, my guy would have been stuck back at home with his girlfriend and they might have gotten bored with all of the snow and had an argument. He might have gotten mad during the argument and said he was going to Los Angeles where people would appreciate him and I'd be looking at Brad Pitt instead of Doug Brenner.

I look up to see Cassie walking toward us.

"Are you all right?" Cassie says to me as she looks

down at Doug who just sat on a folding chair next to the ferns. Cassie must have heard from Aunt Ruth already that Doug and I are having problems.

Doug scoots his chair back into the leaves.

Cassie wears glasses and she pushes them farther up on her nose. She has her hair pulled back with one of those new glitzy clips. She decides to ignore Doug and focus on me. "We should call my cousin Bobby. He can just explain to his wife that he owes me a favor that he didn't get a chance to do before he got married. I'll bet she'd understand if he comes down."

"Would you understand if your husband decided to go on a date less than a week after you married him?"

"Well, no, I guess not."

"Besides, there's no plane that would get him here fast enough. I should have hired an actor to be my date."

"You were going to hire someone?" Doug lifts his head up. I notice some of his color has come back. "How much were you going to pay?"

"Don't get your hopes up," I say to Doug. "If I had hired an actor, I would have expected some acting."

I would have at least expected him not to faint when my aunt asked a simple question.

"You don't need an actor to pretend to be your date," Cassie says loyally. She looks Doug in the eye. "Any man should be happy to be your date—it's a privilege, not some dreaded *commitment* hanging around your neck."

Doug swallows nervously and then stands up. "I think I'll go outside and check my cell phone—maybe I…ah…got a message from work." Doug glances over at me with a tight-lipped smile. "If they need me at the hospital, maybe…ah…you were going to ride back with Cassie anyway, weren't you?"

I smile right back at him. And, I don't show any teeth, either.

The coward. He doesn't even wait for me to finish my smile before he slinks away. Unless I miss my guess, he'll pile one of those little paper plates high with some of those crab-stuffed mushrooms that have just arrived and then head out to his car. I doubt he even looks at his cell phone. I would have expected more fortitude from a man who wanted to plunge into ice water.

"You're still good with me getting a ride home with you?" I ask Cassie.

"Of course."

Going home with Cassie makes sense anyway. I've been staying with her in her apartment in Hollywood ever since I got laid off from my job at the bank in Blythe six weeks ago. Outside of Aunt Inga, the one person I can always count on in my life is Cassie. I thought she was my cousin when I first met her. The whole town of Blythe, or as much of it as I knew in my five-year-old world, seemed to be related to me so I just assumed she was, too. I was really quite pleased when I discovered she wasn't a cousin, but was prepared to be my friend instead.

My cousins weren't always that nice to me.

My mother explained to me that the reason my cousins weren't always nice to me was because I'm a black sheep. Being a black sheep is hereditary in our part of the family, she told me. Just the way she said it made me feel important. I was fine with being a black sheep if it made me more like my mother.

My mother said that she was the original black sheep. She was born to that role simply because she had a different mother than the aunts. My grandfather married my grandmother ten years after his first wife, the aunts' mother, had died.

The aunts' parents had both emigrated from Norway and the aunts thought that, if their father did remarry, it would be to an older Norwegian woman like their mother. They never expected him to marry a young beautiful American woman like my grandmother.

To make it even worse, my grandmother didn't know how to cook anything, let alone anything Norwegian. She'd never heard of lefse or lamb and cabbage stew or any of the foods that the aunts' mother had cooked. She didn't know how to darn a sock. Or kill potato bugs. I'm sure the aunts could give you the complete list of what she couldn't do.

What my grandmother could do was wear a scarf in a hundred ways and she had a hatbox filled with sheer floating scarves. If the aunts saw anyone dress up, it was on a Sunday. They were shocked when my grandmother wore her scarves every day of the week, but my grandmother said a woman needed to live her life with flair.

I've often wondered what my mother's life would have been like if my grandmother hadn't died when my mother was nine years old. The aunts raised my mother after that. The aunts took good care of my mother even if my mother said that Aunt Ruth was forever calling her a half sister. It made my mother feel as though she was halfway in the family and halfway out of it. She didn't like it.

My mother was seventeen when she met my father. She left high school and married him a few months after meeting him. My mother had seven years with my father and then he died, too.

When that happened, my mother told me later that she hadn't known what to do so she went to Aunt Ruth. My mother had never held a job in her life and Aunt Ruth told her she'd never find a job, either, because, as Aunt Ruth apparently saw it, my mother was just like my grandmother and so it was pointless to expect her to know how to do anything useful.

Before my mother could say anything, Aunt Ruth said that fortunately my mother didn't need to worry, because she—Aunt Ruth—knew her Christian duty and would take care of my mother just as she'd taken care of my grandmother before her. That's when Aunt Ruth offered my mother a job cleaning her house.

If Aunt Ruth had said she was doing it because my mother was her sister, my mother might have taken the job. But Aunt Ruth said she was doing it because my mother was her half sister.

My mother said she didn't need a charity job.

Then Aunt Ruth said that my mother shouldn't be foolish. The only job my mother could even get without a high school diploma, according to Aunt Ruth, would have to be a charity job and, if my mother was going to be so picky, she could just go ahead and starve because she wasn't likely to get another offer of employment.

My mother said she'd rather starve than work for Aunt Ruth. Well, you can imagine the rest. From what I've heard, by the time the argument was over, my mother was stomping out of Aunt Ruth's house leaving me with Aunt Inga. Aunt Inga is the oldest of my three aunts and the only one who is unmarried and, except for me, childless. Two days later my mother sent word that she'd gotten a job as a hatcheck girl in a casino in Las Vegas. She also said she still needed a little time to get settled before she took me to live with her.

Aunt Gladys, my third aunt, said my mother got that job just to spite my Aunt Ruth and they all expected my mother to give it up after a few weeks when she'd made her point. But I knew my mother wouldn't be giving it up. A hatcheck girl might not make a lot of money, but at least she didn't have someone reminding her she wasn't really part of the family all the time.

My mother eventually became a dealer in Las Vegas. When I was young, Aunt Inga used to take me to visit my mother around Mother's Day every year. We'd spend the night at one of the small hotels off The Strip and we'd have dinner and breakfast with my mother. Now, I am perfectly able to make the trip by myself, but I still like having Aunt Inga come along, so we both drive up to see my mother for that one weekend. My mother drives down to visit us some, too, but that one visit is a constant.

I sort of understood back then why my mother had to leave rather than let Aunt Ruth make her feel like a charity case. I didn't understand, however, why my mother couldn't take me with her. I was only five, but I was on my mother's side. She and I were both black sheep together. I believed she wouldn't leave me alone for long in Blythe. She couldn't. I was no more fully part of the family there than she was. I belonged with my mother. I only half belonged with the others.

Every night, after my mother had left, I got down on my knees beside my bed and prayed that God would make my mother come back soon and take me to live with her. At first, my prayers were very calm and ordinary. I managed to pray for a puppy in the same prayers. I really didn't even think I needed to pray. I figured my mother would be back at Aunt Inga's doorstep soon enough anyway with an open car trunk just ready for the suitcase I kept half-packed in the closet.

I wasn't asking God for a miracle in those days as much as I was just asking Him to help nudge everything along a little faster so that I would be settled in my mother's home when He chose to send me that puppy I had also been praying for.

As the years passed, however, I forgot all about the puppy and my prayer to live with my mother became more intense until finally it felt as if I was praying for the biggest miracle in the world. I screwed up my face and prayed as hard as I could, hoping God would notice and have mercy on me. He had to see my desire. I had certainly told Him what I wanted. I repeated my request over and over and over again.

Finally, I realized no one was going to answer my prayer. Just like that. One day, sitting in church with Aunt Inga, I knew it was pointless to continue. I was about nine years old and I had been praying that same prayer for years. Nothing had ever happened.

It became clear to me that day that God simply didn't care enough to answer my prayer, even though

He seemed to listen to the prayers of other people and I had no doubt He heard me, too. I mean He wasn't deaf, so He had to have heard all those prayers I'd said. No, He just wasn't bothering to answer me. Somehow, I wasn't important enough to Him. Maybe I was a half and not a whole with him, too.

These days, I don't talk about my mother much and no one else in the family, except Aunt Inga, talks about her at all. It's one of those Delicate Subjects that we don't discuss. Like the fact that Uncle Howard is becoming bald and that the doctor says he's under too much stress.

Cassie says that, with all the silence about my mother, I might as well be adopted as she is. It's funny. Back in the days when I believed my mother was going to come back for me, both Cassie and I thought I was the lucky one because I had a real mother. These days, I'm not sure who had it easier.

Those first years, whenever Aunt Inga took me to Las Vegas to see my mother, I would ask my mother when I was going to live with her. At first, my mother would give me a hug and tell me she just needed a little more time to get a place that was big enough for both of us. Eventually, one year when I asked, she couldn't look me in the eye and didn't offer me a hug. I didn't give up hope quite then, but it wasn't long after that when I sat in church that day and gave up praying. I had finally figured out there was going to be no happy ending to the story of my mother and me.

But that's all history. I have enough problems right here and now to keep me busy without worrying about the cosmic problems of relating to a God who is silent and a mother who has no room in her life for a daughter.

"I don't suppose Elaine and what's-his-name will break up again and call everything off," I say as I take a long look around the party. "That way I wouldn't need to worry about having a date for the wedding."

I am already regretting Doug's leaving. I don't know Doug well, but I know him better than any other guy I've met in Hollywood. I'd counted on him to be my date for the rehearsal dinner and the wedding, too.

"You don't need a date for Elaine's wedding," Cassie says.

I blink at Cassie. "Of course, I do. I took a vow. You remember."

"I'd be surprised if Elaine even remembers the doctor part of it, though," Cassie says.

"Oh, she remembers," I say.

Elaine had reminded me of my vow in the invitation she sent to her engagement party. Her exact words were "dated any doctors lately?" She'd scrawled it right over the embossed black lettering saying what a fine hotel the Grand Carlton was and what a lovely party it would be.

"But that was years ago. What were we—ten at the time?"

"We were eleven. But it doesn't matter. A vow never expires."

Especially not when it has been vowed in front of my cousin Elaine.

It had all started with a pair of black high-heel shoes my mother left behind on one of her visits to Blythe. My mother said I could keep the shoes and, when I strapped them on my feet, I felt grown-up and incredibly tall. Aunt Inga fretted when I wore those shoes, but she didn't have the heart to take them away from me. She knew how much I missed my mother; I guess she didn't want me to miss those shoes, too.

One Saturday, when Aunt Inga was busy doing something else, I decided to walk down to the grocery store with my high heels on and get some eggs. Instead of eggs, I got Elaine.

When Elaine saw me in those shoes, I could see right away she was jealous. Aunt Ruth had gotten her a pair of short, stubby trainer heels, but Elaine was a long way from getting real high-heel shoes.

"You can't wear those," Elaine said. "You'll fall and hurt your insides and not be able to have babies."

"I'm going to have babies," I had told her as I picked up a carton of eggs off the shelf.

"You'll probably never get married, either," Elaine added calmly once she had my attention.

"I will so." I started walking to the counter to pay for the eggs. By this time in my life, I had learned to ignore Elaine's taunts most of the time.

But then Elaine said something I thought was forbidden. She said my problem was that only the saints and a few special mothers could tolerate my red hair. If my mother didn't want me or my hair with her in Las Vegas, why would I think any man would want me around when I was grown-up?

I had bright, unruly carrot hair. Somehow the hair didn't bother me as much as Elaine always thought it should. I couldn't believe, though, that Elaine had said anything about my mother not wanting me with her.

That was supposed to be one of those things that the family didn't talk about, at least not in a public place like the grocery store. We might have our problems with all the half sister and half cousin stuff, but we kept them to ourselves.

Anyway, that's when I had made my vow.

"You just watch and see," I had said. I must have crossed my heart and hoped to die, I was that determined. "I'm not *just* going to get married—I'm going to marry a doctor. And I'm going to do it before you get married, too!"

It had been a foolish vow, but I never took it back. Even now I'd rather eat worms than give Elaine the satisfaction of seeing me admit defeat. When she was giving me the eye a minute ago, she looked happier than when her fiancé got up in front of everyone here and announced their engagement.

Which might be a surprise to someone else, but not to me. Elaine has enjoyed making my life miserable all our lives. And not just because she is beautiful and I am not. Oh, no, it goes far deeper than that. It goes all the way down to clothes.

When I was growing up, I was always well dressed. That's because I got all of Elaine's hand-me-downs. Uncle Howard is a doctor and that has made Aunt Ruth, in her own words, "the richest woman in Blythe." When my mother refused the job as Aunt Ruth's housekeeper, my aunt Inga asked to take it instead. One of the job perks was that Aunt Ruth gave all of Elaine's old clothes to Aunt Inga so she could give them to me to wear.

You'd think from the way Aunt Ruth gave the

clothes to Aunt Inga that they had come off of the back of some royal princess instead of Elaine's scrawny back. I'd rather have worn Aunt Inga's old bathrobe to school than Elaine's charity clothes. But Aunt Inga was so proud when she gave me the clothes that I couldn't refuse to wear them.

The creepy thing was that whenever I was walking around in Elaine's clothes I felt as if I was trying to be someone I wasn't. As if I was a peasant pretending to be a princess. I think Elaine felt the same way only it was easier for her because she always got to be the princess in the story.

The whole thing with the clothes never should have been possible in the first place. That's because I am older than Elaine by five months. Older kids are supposed to be taller. Elaine's hand-me-downs should be too small for me. It just shouldn't work.

Unfortunately, I have always been three inches shorter than Elaine so her old clothes always fit me just when they no longer fit her.

I hate being shorter than Elaine. I used to think that shortness was one of the old Biblical plagues like pestilence and famine. I know now that my theology was a little misplaced, but back then I figured God's punishment on me was to keep me short enough for Elaine's hand-me-downs. I figured He knew I was mad at Him and He was dealing with me in His Own Way. I couldn't even say much about it without looking like a whiner—if He had sent me boils or the palsy than I might have gotten some sympathy. But my shortness looked deceptively ordinary.

The reason I knew God had thwarted me, however,

was because my mother was tall, willowy and beautiful. I might not have inherited my mother's beauty, but I figured I was at least entitled to her height. And, inside, I felt tall. Much taller than Elaine. I don't know what had happened on the outside of me that I didn't grow to the height I was supposed to be.

It was bad enough having to get the hand-me-downs, but what was much worse was that on the first day that I wore any of the clothes to school Elaine would announce where they came from in front of everyone.

"That's the dress I got in Palm Springs," she'd say. "Now my half cousin gets to wear it."

Then Elaine would give me The Look, the one that said she knew she was better than I was and I'd best know it, too. That's the same look she just gave me today. She doesn't call me her half cousin when she gives me The Look anymore, but she doesn't need to. I know she's saying it inside.

I don't even know if there's a word like half cousin, but I knew Elaine wanted it to be clear that I was not her real cousin. Somehow the half part always made me feel as though I didn't quite measure up to a full anything.

If I hadn't been convinced God hated me back then, I would have gotten down on my knees and prayed for some clothes that were all mine. I almost did once when the minister at Aunt Inga's church read that verse about the lilies of the fields not needing to worry about what they were wearing. That was one sermon I listened to with hope.

But it had been a long time since I'd even tried to pray and so no words came. I knew God didn't like hypocrites and I couldn't bring myself to pray for clothes one minute and blame Him for not listening to me the next. Finally, I let the urge to pray pass. I decided to be content with the prayers Aunt Inga said for me. At least she didn't call me half anything.

I don't know why Elaine's engagement party is bringing back all of these memories. It should be a time for looking forward. I decide I will, at least, enjoy myself with what's left of the evening.

Chapter Two

Oh, no, here comes Elaine walking across the ballroom with me in her sights. Her evening gown is a shimmering pale blue sheath and, if it was on anyone but Elaine, I would say it made her look like an angel.

"Tell her Doug got called in to work," I whisper to Cassie, who is still standing beside me.

"I know. That's what he said he was going to check," Cassie says.

"Perfect."

Then we both turn around to face Elaine.

"I'm so glad you could both come," Elaine says.

Elaine is tall, blond and should be a model, at least according to Aunt Ruth, who swears, if Elaine weren't so delicate, she would be on the cover of the JCPenney catalog by now. That's because our local grocery store once ran a picture of Elaine in the paper eating broccoli along with their advertised special on the vegetable.

The clerk in the grocery store said she'd never sold

as much broccoli in one week as she had because of that picture of Elaine. Aunt Ruth had a copy of the ad enlarged and laminated so it wouldn't fade when she put it in her scrapbook. No one could talk to Elaine for weeks after that without her giving them that broccoli smile of hers. To this day, I can't eat broccoli.

"Congratulations," I say as I hold out my hand.

"Thanks," Elaine says as she takes my hand and gives me The Look.

Even Cassie can see The Look so she interrupts. "I'd love to meet him."

"Him?" Elaine's face goes blank for a moment and then she remembers, "Oh, yes, Gary—you'll love him." She looks over at me as if she doesn't realize I've already heard story after story from the aunts about her wonderful Gary. "He's studying to be a dentist you know. Mother says that marrying a dentist is even better than marrying a doctor—he'll make the same income, but he won't have to work weekends."

"He's a student?" I latch onto the weak part in Elaine's story.

Elaine flushes. She knows it's the weak point. "Yes, but he'll finish his classes soon and be accepted into his internship before Thanksgiving. That's why we set the wedding for Thanksgiving weekend."

"So soon?" It's only three weeks away. I can't help but needle Elaine. She has to know everyone in the family already knows the details, right down to the Lenox china pattern that she has picked out. I might be living in Hollywood, but even I'm in the loop. "I hope that gives you enough time to prepare. I mean for such a big wedding and all. I heard you've rented that church in Palm Springs with the fancy windows. It should be perfect for bridal party pictures."

Bull's-eye.

Elaine blushes and looks at me. "I hope Mother told you that I'm limiting my bridesmaid group. Gary's sister, Lynda, is going to be my maid of honor. I don't know her, but, well, she's family. And for the bridesmaids—well, I have so many friends and cousins I can't ask everyone to be in the wedding party."

"Not a problem," I assure her although she and I both know she may have an excess of cousins—all of them male except for me—but very few friends.

"I still want you to come to the rehearsal dinner," she offers.

"I'll be there."

"It's not like you'd be able to wear the bridesmaid dress anyway. Not with your hair."

My hair has mellowed into a very nice dark bronze color, but Elaine still says it clashes with things—and she's right about it clashing with the color she picked for her bridesmaid dresses. She wants a fall theme so she's going with orange and brown. Brown I could handle. But she picked orange for the dresses. Her bridesmaids are going to look like pumpkins, but there won't be a redhead among them. I try not to be paranoid about Elaine picking the one color I can't wear.

Except for Lynda, I wonder who Elaine will even ask to be in the bridal party. I know Lynda, who lives in Boston, wasn't planning to be here tonight, but I heard a rumor that some bridesmaids were here tonight. That was my cousin Jerry talking, though, and he may have just been hoping they'd come so he could look them over.

"Of course, I want you to be available in case Aunt Inga needs help assisting Aunt Gladys as they cut the cake," Elaine says a little too sweetly, "so you will have an important part."

"I'll be honored," I say as I smile. I'm the assistant to the assistant cake cutter. It doesn't get better than that.

Elaine's eyes narrow a little. She's thrown off balance by my smile and good cheer. She looks around. "I wanted to meet your date. And, of course, he's invited to the rehearsal dinner, as well. I don't see him, do I?"

"I don't know where he is," Cassie says.

"He's headed back to Los Angeles," I say and then I pause. "Sometimes the hospital calls and needs him to come in to help with a procedure."

Those are both true statements. They may not relate to each other, but a conversationalist who was able to think up the word half cousin when she was only seven should be able to take note of the pause.

Elaine frowns. "I didn't know he was in medicine."

"Well, he's more of a specialist than anything," I say airily. "Very important in the field of radiology."

"Well, Gary would like to meet him then," Elaine says. "We'll have to make time to sit and talk at the rehearsal dinner. Wouldn't that be nice?"

I smile and nod. It could happen. It would certainly be nice if it happened. Doug might even agree to come with me again. "What are you serving at your rehearsal dinner?"

"Prime rib and lobster."

See? The odds of Doug coming to the rehearsal dinner are improving all the time.

"Oh," Elaine says and I notice she's not looking at me anymore. I turn to see what she's looking at and I understand why she's looking a little nervous. The aunts are all coming over.

"I brought some punch for your young man," Aunt Ruth says as she holds a cup outward and looks around. I can tell she's determined to be supportive of my relationship even if she doesn't understand it. "Where is he?"

"He had to head back to Los Angeles," Cassie says in a rush. "Something came up."

"Oh, that's too bad," Aunt Ruth says as she turns to me. "I hope it's nothing serious?"

I shake my head. That much I know.

"Well, good, because I thought he was nice," Aunt Ruth continues. "He certainly has exquisite manners."

Aunt Inga nods and beams. "Not many men know how to properly escort a woman these days. Even from across the room I could see what fine manners he had."

Aunt Gladys just nods. She has five sons. She may have forgotten what manners are.

"Where did you meet your young fellow?" Aunt Gladys asks.

"Oh, Cassie met him at the coffee shop next to where she works."

I wonder why it's grown so silent and then I see that everyone has their eyes downcast.

Finally, Aunt Ruth says heartily. "Well, there's no need to worry about who has a job and who doesn't— not today on such a happy occasion."

"I'm going to get a job," I say. It was just my luck that I lost my job before Elaine got engaged. "You don't need to worry. It'll be soon, too."

"Of course you'll get a job," Aunt Gladys says. "And it's good that you're taking your time."

"It's only been five weeks," Aunt Inga says.

"Six," I say.

"Oh."

"Elaine doesn't have a job," I finally say, even though it makes me feel as though I'm three years old again. But I know for a fact that she's not even looking for one.

"Of course not," Aunt Ruth says in shock. "She's got a wedding to plan."

I don't have anything to say to that.

But Cassie, bless her heart, does. "Julie is good at planning weddings."

Cassie is remembering that we used to play wedding when we were little. Cassie loved the "who gives away the bride" part because we always pretended her real mother stepped forward to answer and say how very sorry she was that she'd given Cassie away when she was a baby. I loved the rest of the ceremony, from the songs to the flowers to the "I do."

"Oh, we've hired a professional wedding planner to help with Elaine's wedding—the poor woman's been working away for months already," Aunt Ruth says. "It's such an important day—we don't want to leave anything to chance. I mean, for some weddings an amateur planner would be fine, but not for one as special as Elaine's."

Elaine gives me The Look.

I don't know what it is about that look that drives me crazy, but it does. That's my only excuse for saying what I say next. "I'm getting a job as a wedding planner in Hollywood."

"Really, dear?" Aunt Inga looks proud as she turns to her sisters. "See, Julie, is going to be a wedding planner. And in Hollywood! She might even get to meet some of the movie stars. Isn't that wonderful?"

I can see The Look fade a little on Elaine's face before she asks, "Movie stars? You might plan weddings for movie stars?"

"Well, I might have to start out as an assistant wedding planner," I say, feeling pleased that Elaine is a tiny bit jealous.

"Of course," Aunt Inga nods. "Everyone starts out as an assistant so they can learn."

"I haven't actually found the job yet," I feel compelled to add.

"But she will," Cassie says confidently at my side. Cassie never did like The Look, either. "And she'll plan great weddings for movie stars. There will be pictures in all of the newspapers."

Aunt Inga continues to beam. She's probably thinking about her scrapbook. I always did wish I had more things for her to put in her scrapbook. Hers is skinny compared to the ones Aunt Ruth and Aunt Gladys have. Of course, Aunt Ruth has Elaine and Aunt Gladys has all the boys and their sporting honors. I did get my name in the newspaper once for breaking my leg in a school track meet when I was ten, but it wasn't much of a write-up.

I try to smile confidently. Life isn't all about scrapbooks. It would be good, though, if I didn't need to answer any more questions right away. What I need is an earthquake. Everyone is always talking about how California is going to have The Big One. What's wrong with now?

"Isn't that Gary over there?" I finally say as I point in the opposite corner of the room. And Gary, the blessed groom-to-be, *is* there by the way. "I thought he wanted to make a little speech."

Gary had said at the announcement time that he wanted to make a few remarks later. Whatever he has in mind probably isn't of the magnitude of an earthquake, but it does manage to unknot the aunts. Aunt Ruth takes Elaine with her and they go over to talk to Gary. Aunt Gladys goes over to the punch table. And Aunt Inga goes to find a comfortable chair to sit in.

"Well, now I've done it," I say when it is just Cassie and me again. "Everybody's going to expect me to get a job as a wedding planner, in Hollywood no less."

"It'll be easier than finding a doctor to date before Thanksgiving."

I have to admit that Cassie has a point. Strange as it is, it cheers me up. You know, I might actually find a job like that.

"When we get back, I'm going to look at the ads in the *Times,*" I say.

"Get one of those throwaway freebie papers like the *Hollywood Reader.* That's where you'll find those kinds of jobs."

Just knowing I have a plan makes the rest of Elaine's party bearable. Gary, who I don't know all that well since I haven't been around to watch the blossoming of their true love, makes his speech about how grateful he is that Elaine said yes to his proposal and how sure he is that eternal happiness awaits them.

Gary's parents are sitting at a table near where he and Elaine are standing. I can't help but notice that his parents both have smiles on their faces that don't move. Seriously. Their lips are frozen in place. If you just glance at Gary's parents, you'd think they both are happy. But if you keep looking at them for a minute or two, you see that their expressions don't change. It's kind of eerie. Maybe it's a rich person's thing. I'd give odds, though, that they are thinking Gary and Elaine won't have happiness that lasts past next week, much less throughout eternity.

Of course, I should talk. I don't give their marriage great odds, either. I suddenly wonder if my smile is wooden, too. I keep smiling all through Gary's speech so I will look friendly, but I am careful to move my lip muscles some so I look sincere at the same time. After all, Gary might not be such a bad guy. All I really know about him is that he was born wealthy and wants to be a dentist. Neither one of those things is a crime. Of course, I also know that he's a boring guy with no personality, but maybe he can't help that. And, at least he's a *rich* boring guy—with parents.

If my interpretation of their forced smiles is correct, Gary's parents aren't exactly planning to sweep Elaine into their hearts. But, lots of married couples begin their lives together with some kind of in-law trouble. Maybe Elaine and Gary are better off to just get the bad times over right up front. For all of Elaine's faults, she is not the worst person in the world. She and Gary should be able to work it all out fine.

At least Elaine doesn't make speeches and, about now, I'm thinking there's some virtue in that fact alone.

I try to concentrate on the rest of Gary's speech, which continues on about happiness, although he doesn't mention eternal happiness anymore, to my disappointment. I've always wondered about eternal happiness and am not opposed to hearing someone else's thoughts on the matter. I have these questions. I mean, would you know you were happy if you were eternally happy? Does a goldfish know that it's wet if it's always swimming in water? Or does a bird know it's in the air if it's always in the air? Do people need to see unhappiness to know that they are happy? Or do they need to see happiness to know they are unhappy?

Well, Gary isn't going into any of those questions and you can see why the rest of the party is fading off into a blur for me. I am going cross-eyed trying to figure out this eternal happiness business. That's the problem with speeches. Sometimes they make a person think. I take a closer look at Gary. Eternal happiness is quite a goal for an adult, but he looks confident he can meet it even with his two parents sitting there frozen in time beside him. Maybe the thing between parents and their children is never just a slam dunk where everything works out right and everyone is happy.

I used to think I'd live happily ever after when my mother came to take me to live with her, but since she never came, I never knew what that would feel like. I wonder if it's too late to have everlasting happiness with a parent when you're an adult yourself.

I know it's too late to go live with my mother even though a few months ago, when Aunt Inga and I made our trip up there, we were able to stay in my mother's guest room. It's the first time my mother ever had an extra room for us when we came to visit. The spare bedroom was big enough for two twin beds and a dresser. My mother told us she'd just gotten a big promotion and was an assistant manager at the casino now. She said that was why she could afford a bigger apartment.

I was cynical enough to ask myself if it was really true that she couldn't afford more space until recently. It was very convenient that she had the big apartment now that I was too old to live with her.

Of course, I didn't say anything to my mother. I had stopped asking my mother about me and her years ago. I'd stopped talking to her about real things about that time, too. I never even told her about Elaine calling me "half cousin" for the first time.

I'm feeling a little sad now and decide I should go visit my mother again soon. I don't feel close to her when I visit, but I still feel we're on the same team. She is the only one who is full-family to me. Sometimes, I think that's what hurts the most about my mother leaving me in Blythe. Aunt Inga has been loving and wonderful, but she's not really on my team. She tries to be neutral in our great family divide, but she wasn't born a black sheep as my mother and I were. She's not a half anything to the others.

Of course, no one in the family says too much about the different sides. Aunt Ruth is always polite to me. I'm not even sure that she knows that she treats me differently than the other cousins. She doesn't scold me like them, but she doesn't brag about me, either. I'm not quite her niece in the way that the boys are her nephews.

Finally, Gary finishes his speech and sits down. I think everyone is relieved, even Elaine. Maybe she finds it hard to believe in that much happiness, too. Either that or she's gotten a good look at her new in-laws and knows the road won't be as smooth as Gary says.

I look at Aunt Inga. She's the big pray-er in the family and I wonder if she's praying for Elaine these days. I'm not saying I want her to be praying for Elaine. I'm just wondering, that's all.

Chapter Three

The very next morning I announce to Cassie that I'm going to look for that job. We're back in Hollywood by then and we're sitting at the table in Cassie's small one-bedroom apartment eating yogurt and whole wheat toast for breakfast. I like the smell of toast in the air and the sunshine is coming in the large window next to the table. It might not be eternal happiness, but the day is full of possibilities.

The apartment Cassie rents is in one of those old Hollywood brick buildings that have rows of identical windows—you know like the ones Hitchcock filmed in those classic movies of his. I love the big windows in Cassie's place. We're on the third floor so we're high enough up that we look out into air—which is kind of cool if you've spent your whole life looking out windows that face the desert around Blythe.

Not that all you see is air outside of Cassie's windows. If you lean to the right and look down from the window in her living room, you can see the big pots of various plants she has on the fire escape landing outside that window.

You'd think Cassie would be anti-mother because of her real mother putting her up for adoption, but she's not. She's the most motherly person I know. That's probably why she likes to grow things. And why she approaches life with so much hope. Like now, she finishes up her yogurt and then tells me she knows I'll find what I'm looking for. Some people would say that kind of thing and sound phony. But Cassie really believes in me. So, what can I do? We walk out of the building together and, when Cassie walks in one direction to catch a bus to her job in the floral shop, I start to walk in the other direction.

I walk for a couple of blocks and then I see the sign for the Coffee Spot. I know they have the *Hollywood Reader* on a table just inside their door. Since it's a free paper, I won't even have to go up to the counter.

Not that it's bad to go up to the counter. It's just that this part of Hollywood isn't the fun part that people think of when they think of Hollywood so there's no real reason to sit down and have a cup of coffee. No new movie stars are going to be discovered here, that's for sure.

The first clue that you're not in the glamour part of Hollywood is the smell. It smells like fish. And, instead of movie studios, you see Thai fish markets and fortune-tellers who have neon signs blinking away in their shaded windows. The street looks grimy and there are too many cars inching their way down it to make it pleasant.

Anyway, before you know it, I am back at the apartment and I am sitting down at the table once again. I have the want ads in one hand and my pen in the other hand. I'm ready to circle the job I hope will be there. Before I open the paper, I close my eyes.

Now, this is a little weird, but I want you to know me so here it is—as you know, I've gone to church for years with Aunt Inga even though I don't pray anymore. I know most people who go to church take church seriously, but I attend for Aunt Inga because *she* takes it seriously. Anyway, I figure God gets me and understands why, when I bow my head in church, I do not talk to Him. I make lists of books I want to read and movies I want to see, but I carefully do not talk to God. That's our agreement.

Still, even though I don't pray, I sort of got into the habit early on of closing my eyes at times like now because—when I figured out that my mother wasn't going to take me to live with her, I started to pester Aunt Inga for information about my father.

My father had been sick for a long time before he died. Maybe that's why Aunt Inga couldn't think of much to say about him. Mostly, she just said that he was a man who prayed and she was sure he was watching out for me and asking God to do the same. I think she meant to comfort me, but it kind of creeped me out at first. I mean, I wanted a father, but I didn't want one who spied on me, especially if he brought God along when he did it. I mean, how intimidating is that? It's even worse than a living father bringing in the police every time he wants to see you.

But then I thought, well, maybe it's okay if my father is watching over me even if he has to bring help with him. You know, in case I am about to be run over by a car or something. So, now, just in case my father is watching, I bow my head. I guess you could say I pretend to pray. You see, I wouldn't want my father to see me not praying and be disappointed, especially if he's putting in extra time to protect me from accidents. With that toppling thing I have going for me, I could use someone looking out for me and it feels good to think it's my father. So I bow my head and keep my mind blank. I know it is complicated, and a little weird, but that's me.

Anyway, when I open my eyes, I flip the paper open and there it is.

Wanted: An assistant to coordinate music, flowers and filing. Help our clients arrange the ceremonies they want and deserve for one of life's most important days. In the heart of Hollywood. Church setting. Please be understanding and organized. No need to call first—just stop by for an interview.

Whoee! I do a mental high five. This closing-the-eyes business must work. I've seen enough ads to know that the bit about just stopping by means they're desperate for someone to take the job. I can already hear someone saying "my dearly beloved, we are gathered together…" Oh, I love a good wedding.

I'm feeling pretty good by now so I put on this pale pink summer suit I have that's just perfect for afternoon weddings. Then I give Aunt Inga a call. Just in case my dad is on a coffee break about now, I know Aunt Inga will pray that I get the job. I should explain that just because I personally don't pray that doesn't mean I don't think that prayer works. I think it works just fine for people like my dad and Aunt Inga. It just doesn't work for me.

Anyway, after I call Aunt Inga, I put on some lipstick to match the pink suit and fluff up my hair a little extra so I look as though I am ready for a wedding.

I take a bus over to the address on Hollywood Boulevard, feeling more hopeful all the time. First, I see the address on the curb and then I see the church. It is an old stone church with ivy growing up the sides of it. It's the kind of place where movie stars would want to get married. I would want to get married there. There's a tall thin steeple and a series of little carved entryways to what looks like a courtyard. There are even rosebushes around the church.

I take a peek into the courtyard. Wow—what a place for a wedding reception. There are trees with all these deep green leaves and lots of bricked area where you could set up a dozen or more of those large round tables. I can just see the place at night with candles on the tables and some of those tiny white lights strung from the trees. The air is fragrant from the roses and, if the wedding is at night, you could look up and maybe see a star or two. How romantic is that?

I look up at the sky so that my father can see I'm excited and hopeful. I've also noticed that there aren't many cars in the parking lot so there aren't hordes of other people here applying for the job. This could be my day.

I suppose if I hadn't been drooling over the church,

I would have paid more attention to the signs and would have been better prepared for the job interview.

Not that you need to worry—I didn't blow the interview. I know you're in suspense so I'm going to tell you flat out. I got the job.

Now, before you sing the "Hallelujah Chorus," there's something else I need to tell you. It's not the kind of job I was expecting. You see, this place isn't a wedding chapel at all. It's a mortuary. That's right. Dead people all over the room. Well, maybe not in this room, but definitely nearby.

I'm not so sure any of my aunts would approve of me working in a mortuary. I'm not so sure I approve. My dad might think it is okay, but then he's dead so he's got a different perspective.

Anyway, I did a double take when I got inside the mortuary. I still can't believe I didn't notice it was a mortuary from the outside. Actually, there is a very discreet sign on the building—I went out and checked later and, sure enough, there was one of those weathered brass plates with the raised lettering that said Hollywood & Vine Mortuary.

As I said, I didn't know it was a mortuary until Mr. Z, that's the owner, came over in the lobby and asked if he can help me. He's about seventy years old and he was dressed in a black suit. His face was so sorrowful I wondered what kind of weddings they had here.

Well, that started our interview. Me with my surprise showing and him just talking away as if it's every day someone walks in wearing a pink suit and asking to work with the dead—well, at first, we got real tangled and he thought I only wanted to work with the married dead people. He must have thought I was some kind of strange guru or something. I told him that wasn't the case, but I was still at a loss to explain why I was hesitating.

"It's not that I have anything against any of the dead people." I finally just blurted it out in the middle of him telling me about the hours the staff work. I mean I pride myself on being open-minded. I like all kinds of people. Besides, I know what it's like to have someone think they're better than you because of something you can't help and I wouldn't wish that on anyone. So I don't worry about skin color or marital status or religious preference. I'm supportive of handicapped people. I must admit, though, that the dead thing gives me pause.

That's where we are now in the interview. Me stuck with nothing to say and Mr. Z looking at me.

"Don't worry about the dead people," Mr. Z finally says with a wave of the hand. I notice he's wearing a big diamond ring. I'm glad to see he's not all black suit, but I'm a little taken aback. I look around, hoping he's not going to say something loud and offensive about dead people. Men with flashy jewelry sometimes do things like that. He doesn't. Which makes me realize I don't even personally know any men who wear flashy jewelry so I must have a prejudice against men who wear flashy jewelry—which is not good. Something tells me this job isn't the place to have prejudices of any kind.

Mr. Z just keeps going on. "Dead people are easy to work with—it's the families that will give you problems." I almost laugh, but then I realize he's not joking so I sort of choke instead. He's looking at me now as if I'm a juvenile delinquent. "You have any family?"

I think about my mother, but we don't really live together so I figure there's no need to list her. "I have an aunt—Aunt Inga. But I don't need to worry about my family. You see, I—"

Mr. Z isn't listening. "I remember when it seemed like everyone had big families. Now, we see smaller and smaller funerals every day. The relatives just don't come. And, young girls like you—they live thousands of miles away from their families."

He looks at me as though I'd just run away from home in addition to being a delinquent.

"I'm twenty-three."

He doesn't look impressed. "And where is this Aunt Inga of yours?"

"She lives in Blythe."

He looks at me as if I'm trying to be clever and that there's really no such town except in my mind.

"You know, Blythe—it's on the 10 freeway just this side of the Arizona border—a couple of hundred miles from here."

He still looks skeptical, but nods his head and calls for the receptionist to come over.

"This is Miss Billings." He introduces her to me. "She'll measure you for your suit."

This is it? Doesn't he even ask if I'll take the job?
"Oh, I don't need a suit." *One of us needs to speak up.* "You see if I decide to take the job, it'll only be temporary until…"

Until what? Until I can figure out what do with my life?

I get ready to say something, but Mr. Z doesn't give me enough time. He just grunts and turns to Miss

Billings. "Measure her anyway. You never know when she'll get a part that calls for a black suit."

Miss Billings giggles. She has steel-gray hair pulled back into a crooked bun that she keeps clipped down with a black plastic barrette.

"We know all you young girls really want to be in the mov-i-es," Miss Billings whispers to me as she pulls a tape measure out of her pocket. She doesn't say movies like an ordinary person. She draws the word out and she has a proud smile on her face when she says it. "That's why I told Mr. Z he needed to rewrite that Help Wanted ad to make it sound more exciting. Not everyone realizes the potential of working here. We *are* the Hollywood & Vine Mortuary, you know. The Paramount studios are just down the street. The relatives of some big stars are buried here."

I don't want to know what she means by *here*. I need a change in the conversation. "I don't want to be a movie star."

"Of course, we don't blame anyone for wanting to be in the movies. We always let any of the girls rear-range their schedule if they have an audition or some-thing. I used to be a makeup girl for the movies myself." Miss Billings just keeps on talking.

Doesn't anyone listen around here? "I want to be a bridal consultant."

Miss Billings puts the tape measure across my shoulders. "I've done the makeup for many a bride in my day—on and off screen." Miss Billings measures my arm from elbow to wrist. "Now I'm in charge of the final picture of repose."

"Huh?" I look up for this one.

"You know, the final resting pose."

Yikes. "You mean in the casket?"

Miss Billings nods as she measures my shoulder to my elbow. "You'd be surprised how a good hairstyle and a little makeup can make a difference. There's this certain shade of blush that, I swear, makes a dead person come to life—for the viewing that is. It's called Pearly Pink—isn't that lovely? I've always wondered if the manufacturer of that blush had dead people in mind when they made it—you know, sort of a heavenly reference with the pearly gates and all."

I can't believe I'm having this conversation. Would somebody actually develop a makeup for dead people? Maybe they would. I don't know anything about this business of working with the dead.

"Do you have to touch them?" I finally ask.

Miss Billings lets go of the end of her tape measure and the thing spins back into its little box. "Not everyone likes to be touched."

This is even getting creepier. "But how—"

Miss Billings looks at me and just smiles. "We have a form that people and their families can fill out before they need our services. Some people prefer the natural look and don't want to have makeup." She walks over to the receptionist desk and writes something on a piece of paper before looking up at me again. "That's always a mistake in my opinion. People wear makeup when they're alive. They need it even more when they're dead. I mean, just because you're dead that's no excuse to look bad. It's your big day—you've got the final viewing, then the funeral. People might want pictures. No, you need to look good."

I nod. I could probably use some of that makeup about now myself.

"I won't have to?" I swallow.

"Oh, dear me, no," Miss Billings says. "You would need to have experience before you could do that."

That's not totally reassuring, but I'm not going to press my luck.

Mr. Z decides I can start even without the suit as long as I stay in the back and don't interact with the customers. That is just fine with me.

"I'm a size ten," I tell Miss Billings as I head toward the back room where Mr. Z is leading me. "I bet you get lots of size ten women coming in to look for work."

Miss Billings nods and I feel relieved. I mean, just in case my temporary is even more temporary than I suspect, I wouldn't want them to have a suit made up that no one else could wear later.

Now that I think of it, isn't it kind of odd that Mr. Z makes suits for everyone? What kind of an employer makes suits for his employees? I know restaurants sometimes do that, but that's if they have something peculiar like chicken costumes or those red fish-head masks.

I'm not that wild about wearing a black suit all the time, but I've got to tell you I'd rather wear that than a fish head.

I'm almost through the lobby before it occurs to me that Mr. Z might also be making suits for the dead people. Maybe that's why he has a system all set up with a tailor and everything. I wonder if, when I leave, a dead person will wear the suit I leave behind.

"Do people have their own clothes when they come to be buried?" I ask Mr. Z.

"We pride ourselves on having a well-dressed clientele," Mr. Z says as he opens the door to the back room. "We don't let clients go on view unless they are appropriately attired."

I decide I should buy some clothes with my first paycheck. I haven't thought much about preparing for death, but I can tell you this, I don't want a Mr. Z somewhere deciding what I wear for the—you know, my big day. These black suits can't look that good no matter how much Pearly Pink makeup someone uses on your cheekbones. Besides, if I die anytime soon, I want to look as if I was a fun person while I was living. Maybe Cassie would promise to ask Aunt Inga to bury me in this pink suit I'm wearing now.

I never knew a mortuary could have so many forms. There are two rows of file cabinets in the back room, which is also the break room. One whole side of the room is covered with this big white board that you can mark on. It has the work schedule on the right side and the funeral schedule on the left side with little numbers here and there as though someone calculated a worker to funeral ratio.

I am not sure I like having my name there, but Mr. Z marks me in for the day anyway. There is my name in big black letters not two feet away from the listing of who is up for their final viewing. I wonder if Mr. Z ever gets the rows confused and puts an employee on the dead list or a dead person on the employee list. Wouldn't that be creepy if I came in some day and my name was on the wrong list?

I don't like thinking about the board so I look down at the basket of forms Mr. Z has given me to file. One basket has forms the family has filled out describing their wishes for the services at the mortuary. The other basket is signed contracts for financial arrangements.

I take a peek at one of the financial forms. Yikes. I can't afford to die yet, that's for sure.

I decide to file the Request for Services forms first and leave the financial stuff for last since it's a little alarming.

I am halfway through filing the requests when I notice that some of the forms have little handwritten notes at the bottom. Here's one of them: A Mr. Weston asks that his wife's hair be dyed blond for the ceremony. "She always wanted to be a blonde," he wrote. "I regret now that I didn't encourage her to just do it. I regret a lot of things I didn't encourage her in."

As I'm reading Mr. Weston's note, I have one of those moments of understanding. That note could be coming from my husband fifty years from now—not that I even know who that will be, but I do know myself. I know I am impulsive about some things, but they are mostly the small things like deciding to paint my toenails purple.

When it comes to important things like my relationship with mother, I have never done anything impulsive. I wanted my mother's approval so much I could barely move when I saw her. I certainly never had the nerve to ask her what she thought about me or why she never took me to live with her. I was a coward with her. Not knowing if you are loved can make you feel so insecure you don't do anything. Would it be that way for me around my husband unless I knew he really loved me?

Would I someday be like Mrs. Weston and not even have enough confidence to dye my hair a different color without fretting about it and wondering if the person I loved would like it? I feel sad for her, and even a little bit for Mr. Weston.

Then I think about Elaine. The way Aunt Ruth has always bragged about Elaine, I bet Elaine will never hesitate to do anything because she is afraid she will lose someone's love. I don't think even Gary will make her question herself. I've wondered all along if Elaine loves Gary, but I've never wondered if she believes *he* loves *her.* Elaine probably believes the whole world, except for maybe me, loves her. She doesn't know what it's like to be a half anything to anyone. She's always important.

I wonder what that kind of confidence would feel like. I'm sure Elaine doesn't question whether or not God likes her well enough to do her bidding. She is probably always praying for things. She's never known my kind of insecurity. Knowing her, she probably even thinks Gary's parents are going to be her fans once they get to know her a little better.

I decide to stop on my way back to Cassie's and get some of that wash-in hair gel. I may not be able to change myself, but I can look more confident. Even though my hair has outgrown some of its redness and is a nice auburn now, it wouldn't hurt to have some of those red sparkly streaks in it to really liven it up. I might even get some of those cheap sunglasses that have all kinds of colors around the rim.

The more I think about it, the more I decide Mr. Weston is on to something. His wife should have dyed her hair. If you look exciting, it's easier to be a confident person. I set the Weston form aside. I want to be sure Miss Billings knows about the hair color. Maybe she'll even go with a brighter blush on Mrs. Weston. I'll have to ask her—Miss Billings, that is.

Chapter Four

I've been at the Big M—that's what everyone calls the mortuary—for a week and a day now and I've told Cassie all about it. We still can't believe I'm working in a mortuary. That's part of the reason I haven't told anyone but Cassie yet. I figure I should be comfortable with my job before I go announcing it to the world.

We are at Cassie's apartment and she looks up from the plant she is repotting. She has sort of a plant rescue thing going with the floral shop that she manages. She can't stand to see plants thrown out when they become damaged so she brings them home and nurses them back to health. Cassie usually does the repotting on the weekend, but she got a no-information letter back from some network where adopted kids can leave word for their real parents to contact them and, when Cassie is upset, she needs to repot something, so here we are.

Cassie is sitting on the floor close to the wooden

crate that serves as a coffee table. Her wooden floor has lost its shine, but the grain of the wood gives her small apartment the feeling of home. Cassie made some rag rugs for her floor and we are each sitting on one with our legs crossed.

I'm wondering if I should say something more to Cassie about her letter, but she's already told me twice tonight that she's okay so I figure she doesn't want to talk about it yet, even though I know it has to be discouraging to know her mother hasn't been looking for her the way Cassie has been looking for her mother.

It is Monday evening and we've both had a long day. The root-bound ficus Cassie is pressing into a new pot still doesn't look too happy and I am filing my nails and feeling guilty that I'm not doing more to save distressed plants. Of course, I'm saving my cuticles so that should count for something even if my cuticles aren't another living thing and didn't appear all that distressed to begin with, even if the puce polish was starting to chip off my nails.

"Anything happen at work today?" Cassie asks as she puts some more dirt around the ficus.

"Mrs. Weston's daughter came by to thank Miss Billings for making her mother look so nice for the final viewing." I had already told Cassie about Mr. Weston's request that his wife's hair be dyed blond and Cassie agrees I should wear more red streaks in my hair. "The daughter seemed real nice. You could tell she had been close to her mother just by the way she talked about her."

I figure this is Cassie's chance to bring up her mother if she's ready to talk about it.

"Real close to her mother," I add.

I am silent for a minute to let Cassie say something about her birth mother, even if it's just to say that the woman doesn't deserve to have a daughter who wants to know her.

"Doug stopped by the floral shop today," Cassie says instead.

"Oh." I grunt and decide to file the nail on my little finger again. You can't be too careful about getting your nails smooth. Apparently, Cassie doesn't want to talk any more about her mother right now. But that doesn't mean I want to talk about Doug, either.

"I thought he looked a little sad," Cassie adds.

"Did he say he was sorry?"

Cassie is quiet for a minute. "I thought maybe you would say you were sorry to him."

"Me? I didn't leave me standing at my cousin's engagement party without a date. He backed out of our agreement. If there had been any money involved, I could take him to small claims court and get a refund. That's how much he let me down."

Cassie is patting a little more dirt around the ficus plant. As I said she is a mother to any plant or creature that needs help. That's why I'm not surprised she says what she does next. "I think he was hurt. He made this big speech about people not saying thank you anymore—something about it showing the decline of civilization as we know it."

"I don't think bad manners will doom a civilization."

At least I hope bad manners won't doom a civilization. It's an awful lot of pressure to put on a casual thank-you.

Cassie shrugs. "I told Doug how things were between you and Elaine. I don't think he knew how important that party was to you."

"You *what?*"

Cassie waves her hand to reassure me. "Just in very general terms. Nothing specific, but I think he might have got it. He might even agree to be your date for the wedding. If not, I can always ask my cousin Bobby to come down for that."

You might have noticed that Cassie is always looking for reasons for Bobby to come down. Her favorite relative is Bobby. He's adopted her better than anyone else in the family. He doesn't worry about whether she's an adopted cousin or a real cousin; he just really likes having her for a cousin. Some people I know could take a lesson from him.

Still, I hate to have Cassie ask him for another favor, even if he did back out of the last favor she requested. Besides, there's the whole wife thing and I don't want to cause some woman somewhere any unnecessary pain.

"Did Doug actually say he would go with me again to something?"

"No, but he seemed very open about things," Cassie says. "He told me to tell you to give him a call and he left his number. I was impressed that he stopped by my work. He could have just gone to the coffee shop and then left with a to-go cup or something. But he opened the door to our shop and just walked up to the counter and asked for me."

"He probably found it morally bracing to demand an apology."

I had told Cassie about Doug going to the rally so she knew all about the morally bracing time he had there.

"I don't think he was demanding anything, "Cassie said. "Even when he was going on about civilization, I could see his heart wasn't in it. I think he just didn't know what to say."

We were silent for a moment.

"I could write him a thank-you note I guess," I finally say. "Just in case he comes by your shop again. Then you could give it to him."

If Doug was going to be braced up morally, I could be braced even more. "And a coffee coupon. I could give him a coffee coupon."

I always think those coffee coupons make such a classy little gift, don't you? I'll show Doug that civilization has nothing to fear from my lack of social graces. Besides, I may become desperate again. It's not as though I have many other options if I want someone to be my date for Cassie's wedding. If he and I did go, I'd definitely make it clear that we are only in this until after Elaine's wedding, though. I don't need a repeat of the dumping scene.

Cassie doesn't respond to my comment about the coffee coupon because the phone rings. She'd already agreed not to answer it, but I can see her hand almost twitching to do so. We've had a hard time with the telephone this week.

"You've got to tell your aunt about the job eventually," Cassie says.

For the past week, I've managed to just leave messages on Aunt Inga's telephone. Every time she's called I've returned the call when I've known she

wouldn't be home and left a message for her. Neither
Cassie nor I have answered the phone since we got
back from Palm Springs. The good thing is that,
because of the messages I leave her, it looks as if I'm
trying to talk to Aunt Inga even if I'm actually carefully avoiding her. I've called her when I knew she was
at choir rehearsal and when she had a dental appointment. Today is a bad day, though. She normally
wouldn't be going anywhere today and I don't want
her to worry that something has happened to me.

"You can't avoid talking to her forever," Cassie
says.

"I don't even know if the mortuary job will last very
long," I say in my own defense. I've thought about this.
"There's no point in upsetting the aunts for something
that might just be a funny memory by the end of the
month. They might never need to know."

I hear Aunt Inga's voice come in on the message
machine. "Julie, Julie, are you there? It's Aunt Inga. I
need to talk to you. Call me when you get a chance."

In my messages, I've told Aunt Inga about the beautiful old church and the cousin of a movie star who came
by the other day. He was Very Good-Looking, by the
way. Miss Billings swore the man looked like a young
Cary Grant. He was a safe topic for a message to Aunt
Inga. I have carefully avoided any mention of either
brides or dead people in the chatty messages I've left for
her. Architecture and visitors I considered safe. I mentioned the roses and the courtyard. I didn't lie, I just
didn't tell Aunt Inga every little bit of the whole truth.

Cassie frowns. "You're going to have to tell your
aunt what you're doing pretty soon."

"I know."

I must admit it is not as bad as I thought it would be working at the Big M. I mean there are no ghosts walking around and you smell roses all day long. Plus, it seems noble somehow to help people arrange the way they want to pay their respects to the dead—or the "dearly departed" as we are taught to say.

I got my black suit late last week and have actually been talking with the bereaved. I have done pretty well, except I got confused at first. Instead of "dearly departed," I said "dearly beloved" a lot. But no one seemed to mind and now I've got it down. I bet I'm going to say *dearly* more often at the Big M than I would if I were a wedding planner. As I said, I kind of like it there.

Of course, even if I actually have to tell my aunts that I work in a mortuary, I could never tell them that I've come to like my job with the dead. That's even worse than having the job in the first place.

Besides, I'm not giving up my dream of being a wedding planner. I'm carefully keeping track of the things I do at the Big M so that when I do apply for a wedding job, I'll be able to say I helped place the flowers where the family wanted them and coordinated the guest seating or arranged the receiving line.

It's amazing how much the two jobs are the same— you have the processionals, the tears, the flowers, the special music. Substitute bridesmaids for pallbearers and you have it made. If I keep seeing my job at the Big M as a stepping-stone to my real future as a wedding planner, that helps me keep things in focus.

"I thought your aunt sounded a little stressed in the

last message," Cassie says. "Maybe you should just call and be sure she's okay."

"You don't think something's wrong?" I stand up and am already walking toward the phone. I never thought that something might be wrong with Aunt Inga. I was just worried that she'd be worried about me. I mean, I'm in Hollywood and she's in Blythe. Nothing ever happens in Blythe. Unless… "Maybe that dentist appointment I remembered was really a doctor's appointment."

Cassie is frowning now, too. "I don't think—"

"For all I know Aunt Inga could be dying," I say. I know it sounds melodramatic to think that she's dying, but one thing I've learned during this past week is that people do die. All kinds of people die. And, in too many cases, the people next to them don't even suspect the person is going to die. That's one of the reasons everyone has so many regrets.

I'm dialing the phone and trying to remember the types of pills that Aunt Inga is taking.

"What did the doctor say?" I ask Aunt Inga the minute she says "hello."

"Julie? Is that you?"

The relief in my aunt's voice makes me wish I'd called her back sooner. "I'm here now. I can come home anytime you need me. Remember that. I can quit my job in a heartbeat."

"But you can't quit your job," Aunt Inga protests. "What would we do then?"

"Well, I'd only quit if you were sick."

"Who's sick? Nobody around here has time to be sick. Not since we got the bad news."

I knew there was a problem here somewhere. I brace myself. "What bad news?"

"I guess it's not so terribly bad," Aunt Inga continues. "I mean Aunt Gladys has her boys folding some origami flowers to be scattered on the bridal tables. I'm crocheting some of those roses to be used for petals in the aisle if we need them—I was going to do pink, but Elaine wants orange so I'm doing orange."

"You're crocheting roses and the boys are folding origami flowers? The boys—my cousins?" I can't picture my cousins doing that. They all played football in high school. All of them. And they won. They're built like tanks.

"Well, I think Jerry might be out trying to buy a hundred orange taper candles at the moment so he's not folding right now. Do you have any idea how hard it is to find orange taper candles?"

"I can imagine."

"I'm worried your uncle Howard is going to have a stroke. He's been staying in his room and he won't come out. I haven't seen him for two days."

I know Elaine's wedding is going to be elaborate, but I can't understand why everyone in the family is in such a panic. "I thought that's why Aunt Ruth hired a professional wedding planner—I thought the planner would do all of these things so no one else would have to worry about them."

Aunt Inga is silent. "It seems the wedding planner was—well, I always thought Ruth got recommendations, but…"

Aunt Inga is silent again.

"Did the wedding planner quit?"

"I don't think you'd call it that exactly, but she's definitely gone."

I'm beginning to feel a hot ball of something in my stomach. I'm a little glad that, for once, everything isn't going smoothly for Elaine. But I'm also a little worried about Aunt Inga and my cousins and even, to be honest, Aunt Ruth and Elaine. Worrying about them makes me feel a little disloyal to my mother, but I figure it's only a short-term worry. And, really, I don't need to worry too much. "Even if the wedding planner is gone, I know she already made all of these plans. She got everything lined up—the church and the caterer and the band for the reception. Elaine told me how much each one of those things costs so I know the woman got those things arranged at least. Even if she left before every little thing was done, you can hire someone else to just follow her plans. It might not go as smoothly as it would have with the original wedding planner, but no one needs to be crocheting flowers."

Aunt Inga takes a deep breath. I can hear her inhale over the phone. Then she lets it out. "The crocheting is just to keep me busy so I won't worry. I just feel like I should be doing something and I don't know what else to do."

"Well, what you shouldn't do is worry. Nothing good comes from worrying."

"How can I not worry? You see, the wedding planner made the deposits for everything and showed Ruth the receipts. The invitations were all printed with the church on them and everything. Who knew the wedding planner could cancel all of the deposits last week and get the money back in checks? She forged

Aunt Ruth's signature and cashed them. By now, she's gone off to who knows where? Some island probably."

"What?"

"Nineteen thousand dollars and she took it all with her so I'm sure she can afford a trip to some island. Ruth has been lying down with a cold washcloth on her head ever since it happened. Of course, she's in the living room, because Howard locked himself in the bedroom and won't let anyone else come in. I don't think he knew how much Ruth had already spent on the wedding."

Uncle Howard wasn't alone in that. Nineteen thousand dollars. Wow. I knew from the bragging Elaine had done that the wedding was going to be expensive, but Elaine could buy a car with that. Of course, Uncle Howard had bought her a new car last Christmas so I guess she doesn't need a car like I do, but still that's a lot of money.

I swallow. "Well, I'm sure the police will find the wedding planner and get the money back."

"Even if we got the money back today, there's no place for the wedding now. The date that we had reserved at that beautiful church has already been given away and the wedding coordinator at the church refused to tell the other people that Ruth had booked there first. The coordinator said she was following policy and the other people had been on a waiting list and they won't budge. So, there's no church in Palm Springs for a wedding until next March. Gary lined up his internship this past week. He can't put off marrying Elaine until March."

Okay, so now that red ball of emotions is really jumping around. I mean, I hope Elaine gets to have her big day; it's just nice to know that no one's going to be scrutinizing me on that day and wondering why I'm not following in Elaine's rose-strewn path.

"There's the church in Blythe," I say. I know Aunt Ruth would consider that a step-down, but it's not a bad church. Granted, it's a little old and the carpet needs replacing, but every church can't be a showplace.

"Remember that remodeling project the church was raising money for?" Aunt Inga asks.

"All the bake sales?"

"That's the one. It's happening now. The church is all torn up inside. We aren't even meeting there for regular church services now."

I can afford to be generous. "Well, I'm sure Elaine will find someplace nice for her wedding."

Aunt Inga is silent a little longer this time. "I told everyone about the chapel where you work. How the ivy grows up the walls and there are roses all around and that the movie stars come there. Elaine even stopped crying at the mention of movie stars."

"Oh, but my chapel isn't—I mean—Elaine wouldn't want to have her wedding at the place where I work."

"She's desperate."

Not as desperate as I am about now. "Can't she have it in the place where your church is meeting while the remodeling is going on? I know you must be meeting somewhere."

"We're using the school gym on Sunday mornings before the basketball team has their practice."

"Oh."

I don't have the nerve to suggest it, but apparently Aunt Inga thought of it anyway because she continues, "The coach said there is a basketball clinic during Thanksgiving weekend so there's no time for a wedding. Especially not on the Friday evening after Thanksgiving."

I take a deep breath. This can't be happening. "But I'm new at my job. The boss won't just let me use the place. Besides, it's probably already booked."

"You could ask...."

The red ball in my stomach is sinking like a hundred-pound bowling ball. I am forever in Aunt Inga's debt. Not that she's ever asked me for much in return for supporting me since I was five years old.

"I'm pretty sure it won't work..." I swallow. That red ball is sitting like lead in my stomach. "Of course, I'll ask but I don't think—"

"Just asking is the important thing," Aunt Inga says with the kind of confidence that lets me know that she has no doubt it will all work out. "Elaine is wondering if you have one of those Elvis impersonators at your chapel."

"Tell her we don't have any impersonators."

"But you must have people who sing at your place."

"Sure, there are some vocalists that we use, but they're mostly—ah—slower than Elvis. They do a lot of hymns." I don't mention that Mr. Strett, the male vocalist at the Big M, got a little tipsy at the last funeral he worked and was even slower than usual as he sang about gathering at the river.

"Most of the people who use your place must be older then."

"That's right," I say in relief. "I really think Elaine would like someplace else better."

"Elaine says the gym smells like dirty socks."

"Well, of course, not the gym, but there must be someplace else she could use. How about the hotel where they had the engagement party? Elaine could have a small wedding there. I thought the place was very nice."

"They told Ruth she was never to come to their place again," Aunt Inga says indignantly. "Not even for lunch."

"Oh."

"I think some of their staff quit after the party we had there. They said Ruth made them wax the floor and then she complained that it was too slippery."

"There have to be other hotels in Palm Springs," I say. "That one isn't the only nice place there."

Aunt Inga is silent. "I think the hotel people all talk to each other."

"Oh."

"No one said yes we could come," Aunt Inga says. "All because of that wax on the floor. And maybe the problem with the punch cups. Or maybe the stuffed mushrooms Ruth sent back to the kitchen. I can't believe they would make such a fuss over a few little things. Every mother wants her daughter's engagement party to be perfect."

"Wow." This can't be good. Not even I mess up that badly. I never thought Aunt Ruth and I would have anything in common. "Everyone said no?"

"I'm going to pray for your boss, what's his name?" Aunt Inga asks me a question instead of answering my question. Although, I guess there's no need to answer my question. It's all too obvious.

"We call him Mr. Z," I say.

Cassie has been sitting on the floor and watching me. She has looked a little puzzled for a while. Probably because of the Elvis reference. Once I mention Mr. Z though, she smiles encouragingly. She thinks I'm going to tell Aunt Inga about where I work. But I can't tell Aunt Inga, not now.

"What kind of name is Mr. Z?" Aunt Inga asks. "He's not a movie star, is he? Elaine would really like it if a movie star came to her wedding. Maybe it would make up for some of these last minute problems."

"No, Mr. Z is not a movie star. It's just a nickname."

"Oh." Aunt Inga brightens anyway. "Well, a man with a funny nickname must be a nice man even if he's not in the movies."

"He's very nice."

"And you promise you'll ask?"

"I promise."

"Tomorrow?"

"Tomorrow."

"Good," Aunt Inga says with satisfaction in her voice. "I told Ruth we would work everything out. The family's counting on you."

Only I know how much Aunt Ruth must hate asking me for help. Well, I guess my mother would know, too. And her mother before her.

Suddenly, I realize Aunt Inga said we'll work it out. That word *we* covers a lot of territory. "Did Aunt Ruth say she wanted my help?"

"She needs your help," Aunt Inga says. "It doesn't matter what she says."

It matters to me. "Unless she asks me, I don't think I should be getting into her business."

"This is family business," Aunt Inga says. "We're all family."

Aunt Inga never knew all of the times Elaine called me her half cousin when we were growing up. Even then I knew Aunt Inga felt pulled apart with her love for me and my mother on one side and her love for her own family on the other. No one should ever have half families. Sometimes I think even a stepfamily has it easier. At least with a step, you're going forward. With a half, you're coming apart.

"I'll call when I know anything," I finally just say. It is pointless to upset Aunt Inga by refusing to ask Mr. Z when I already know the answer has to be no.

I can see Cassie is puzzled. Either that or she's looking worried because I'm probably turning a little green.

"Well, I better get back to my crocheting," Aunt Inga says. "How many petals do you need for the aisle anyway? I have sixty-four."

"That sounds like plenty," I say. "Don't strain your eyes with all that crocheting."

"I won't. You're sure you'll call tomorrow?"

"I'll call."

I stand still and just hold the receiver in my hand after Aunt Inga has hung up.

"Are you okay?" Cassie asks.

"I'm doomed."

Cassie is worried about me so I tell her about the conversation I just had with Aunt Inga.

"Of course, Elaine's wedding is planned for Thanksgiving weekend so there's probably already a funeral booked," Cassie says to be comforting.

"There will be a funeral," I agree. "It's eleven days

away yet so the person is probably not even dead at this point, but someone will want to be buried then."

Surely someone will die a week or so from now. That's one of the challenging things about the funeral business. No one plans too far ahead. Although Mr. Z does have a prepaid plan that is popular with people, no one actually schedules their funeral in advance like couples do who are planning a wedding. Actually, if the Big M were a wedding chapel, it would probably not even have an open date for Elaine's wedding. I'm surprised Aunt Ruth didn't think of that. I guess Aunt Ruth is too desperate to think. She's probably still hoping that one of those Palm Springs hotels will decide she's not so bad to deal with after all.

"Maybe you should call Doug," Cassie says.

"He won't know if there will be a funeral in eleven days," I say in surprise.

"No, but he sounded like he was under a lot of stress when I talked to him," Cassie said. "I know he's young, but stress isn't good for anyone."

I'm sure Cassie was thinking about the man I talked to at the Big M this morning. His name was Robert Cameron and he said almost those same words about his brother, James, who had died unexpectedly. The two brothers hadn't talked to each other for three years because they'd had an argument over their mother's will.

Robert shook his head as we talked about what he wanted for the final viewing arrangements for James. Robert kept talking about their argument as if he couldn't let go of it. He said that, if he had known the stress his brother was under because of problems with his business, he would have given James every single dime of both of their shares of the estate just to ease his troubles. Robert said he'd rather have his brother around than all of the money in the world. He didn't know why they had been fighting so long about it all anyway. They'd wasted some of their best years together.

"I'll call Doug in the morning," I say. I don't tell Cassie, but I'll even apologize to him just to show him how civilized I can be. "And I'll do what Aunt Inga wants and ask Mr. Z about using the mortuary."

All of this worrying about people dying is getting to me.

"The mortuary is a beautiful place," Cassie says. "With all those roses, the courtyard would be a lovely place to get married."

"It's an even better place to have a funeral. It's probably not booked now, but Mr. Z knows it will be booked so he'll say it will be busy that weekend."

"But what will Elaine do?" Cassie is worrying the way she does over people, even Elaine.

"I don't know. There's got to be a big hotel or something around here. And, if not that, we can try parks. People have had beautiful weddings in parks and there have to be dozens of parks in Los Angeles."

"Would they let her put up a tent or something?" Cassie asks.

I sigh. "Probably not. And I can't see Elaine doing a picnic-style wedding where all of the guests sit on the ground behind some trees. For one thing, she wouldn't have an aisle."

"Oh, she has to have an aisle. The most important

part of the place where you get married is the aisle. You have to be able to walk down an aisle so you can be given away by your parents."

Cassie is starting to look as though she might cry. I know it's not about Elaine's wedding anymore.

"I bet your mom didn't want to give you away when you were born," I say because I know where Cassie's thoughts are going. I remember all those times we played wedding years ago.

"If my mom hadn't wanted to give me away, wouldn't she have already registered with those adoption places?"

"I don't know. Maybe she doesn't know about them." I know it's not much comfort.

Cassie and I sit there for a while in the quiet of her apartment. This is one reason Cassie and I are so close. We both know the aches of each other's hearts so well we can just sit together with our feelings. I wished I could give Cassie some encouragement, but I've wondered, too, why her mother wasn't registered at any of the agencies. I wonder sometimes if her mother is dead, but I've never said anything to Cassie. That would crush all of her hope. At least I know where my mother is even if it has been weeks since we've talked on the phone.

I scoot a little closer to Cassie and pick up the bag of dirt she's been using. "That begonia plant you brought home needs pruning."

We spend the rest of the evening taking care of Cassie's plants.

Chapter Five

I call Doug on my cell phone while I am taking the bus to work on Tuesday. I know Doug likes to get into the hospital early so he can eat breakfast in the cafeteria before his 10:00 shift begins for the day. He told me that much on our drive to Palm Springs for Elaine's party.

I hear the call go through and then a voice answers, "Doug here."

Okay. The sun is shining into the bus windows so brightly that I squint. The bus must have gone through a car wash of some kind recently because usually the coat of dirt on the windows keeps the sun from bothering my eyes. "Hi. This is Julie—Julie White."

"Hey, how's it going?"

Doug's voice isn't warm, but it's not cold, either. It sounds restrained. I try not to think about what that might mean.

"Good. I'm good." I'm sitting on the backseat of this Metro bus and there aren't a lot of other people around me. My work hours start a little later than those of most commuters so the big crush of workers has already been bussed to wherever they need to be. Still I look around to be sure I have some privacy for my apology. There's a girl two seats ahead of me, but she has headphones on so she can't hear me.

I decide to dive in. "Yeah, well, I'm calling about the other day at my cousin's party last week. I wanted to say I'm—"

"I'm sorry," he interrupts. He pauses for a second and I wonder if we've lost the connection. "I didn't realize what I was doing when I left that party until Cassie explained it."

He actually sounds sincere.

"What did Cassie say exactly?"

"Nothing that I shouldn't have figured out if I'd been thinking. I hadn't realized that you had been raised by your aunt."

"That's not a big deal." I don't like people knowing my mother left me so I don't go around announcing the fact that my aunt Inga had to raise me instead. Still, it's nothing for Doug to worry about.

"It *is* a big deal," Doug says. "I know. I was raised by my aunts, too, so I know something about how that feels. It's always made me a little touchy about things like family get-togethers."

"Oh." I'm not so sure I want to share the same problem with Doug. It's not so easy to be angry with someone if you share even one trouble with them.

"I know your situation was different because you got to stay with just one of your aunts," he says.

I'm glad he realizes we didn't really have the same problem. "My aunt Inga is great."

"That's what Cassie said. I rotated between three of my aunts."

Wow, I had never thought about it, but that is what could have happened to me. There was nothing that required Aunt Inga to keep me full-time. She could have asked Aunt Ruth to take me part of the year and Aunt Gladys to take me the other part. I wouldn't have known where I was living if that had happened. Besides, I would have felt torn apart. The only thing I know of that the aunts would have all agreed on was that it was such a shame my mother was wasting her life and neglecting her duty to me. Imagine hearing that from three different households, two of which viewed you as only halfway part of their family.

"So maybe you can understand why I didn't do so good talking to your aunt," Doug says. "I was telling her the truth when I said I had a thing about commitments. Even the word makes me uptight. And all those relatives there."

My mind has already left the problems of Elaine's party. Now that I know our problems weren't completely the same, I am starting to feel a little compassion for Doug. "Where did you even keep your clothes? With all that moving around?"

I know from my own experience how important clothes and stuff are when you're going to school.

"I usually just kept my suitcase packed."

"Wow." I guess I can see why he'd have a commitment problem. "But shouldn't all of that moving around have made you the reverse? Shouldn't you want to be committed to someone? I mean not me. But someone with a closet."

"You would think so." Doug chuckles. "I think I'm a little all over the place with it, but I'm working on it. And, just so you know, I'm grateful the aunts took me in when my parents died. I don't know where else I would have gone."

"I know the gratitude, too," I say. Those of us who are raised by relatives are the almost lost ones. We owe so much to those who took us in when they didn't have to do anything. "And the guilt."

"Yeah," Doug says.

I can't help but put myself in Doug's place. What would I have done if none of the aunts had wanted me? My aunt Inga never made me feel unwelcome, but I was always aware that I might be holding up her life in some way. Aunt Inga was still young when she took me in. I wondered if she would have gone and done something different than work for Aunt Ruth if she didn't have me to worry over. I owe Aunt Inga big-time for all she did for me. And I wasn't even part of her family, not in the way Elaine and the other cousins were.

Most people would agree a mother or father is required to take care of their child; an aunt really doesn't need to care for a niece or nephew. And, in my case, I'm a half niece, so there was even less obligation. I have always wanted Aunt Inga to see me at my best just so she knows she didn't waste her time for all those years.

"It must have been tough to lose both of your parents," I say to Doug. I am feeling it's okay if we have some bond between us after all, so I tell him a little of my story. "My dad died, but my mother just moved to Las Vegas and left me with Aunt Inga."

"That had to be hard, too," Doug says. "It took me a long time to get over feeling bad because I was an orphan. As long as I had the aunts, though, I had somebody."

"Yeah." I know what he means, but I don't want him to think I'm too pathetic so I add, "My mother would have taken me to live with her if she had room for me in Vegas."

"If my parents had lived, I would have stayed in a closet just to be with them. So you're lucky. You get to see your mother. At least, I assume you do."

"Yeah, I do." I haven't felt lucky about that for a long time.

"Anyway, I have been looking at myself in the mirror lately and wishing I was a better person," Doug says. "I might have issues, but that's no reason to let other people down. That goes double for last week. I shouldn't have split on you like I did. I'm really very sorry."

Okay, so I guess I have to forgive him. That doesn't mean I'm going all gooey over him or anything, it just means that fair is fair. He spilled his problems and we talked. He apologized. It's time for me to accept his apology—almost.

"Yeah, well, I just want to say I would never pressure some guy to have a relationship with me." I want to get this into the conversation before Doug apologizes for everything under the sun. "I know I needed a date. But I never thought that meant anything more than that you were doing me a favor. That's all."

"Like I've said, it didn't turn out to be much of a favor."

"Just so you know that I know there's no commitment involved. We're both commitment free."

I'm trying to be as clear here as possible.

"It's not that kind of commitment that was giving me a problem," he says and his voice is soft. "If I'd thought about it for two seconds, I would have known it's the look-at-my-life kind of commitment that's bothering me. That's what's been bothering me for months. I think that's why your aunt pushed my buttons so easy. Not that it's her fault. She seems like a nice lady."

"I haven't heard many people call Aunt Ruth nice. Effective maybe. Nice no."

Doug laughs. "She just comes on a little strong. She reminds me of one of my aunts. I think I could handle her okay next time."

Well, that sounds promising. I don't want to rush in and ask if he'll be my date for the rehearsal dinner and wedding yet, but it is promising. "One good thing about Aunt Ruth is that she always puts out wonderful food at her parties. She never skimps on what she serves. Did you get some of those crab-stuffed mushrooms before you left?"

"I'm afraid I just left when I left."

I don't know why, but it makes me feel better to know that Doug didn't make a stop at the buffet table on his way out of Elaine's party. I would rather be left standing because of honest issues instead of a craving for crab appetizers. "I hear Aunt Ruth is planning prime rib and lobster for the rehearsal dinner."

I'm being optimistic here and assuming there'll be a place to have the rehearsal dinner. Finding a place for a sit-down catered dinner won't be easy, but I'm sure Aunt Ruth will find it.

Doug whistles. "Prime rib and lobster. If you need a date for that one, I'm your man. That is, if you still want me to go with you after the last time. I promise I won't get cold feet. I mean, if you need a date—I wasn't sure after Cassie talked to me later if you needed a date or not."

The tension in my shoulders eases. "Oh, I need one. And thanks. I don't know where the dinner will be yet, but I appreciate the offer."

"No problem. In fact, I need someone to go someplace with me and I thought of you so I'm really glad you called," Doug says.

"Turnabout is fair play. I'll even put up with your Aunt Ruth—the one who you mentioned." Now see, this is how it should be between Doug and me. We can both help each other out, especially now that we have the aunt thing between us. I know being raised by an aunt has left me a little insecure and I'm thinking Doug has had the same feelings, especially if he went from house to house trailing a suitcase behind him. At least I had the same closet for all those years.

"My aunt lives in Texas now so it's not about her, but you might not want to do this anyway," he says.

There's enough hesitancy in his voice to make me stop and think. Okay, so what could it be? Something south of the border? Visiting really sick people who are contagious?

The bus I am on has just pulled into a stop and is letting a couple of teenagers off. My stop will be here soon.

"Is it legal?" I finally ask. "I don't do nonlegal."

"Me, neither. This is a little strange, but definitely legal."

I can hear some bus noises on his side of the conversation so I give up my theory that he is driving himself to work. He's bussing it the same way I am, which makes me like him even better. I always like people who don't put on airs and it's hard to put on airs on a Hollywood Metro bus. Especially because, if you did, people would just think you were practicing a movie role so it wouldn't really do you any good since they would already know that you're not one of the big stars since you're riding the bus and no one even recognizes you.

"I don't have to dig a pit and cook a stuffed pig or anything like that, do I?" I ask. "I'm not a very good cook."

"No, nothing like that."

"Well, then, if I don't have to dig any pits and there's no Aunt Ruth, how bad can it be?"

Doug pauses and then he almost whispers. "I need someone to go back to that rally with me."

I can picture him looking around the bus to make sure no one is listening to him, just as I'm looking now before I talk. "You mean that Billy Graham thing?"

"Well, Billy Graham is not the guy speaking, but yeah, my aunt said it's like a Billy Graham thing."

Doug's voice slowly got back to normal.

"Your aunt's going? The one who went with you before?" I ask more as a stalling thing than because I have any reason to ask. Of course, his aunt is going if Doug is going. She's probably the reason he's going. Doug probably feels the same need I have to make his own aunt glad she'd spent the effort to help raise him rather than let him go into some foster home. Maybe he even gets extra credit if he drags someone else along with him.

"No, she's gone back to San Diego. She doesn't know I'm going to the place again."

I notice the girl in front of me has removed her earphones so I lower my voice. "Isn't the reason for going to make your aunt happy? You'll get extra points if she actually sees you there and doesn't just hear you say that you've gone."

I've got to admit the thought of going with Doug to some religious rally makes me wish it was something involving a stuffed pig instead. Doug may be comfortable at some rally, but I would not be. I've gone many times to the same church in Blythe, but God and I have an understanding in that place. I leave Him alone and He leaves me alone. I don't know what He would think if I showed up at a rally in the Hollywood Bowl. That's a little—well, public—don't you think?

Doug says, "I'm not going there to get points with my aunt."

Okay, so now he's really making me nervous.

"Well, I don't think you need a date for a rally," I say, mentally inching myself away from the invitation. "Not if it's anything like church."

"I don't know if it's like church. I've never been to church."

"Well, trust me, I've gone to church tons of times and you don't need a date for the rally."

"Maybe not, but I need a friend."

"Oh." I don't know what to say to that so I clear my throat.

He keeps talking. "It's tonight. I was going to call you later today. I didn't want to ask too far ahead of time because I didn't want you to worry about going."

"I'm not worried."

"Good. I thought you might be a little afraid to go to something like that. Some people are."

"I'm not afraid. Well, maybe a little. But not like walking into a deserted house in the dark scared."

I hope I'm telling Doug the truth on this one. I tell myself I'm not afraid really. I might be very, very nervous. But that's different, isn't it?

"So you'll go?" Doug says. "I could meet up with you at the coffee shop after work and we could have something to eat before the rally."

I take a deep breath and remind myself that he is the only date I am likely to get for Elaine's wedding. "Sure, that works."

The deep breath helps. Either that or it completely rattles my brain because it suddenly occurs to me that going to that rally might be just the thing I need to do. Unlike Doug, I'd be willing to use this one for aunt approval. Maybe Aunt Inga will be so pleased with me for going to something like that on my own that she won't be quite so disappointed when I tell her that we have to look for another location for Elaine's wedding.

"Is this like an anthropology interest—this going back to the rally again?" I say to Doug. If I can understand why he's going, I might be better with it all. "Do you want me to take pictures? Do they have any strange rituals they do?"

I am not saying that some people wouldn't go to a rally like this just because they wanted to go. But those are mostly people who go to church all the time. Doug doesn't have anything to do with a church.

"Well," he says, "they pass around a big basket and people put money in it. That's kind of primitive, I suppose. I was surprised there were no debit cards or anything. Just checks and cash. I even saw a hundred-dollar bill."

"You do know you can't reach in and take money out when the basket comes by," I say. "That's why they always have big guys passing the basket around. They keep watch over it."

"I know the rules. I know you can't take money out of the basket."

"Good, because the passing-for-money thing is something all churches do."

We're both quiet a minute before Doug talks again. "I just seem to keep thinking about what the guy said. I can't get it all out of my head. Finally, I decided the only thing to do is to go back and make sure I heard him right."

"So, it's sort of a fact-finding thing?"

Doug nods. "Yeah, you could say that."

"I'll take notes for you then." This could work. I'd willingly take notes at a dozen rallies to have a date for Elaine's wedding. Besides, Doug has already met the family so Aunt Ruth won't surprise him again. Plus, there's something to be said for continuity when it comes to fake boyfriends. It makes them more believable in the part.

"Notes are good. That way I can just listen," Doug says.

"Well, then I'll see you after work at the coffee shop."

The bus is pulling to a stop again and this one is mine. After Doug says goodbye, I stand up to get off.

I wait until I am out of the bus to put my cell phone back in its holder and I see that I got a message while I was talking to Doug. I press the button and hear Aunt Inga's voice reminding me that she will be praying all morning that Mr. Z will answer our prayers.

I don't like to think of Aunt Inga praying all morning about anything. It is too stressful. So I call her back. Aunt Inga doesn't answer so I leave a message on her machine telling her I haven't spoke to Mr. Z yet but that I'm going to a Billy Graham kind of a rally tonight. I also mention that if we can't use the chapel at where I work, there are a lot of places to get married. People even have weddings at the beach, I say. Or parks. There are a lot of public parks. I want to prepare her for the disappointment I know is coming.

I'm wearing my usual black suit to the Big M—the suit Mr. Z had made for me—so it's no surprise that no one pays any attention to me when I walk away from the bus step. To attract attention in Hollywood you have to be wearing a nail through your head or snakeskin pants with the snake's fangs dangling from your back pocket. You see some of the weirdest people on the streets around here. I've got to admit though that I like the place.

You would understand why I like it around here if you had spent your whole life in a place like Blythe where nothing strange ever happens. Well, except for the time that my cousin Jerry drank so much grape juice that his eyeballs started turning blue, but that's another story. The aunts said it couldn't happen, but we cousins saw it and we remain convinced to this day. I'm always careful not to drink too much grape juice.

You know, I wonder why none of the other cousins have moved into the Los Angeles area. I think Jerry would be a natural for Hollywood. I guess he's not so adventurous anymore. He has a job as a car mechanic and he seems happy enough to stay in Blythe with all of his brothers and turn wheelies in the grocery store parking lots after dark on the weekends.

I stop to look at the Big M when I am halfway up the walk to the front door. I always stop about here and just look at the building. I like the roughness of the stone exterior. After a cold night, there's a look of dampness to the stone that makes me think of drawbridges and castles and the English moors. I suppose it was all those historical romances I read in high school. I used to love those dark, brooding heroes that walked around in the fog and frowned at anyone who came too close.

Today I take a minute to admire the stone and breathe in the slight scent of the roses that are just inside the courtyard. The chapel is built in a French Gothic style. Miss Billings told me that the place was made out of native California stone in 1915 and was a regular church for many years before Mr. Z bought it in the 1980s and turned it into a mortuary.

I get asked about the building a lot when I'm working there so I've learned a few dates. It has taken me a while to figure out why I like the place so much. I finally decided it is because the whole building looks as though it's reaching for the sky. There is a thin steeple that shoots out from the top, but it's more than that. The whole building has got to be over a hundred feet tall and the arches all come to points that lead up to that steeple. Inside—you can't see it from here—there is a long, narrow stained glass window showing Jesus holding a lamb in one arm and a shepherd's crook in the other.

If you sit on the pews in the chapel, your eyes are automatically drawn to that stained glass figure. I didn't notice when I first saw it that the lamb is sleeping, but now my eyes always come to rest on the peaceful face of the lamb. It's not a very exciting stained glass window, but I'm sure it gives much comfort to the bereaved. It comforts me.

Somehow, though, I can't see Elaine standing under that lamb and saying her "I do's" to her dentist. If Aunt Ruth has a problem with glass cups being too common, she would be real unhappy with a farm animal staring down at Elaine's nuptials.

I feel a sudden urge to protect that lamb from Aunt Ruth's disdain. If Elaine were to get married in this chapel, would Aunt Ruth demand more important artwork? Maybe she'd drape the stained glass window with some orange silk material. It can be done. Mr. Z has a drape that he uses to go over the stained glass picture if the bereaved request it. Of course, that drape is in black, but Aunt Ruth could add some ribbons or something to make it more bridal.

The Big M makes the lamb the focal part of some funerals, especially if there are children in the family of the bereaved. Miss Billings has a box of stuffed toy lambs that she will give to children to hug during the services, too. Once I asked her about the lambs and she reminded me that the Big M is in Hollywood and people expect a few extra touches. She's right, you know. From what I've seen, people do feel their funerals can be more unusual here.

Now that I am inside, I wait for my eyes to adjust to the dimmer light.

The front doors of the chapel are made out of a dark heavy wood, but the inner doors leading to the sanctuary are covered with Italian leather that has mellowed over the years. The leather has been nailed to the thick doors with old brass upholstery tacks. There are brass sconces along the wall of the foyer that are fitted with low-watt electrical bulbs so that they almost look like candles in the dark. The whole foyer makes me think of medieval monks.

I shake my head. Monks and lambs are definitely not Elaine's style.

Then I remember the roses. What bride wouldn't like roses?

The roses in the courtyard are a little scraggly since they're dormant this time of year. Miss Billings says they need to be cut back for winter, but she doesn't do them all at once. It's warm enough in Southern California so that Miss Billings finds a way to have a few roses present no matter what time of year it is.

Mr. Z has left this area just as it was when he bought it—except for some repairs. The business part of the mortuary is all behind a newer door that leads off the left of the foyer.

Before I go through the new door, I push open the doors to the chapel and stand a minute. The arches inside the main part of the chapel all reach up to a series of crown-shaped stones. The curved ceiling inside the sweep of the arches is painted a dark, muted blue. It could almost be the sky.

For a second, I think to myself that it really is a pity that Elaine's wedding couldn't be held here. I shake myself so I don't go soft. I should know better. Quite apart from the lamb, the chapel is too unique for Elaine. She'd rather have the guests talking about her dress than the church and, with this church, that wouldn't be likely to happen.

The budding wedding planner in me thinks it's a shame, though. Elaine's dress would certainly do the church justice. Aunt Ruth ordered some designer dress from a shop in Palm Springs and it is being shipped in from Paris. That's Paris, France. It has probably already arrived. I haven't seen the drawings of it, but Aunt Inga says it will be spectacular.

Miss Billings is on the phone when I go into the main part of the mortuary so I walk over to the room where I check the board Mr. Z keeps up. Sure enough, he has scheduled me in the right column with the employees working today and not with the deceased who are having their viewing today. Actually, there is no one in the viewing column today. I think I'm a little superstitious about his columns, but I feel relieved every day when I find out I'm listed in the correct one.

If someone had told me a month ago that I would be worrying about what day I'd be scheduled for my final viewing, I would have laughed at them. I didn't even know what a final viewing was. Now, look at me.

I take a moment to see what is in the bins to be filed

so I will know how many new folders to get from the supply room. I'm still in charge of filing forms even though I am a customer service rep, as well. I actually like both of these jobs so I'm not in any hurry to be promoted out of the filing part of my job.

I check my hair in the mirror that's on the wall by the microwave. I'm even getting used to the black suit. I generally wear some silver jewelry with it, but I've come to like the plainness of working in a black suit. I've changed my mind from the pink suit and I'm already pretty sure I'll wear a dark suit like the one I work in at the Big M when it's time for my final viewing. Death is one time when a person wants to be dignified and there is something reassuring about a solid black suit. I think it comforts those who are left behind.

Besides, too many people use clothes to define themselves. When I worked at the bank in Blythe, I would spend the first fifteen minutes of every day checking out what everyone else was wearing just as they were looking at what I was wearing. At this job, no one notices. We're all wearing the same kind of thing. There's a strange way in which that lets us truly be ourselves. We know each other by our personalities, not our wardrobes.

I wish I had known more about clothes when I was growing up in Elaine's hand-me-downs. I let those clothes define me and they were really just pieces of fabric on my back. I have wondered in the past day or two if Elaine had as hard a time with the hand-me-downs as I did. Maybe she felt as though her identity was being ripped off her back and handed to me with each blouse her mother gave Aunt Inga.

I've never really thought about things from Elaine's point of view much before. Maybe we both should have worn the equivalent of black suits and been done with it. I smile just thinking of Elaine in a plain black suit, but the smile doesn't have the sting it would have a week ago. It's funny how much a person can learn about living when they hang around dead people. If I keep working here, the day may even come when Elaine doesn't bug me so much. Maybe she even had some reason for seeing me as her half cousin instead of her cousin.

Miss Billings is off the phone when I come back into the reception area. There is a huge potted orchid on the coffee table in front of the sofa where visitors sit. Sometimes there are flowers leftover from funerals and they are placed in the reception area so the whole building often smells of flowers.

"Hey, good morning," I say. I've come to like Miss Billings. I'm not quite ready to take her up on her offer to show me how to apply makeup to the deceased, but I do really like her. I might even ask her to give me some makeup tips for me to use while I'm alive.

Miss Billings looks at me as if she's got a secret she can't wait to tell me.

"We've got one in Room B," she finally says to me in a hushed voice when I've walked over to her desk.

I look over my shoulder and down the hall to the various rooms we have. "A viewing?"

As I said earlier, I didn't see any morning viewings on the scheduling board. That is the first thing I check because we're all supposed to know how to direct any visitors to the correct viewing room. Maybe there's some separate list Mr. Z keeps, though, that I haven't learned about yet.

Miss Billings shakes her head. "No, it's a movie star—that new young doctor on the emergency room show. What's its name? It comes on late on Thursday nights. Anyway, he's in Room B."

"Isn't Room B where Mrs. Malote is going to be?" When I went through the files a few minutes ago I noticed the file on Mrs. Malote particularly because she was only thirty-seven. That's too young to die and I read a little about her in the notes. "She's not ready for her final viewing."

"The man's not here for the viewing. He came to bring the clothes for Mrs. Malote to wear when she has her formal viewing," Miss Billings says as she picks up a shiny dress box that is sitting on the top of her desk. The gold letters on the box spell out the name of a very upscale department store. "He said her husband sent him with this. I let him into the room to see where Mrs. Malote will have her viewing. He just wanted to sit for a while. The casket is there waiting, but of course she's not in it yet."

"I suppose her husband is too upset to come."

Miss Billings shakes her head. "The man—I remember his name now, it's Aaron Peters—said the husband is in Canada filming something. He's some big movie producer and he's overbudget."

I can tell Miss Billings is torn. She loves the movie business and the box from the department store, but she doesn't approve of something here. We're trained at the Big M to never show our disapproval of any client's family, because grief does come out in strange ways sometimes and we are trained to offer comfort rather than criticism. But Miss Billings has a way of pursing her lips that lets me know when she doesn't approve of something. Last week it was the new purple staples the supply store sent instead of the silver ones she ordered.

"I'm sure Mr. Malote will be back for the actual funeral." I guess that's what's troubling her. I know it's kind of troubling me.

Miss Billings shakes her head. "It wasn't a love match, that's for sure. Him up in Canada and her down here having to wait for a proper dress for her viewing."

"But he sent a dress, just now."

Miss Billings shakes her head. "It's something her husband should have done—going through her closet, picking out a slip to go with the dress and maybe some earrings—that is the kind of thing that should be done by someone who loved the deceased. You don't just ask someone to do that for you—I don't care how important you are."

"Maybe this Aaron guy is her brother," I say. "Maybe he loved her, too."

"I bet he forgot to send a slip," Miss Billings says as she starts to lift the lid off the dress box. "A slip always makes the dress lie—"

"Oh." Miss Billings stops talking and we both stare at the dress. It is fire-engine red and there isn't much of it.

"I don't think you wear a slip with that dress." I finally find my voice. The material looks like silk and the neckline on that dress must plunge to the midriff. It's a dress for dancing, not dying.

Miss Billings looks down the hall at Room B. "I can tell you one thing. That man's not her brother. I'll have to ask Mr. Z about this."

"Do you think Mr. Z will be upset?" I figure there's no reason to try and make sure Mr. Z is in a good mood when I ask him about using the place over Thanksgiving weekend. I know the answer will be no. But I don't want him to think I don't properly respect the Big M.

"Mr. Z has seen it all," Miss Billings says calmly. "He and I have over twenty years in the business. I'll just let him know so he can have something substituted for Mrs. Malote's dress. He has a line in the contract that the family signs about suitable clothing. No one reads it, of course, but it's there when we need it. We both feel a responsibility to the deceased to see they are treated with dignity."

"I suppose they thought a picture of her in that dress in the casket would get them some publicity for the movie her husband is making," I say.

"Probably," Miss Billings says as she stands up and puts the lid back on the dress box. "But then, this is Hollywood. And tabloids love a death almost as much as they love a wedding."

"I don't suppose anyone has ever used this place for a wedding," I say. Maybe I don't need to bother Mr. Z. "There's probably a policy against using the facility for anything but funerals, isn't there? You know, because of the dignity and everything."

Miss Billings starts to walk toward the door marked Private that is across from her desk area. She stops and looks back at me. "There's no policy like that that I know of. Why? Are you thinking of getting married? I could do your makeup."

"No, not me. It's my cousin. I promised I would ask if she could use the Big M for her wedding. She's run into some problems in finding a place and my aunt suggested maybe we could use the Big M. I said I'd ask even though I know it's not possible."

"Well, I'm sure Mr. Z would do whatever he could to help you. He's been real pleased with the way you don't complain about doing the filing."

"I don't mind filing."

"You're the only one of the customer service reps who will do any of it. He and I both appreciate that. It keeps things running smooth."

"I like reading the forms to see who's coming up for their viewing."

Miss Billings nods as she turns back to face the door again. "I'll see what I can do about your cousin's wedding."

I start to feel a little alarmed. "No, that's fine, really. I know there's always a funeral going on."

"It doesn't hurt to ask," Miss Billings says. "That's always been my motto."

Okay, so I'm having a little trouble breathing. I look up at the ceiling just in case my dad is looking down at this one.

Miss Billings comes back out of the office. "Mr. Z has a minute to talk to you. Why don't you go in?"

I take a deep breath and tell myself I can do this. Mr. Z has always seemed like a nice person. I certainly don't need to be afraid to ask him my question.

I take a few steps and I am inside Mr. Z's office for

the first time. Mr. Z doesn't spend a lot of time in his office so I usually see him out and around pointing out the features of a casket or something. He is partial to the caskets that are lined with that new ultrasoft satin.

"Miss Billings tells me you'd like to use the facilities here," Mr. Z says as he looks up from his desk. He has a catalog lying open on top of a folder or two.

"Oh, I know it won't work," I say in a rush. "I just promised my aunt that I would ask you. You see my cousin's wedding plans got messed up and now she doesn't have anyplace to hold her wedding and it's for Thanksgiving weekend and that's so soon everything else is booked and none of the hotels will take her and, well, I promised my aunt I would ask if we could use this place. You don't have to worry about it. I know it won't work. I just wanted to be able to say I had asked."

I take a deep breath when I have finished.

Mr. Z nods. "Is this the aunt you told me about? The one who raised you?"

I nod. "Aunt Inga is great."

"She's out in—what is it—Blythe?"

"That's east of Palm Springs. It's not too far from here."

Mr. Z is looking thoughtful and a little sad. "It's important to stay close to your family," he says. "If I had one thing I could do over in my life it would be to stay closer to my family."

I never thought about Mr. Z's family. "Where is your family?"

"Most of them are buried in the village in Italy where I grew up. Only my brother is still living and he's in Florida. I haven't talked to him in over twenty years."

Mr. Z has a long face and he sort of looks mournful most of the time anyway, but when his eyes look sad, too, I don't like it.

"I'm sorry." I think back to the Cameron brothers, you know the ones who were not talking because they had a fight over who was supposed to be the executor of their mother's estate.

"I've thought a lot about my brother this week," Mr. Z says, so I know I wasn't the only one touched by the brothers' story. Mr. Z might have even talked to Robert Cameron more than I did. Mr. Z continues, "I can't even remember why we got mad and stopped calling each other on the telephone. We used to talk every week."

"Maybe if you talked to him now," I say, and then stop myself because twenty years is a long time and maybe his brother is…well, you know, departed from this world. As I've said before, more people die than you would think—or, at least, more than I ever thought did. I mean, I had my dad die, but that was a long time ago.

"I called directory assistance this morning and got his telephone number," Mr. Z says as he shuffles the folders on his desk and pulls out a small piece of paper with a number scribbled on it. "Do you know I didn't even have my brother's telephone number anymore? How could I not have my brother's telephone number? How did we ever get that far apart?"

I don't think an answer is required, but I'm glad he got the number. I'm sure dead people don't keep their phone bills paid so they wouldn't be listed in any directory.

Mr. Z is still looking at that piece of paper in his hand, so we are both a little startled by the ring of my cell phone. Of course, it's not a ring like a telephone makes. It's more like a happy tune from a kid's song.

"Sorry." I reach down to detach my phone from its place on my belt. "I'll just turn the ringer down. It'll only take a message."

"But it might be important," Mr. Z protests. "Maybe it's your brother calling."

"I don't have a brother."

"Well, maybe it's your aunt," he says with a wave of his hand. "We wouldn't want to keep her waiting if she wants to talk to you. Family is important. You can take the call here while I finish looking at this catalog."

I reach for my cell phone and check the number. Sure enough, it is my aunt Inga.

"Hi," I answer the phone, but I try to keep my voice quiet out of respect for where I am.

"Julie, is that you?"

Aunt Inga always says that when I answer the phone. I don't think she quite trusts the telephone company to get her to the right person. I suppose it is a miracle that they do when you think about how many people have phones. "Yes, it's me, Aunt Inga. How's everything?"

"We've got trouble."

"I know about the wedding plans. I've been thinking there are lots of places in Los Angeles to have a wedding."

"Have you asked your Mr. Z yet?"

"I'm in his office now, but I'm sure he's already booked. Thanksgiving weekend is less than two weeks away."

I hear Mr. Z rustle his catalog pages and I look up to see him looking at me.

"When?" I hear Mr. Z whisper.

"I'm sorry, Aunt Inga," I say into the cell phone. "Mr. Z has a question. I'll be right back."

I put my hand over the mouthpiece on the phone and look at Mr. Z. "What?"

"This wedding, when is it?" he says.

"The day after Thanksgiving," I say. "But I completely understand that you'll be booked."

"Thanksgiving is such a nice holiday," Mr. Z says and he gets a distant look in his eyes before zeroing in on me again. "All the families they get together in this country?"

"Well, yes, they do. Most of them anyway."

"I'll take a holiday," Mr. Z says with a slap to his desk that makes the room shake a little. "If a man can't take a holiday to be with his family, what is the good of living? Yes, I'll close the Big M."

"You're going to close the—" Had I heard him right? "Can you do that?"

"Of course, I can do that," Mr. Z says and then he stands up. "Nothing is already booked for that weekend and you shall have your wedding day."

"It's really my cousin that's getting married." I stammer a little.

"Then your cousin shall have her wedding day here," Mr. Z says with a flourish. "And I'll take the time off and go to Florida."

"To visit your brother?"

"If he will have me," Mr. Z says as he strides over to the door and walks out of the room.

I am stunned. And sit there for a minute before I remember I have my cell phone in my hand.

"Aunt Inga?" I say when I put the cell phone to my ear.

"Julie?" my aunt answers. "I heard everything."

"I'm not sure…" I begin to say and then my words dwindle. What can I say?

"I'm so glad we have the chapel arranged for the wedding," Aunt Inga says in a calm voice just as if a miracle hasn't occurred here. "That will take some worry off everyone's mind now that Jerry's gone."

"Jerry? Where'd he go?" I am starting to breathe again. "You know, Aunt Inga, there are many other places Elaine could get married. The Pacific Ocean is right by here and it would make beautiful pictures."

"It's November. It might rain. Besides, what place could be better than a lovely wedding chapel that is all set up for weddings?"

What place indeed? "I'm not sure she'll like the chapel here. You see, there's a stained glass picture and—"

"We don't have time to look for anyplace else," Aunt Inga says. "Not when Jerry's gone off."

"Did he go somewhere for work?" Jerry has been known to go to Las Vegas now and again for a workshop on carburetors or engines or something like that. He and his friends probably go there sometimes, too, just to look around.

"No, he's run away from home," Aunt Inga says.

"He's twenty-five years old. Technically, I don't think he can run away from home."

"Aunt Ruth says it's all her fault. She thinks he ran off to follow the wedding planner. She says she knew she shouldn't have picked a young stylish woman for a wedding planner, but Elaine said she wanted someone like that planning her wedding."

"But I thought the wedding planner left days ago."

"Well, where else could he be? Who else does he know? He didn't go home last night and we're all worried. He left some kind of a note, but it didn't make any sense."

"But how would he even find the wedding planner? Aren't the police looking for her?"

"Well, she must have told Jerry where she lived before she left."

I got a good look at the wedding planner and, trust me, she wasn't the type to run off with my cousin Jerry. Not that Jerry isn't cute in a mountain bear sort of a way. But the wedding planner looked more like the kind of woman who went for a professional man. Maybe a doctor or a lawyer or at least a white-collar thief. Someone with no grease on their hands, ever. No, I don't see her and Jerry. "I thought you were worried about getting a place for Elaine's wedding."

"Oh, that," Aunt Inga says. "I wasn't worried about that. I'd already prayed that God would touch your Mr. Z's heart and make him open the chapel up for Elaine. I knew that was taken care of."

Well, I had nothing to say to that. I guess I should take a minute to tell you that, even though I try to keep my distance from God, I have seen too much in my life

not to believe He exists. It was never a "does-He-
exist" or "doesn't-He-exist" question in my mind. The
whole thing is more complicated than that and I try not
to think about it. To tell you the truth, God scares me
a little. I'm afraid He's too much like Aunt Ruth.

You know, Aunt Ruth would vote me and my
mother out of the family if she could. After all, we're
the half family. Of course, she's polite, but politeness
can feel pretty cold. I've always wondered what it
would be like if I did get to heaven and found out I was
only half-welcome there, too.

"Well, I'm sure Jerry will come home soon," I say.
He doesn't have to worry about being half family. "He
would miss Aunt Gladys's cooking before long."

"Yeah, I'll tell her that. Maybe she should make a
big pan of lasagna. Jerry always liked her lasagna."

"That's a good idea," I say. "Just be sure and relax.
Don't worry. I'm sure wherever Jerry is, he's just fine."

"You're probably right," Aunt Inga says. "He never
did find those candles you know, the orange tapers that
Elaine wanted. Most of the candles will have to be
white now that we can't find orange ones, but Elaine
did so want a few orange ones to go in some centerpieces for the reception tables."

"I'm sure everything would be fine even without
orange candles," I say.

"You tell your Mr. Z a thank-you from all of us,"
Aunt Inga says. "And let me know when we can come
down and measure."

"Measure?"

"Oh, we'll have to measure everything. How long
the aisle is? How many candles do we need? We want

everything to be perfect. Ruth is so nervous about making sure everything is just as it should be since Elaine is marrying into such an important family."

I can feel a headache coming on. There's no way to keep the business of the Big M a secret if everyone just drops down for this and that. And I've seen enough of Gary's parents to know they won't find a mortuary wedding acceptable. "I'll have to get back to you on that."

Aunt Inga and I say goodbye and I just sit here. I am torn. I could just level with everyone and tell them that the Big M is a mortuary and that our usual clients are dead people. Everyone would freak out and say I'd messed things up again, but I could live with that. Of course, that would cancel any talk of having the wedding at the Big M. If Aunt Ruth couldn't bear the thought of plain glass cups at the engagement party, she would definitely draw the line at using a mortuary for the wedding ceremony.

The thing I'm not sure I can live with, though, is destroying Cousin Elaine's wedding day. Now, if someone else were going to destroy it, I could live with that. I might even sit back and enjoy the show. But I can't do it. Maybe it's all these estranged brothers I've heard about this week, but I've come to realize that I don't want to make Elaine so mad at me that she never speaks to me again. We might be half cousins, but half or whole, she's the only female cousin I have. She's also the closest thing to a biological sister that I have.

I always kind of thought that, when we became older, Elaine and I would be still baiting each other in the way people do when they know neither one takes it seriously anymore but neither one wants to stop, either. Sort of like *The Odd Couple* guys.

As I see it, my only way not to ruin Elaine's wedding is to find a different spectacular place for Elaine's wedding so we don't need to come near the Big M. Wish me luck. Maybe I'll be able to think of some possible places tonight when I'm at the Hollywood Bowl with Doug and his rally.

Chapter Six

I am sitting in the back row of the Hollywood Bowl and Doug is sitting next to me. This is my first time here so I'm glad I have a chance to see what it's like. The Bowl is an outdoor amphitheatre that's built into a hillside so I see trees on both sides of the curved walkways that line each side of the seating area all the way up the side of the hill.

Doug and I are sitting in two of the top seats. There's some kind of a shrub growing behind the back of our section of the bench and I can smell the tiny flowers on the bush. It's cool, actually. The flower is white and I didn't recognize it when we sat down, but the air smells very floral, almost like gardenias, even though I know the flower isn't a gardenia. A gardenia is huge in comparison to these little flowers.

Anyway, we got here early for today's Great Revival Rally, which is very much okay with me. I'm a little nervous and I am glad we have some extra time to check out everything before they turn down the big spotlights that give off the wattage that manages to light up the whole area.

This rally has apparently been happening here every Tuesday night for the past six weeks. I, of course, hadn't even seen a flyer on the rally so I wouldn't have known how long it has been going on if Doug hadn't told me. That's one of the things I haven't gotten used to since I left Blythe. In Blythe, I knew everything that was going on whether or not I personally wanted to go to it or not. Here in Hollywood, I don't know anything about anything that's happening.

I look around so I can at least feel that I know a little more about how things will go tonight at this event. The program the guy handed me when we came in says that the Reverend Johnnie Markum will be speaking tonight. Actually, I think he speaks most nights, but I don't know who he is. I wish he was standing up there on the stage so I could see him.

You can tell a lot about a man by studying the way he stands. You know, whether his hands are in his pockets or by his sides and that kind of thing. I'd like to get a feel for whether or not this Johnnie is an honest man—I figure that goes with hands outside the pockets. But the only people on stage are a couple of guys adjusting some microphones and, while they have their hands in full view, that's only because they are setting things up for the sound system.

While we're waiting for Johnnie, I can pass along a few things about the Bowl that Cassie told me before I came today. Usually, concerts are the main attraction here. Well, I knew that even before Cassie told me. But I didn't know that there are patches of lawn all along the path leading up to the Bowl and Cassie said people sit on the grass having these elegant picnics, often complete with crystal goblets and candlelight, before the concerts start.

Now, that's something I'd like to do sometime in honor of my grandmother. She would have loved doing something like that with one of her scarves wrapped around her neck and her wicker picnic basket beside her while she nibbles on some Brie cheese and crackers.

I wish I could, at least, see other people picnicking, but tonight isn't a concert and people aren't eating. I guess everyone is too serious tonight. Besides, I have to admit that Brie cheese and crackers go better with classical music than with sermons about the soul. The Los Angeles Philharmonic orchestra often plays here, but Cassie said she's heard that other musicians like Elton John and Pavarotti have performed here, as well.

"Do you know if the Great Revival people have always held their rallies here?" I say to Doug. I read in the program that they have these rallies every year. Doug has been looking around just as much as I have, but I figure we should talk—you know, since we're here together. It's almost seven o'clock and it's getting pretty dark even with the lights that are on.

"I don't know," Doug answers. "I hadn't heard about these rallies until my aunt told me. She didn't mention anything about other rallies in the past."

Doug and I are both watching the many kinds of people who are walking up these aisles. I don't know about him, but I find it a bit daunting to be going to church with thousands of other people. Besides, some of the people here are a little scary looking. In Aunt

Inga's church, no one wears black lipstick let alone a leather strip with spikes on it around their neck. That's what the guy and girl who just walked in front of Doug and I are wearing. The guy has the lipstick and the girl has the spikes. Suddenly, Doug's Donald Trump style isn't so bad. There's something to be said for stable.

In fact, I take another glance over at Doug. It might be the light from those spotlights hitting his head, but his hair has a nice golden look to it. Maybe he is more attractive than my initial impression would have indicated. Or, maybe I just like him a little better now that I know he has some of the same problems in life that I do.

Only people like the two of us would even begin to understand what kind of a problem it is to be raised by one's aunts. Other people probably wouldn't think there was a problem; they'd just say we should be grateful that we had aunts willing to take us in, which, while true, isn't all that there is to it. Not everyone necessarily understands that having someone raise you who is not required to raise you means they can quit raising you at any time.

You know, presto; it could be over. Then it's the old "Bye, kid."

It is hard to feel secure with that kind of a deal. At least if you're adopted or have regular parents, you know who has legal responsibility for you. You know they have to keep you even if you mess up here and there. The police pretty much make them keep you if they are your legal guardian—which should make lots of kids sleep easier at night.

Of course, sometimes the police don't help you

out—as in my case, with my mother asking Aunt Inga to take care of me. I'm pretty sure that Aunt Inga taking care of me was legal even though she obviously never adopted me. She still signed all my permission slips at school and everything, though, so she was my day-to-day parent. And, at least she was the same person all the time. Since Doug was passed around among his aunts, he probably didn't even know who to give his report card to if it needed an official signature. Most kids might think they'd like something like that, but—trust me—they wouldn't.

Anyway, it's no wonder he and I have our problems. I mean, there was Doug bouncing around from house to house like a Ping-Pong ball (that's got Big Commitment Issue written all over it) and I have that toppling thing going on which I never seem to outgrow.

I have to admit that, even though I know Aunt Inga loves me, I still feel insecure. Part of me is always waiting for Aunt Inga to leave me the way my mother left me. I've thought sometimes that my toppling thing comes from trying so hard to be sure no one ever leaves me again that I mess up. Sometimes I try too hard to please people because I want to fit in. Or I don't take enough time to really look at a situation before I jump into it, because I'm afraid that, if I hesitate, someone will pull the chance to jump in right away from me.

When I think of Doug's response to Aunt Ruth at Elaine's party, I realize I kind of get the panic he must have felt. You know, when your heart starts to pound and you want to run for the door, but you can't because you don't even know where the door is?

It must have been like that for Doug. The poor guy

probably doesn't even know what commitment really is. He certainly hasn't seen much of it coming his way in life. No wonder he thought about his assets and that ice plunge in Sweden as a way to avoid any thought of a commitment. He probably doesn't sign up for the year-long cable plan, either.

Don't tell anyone, but I have been having these moments when I feel a little closer to Doug now that I understand him better. I don't want him to know I have this close feeling going on, though. That would be weird. Especially because the closeness I feel is for the little boy with the suitcase that Doug used to be, not for the guy who is sitting here beside me now. That little boy would never have embarrassed anyone by dumping them at their cousin's engagement party and I obviously can't say the same for the grown-up Doug.

Okay, so I still have some resentment left that mixes in with the closer feelings. I'm working on it.

Anyway, I don't want Doug to see me staring at him so I look at the guy with the lipstick until he glances up my way. I don't want him to see me looking at him either so I look down at the program. The back of the program has a couple of paragraphs about the history of the Hollywood Bowl and it says that Fred Astaire danced on the stage here and the Beatles played their music here decades ago. Even Judy Garland was here. I wonder what Judy Garland would think of the necklace of spikes.

"I think they're part of a gang," I whisper to Doug when I see a large group of teenagers walk down the row in front of us. They are headed in the same direction as the first guy and girl and I think they all know each other. At least they're all wearing white T-shirts with these low-hanging pants. It's the way they are standing, though, that makes me think of gangs. "They're staking out their territory."

"They're probably just nervous," Doug says. He's looking at his program, too.

I grunt. "I bet they enjoy making other people nervous. Their nerves are probably like steel."

We're quiet for a minute.

"So, have you called your aunt yet?" Doug asks. He's finished looking at the program and is looking around again, too. He's anxious. I can tell by the way his voice is a little more high-pitched than usual. I heard that voice when he was talking to Aunt Ruth at Elaine's party.

The benches are made of strips of wood, but they are fairly comfortable. You can certainly see for a long way when you're sitting near the top. The hills of Hollywood are ahead of you and the white half-circle stage of the Hollywood Bowl is between us and them. There's naturally good acoustics here and that's why they built this place almost a hundred years ago in this location.

"I talked to Aunt Inga today," I say. "She called when I was in Mr. Z's office. He said we could use the place for the wedding."

"What? That's great news."

"It's a mortuary."

"Oh, you haven't told them?"

I shake my head. "I'm not sure what to do. Either way I mess up Elaine's wedding."

"Well, surely she wouldn't hold you responsible," he says although his conviction lessens as he speaks.

I only lift my eyebrow.

"Well, maybe you can have everything in the court-yard," Doug says. He knows the setup of the Big M because he told me he had been to a funeral there once. "If you're just in the courtyard, there's no clue that the place is a mortuary. You might have to tell the aunts, but I don't think you'd need to tell the guests. Let them enjoy the day."

You know, you may not believe this, but my life used to be simple. Sure, I had the clothes thing with Elaine and the disappointment with my mom, but I didn't have to make complicated ethical decisions that involved picking the reason to be on Aunt Ruth's bad list forever.

If I tell the aunts that I'm working in a mortuary, they will think I've messed things up as usual. If I don't tell them and let them continue to think that the mortuary is a wedding chapel, they will, at some point, still realize that I have messed things up as usual, unless, of course, something happens before they find out that the Big M is a mortuary. And, things could happen.

Elaine and her fiancé could get cold feet. They did once before when they had that brief breakup; they could split again for good or maybe just temporarily. Maybe they'll postpone their wedding for a year or so until they're more ready to get married.

I should ask Doug to recite his no-commitment speech to them; that might make them hesitate. It sure convinced me. Who wouldn't want to see the world instead of getting married right away? The other thing that could happen is that another place could be found for the wedding that is so spectacular that all thought of using the Big M simply fades away. And, believe me, there are places like that around here. Maybe Descanso Gardens or the back lawn of the Ritz-Carlton Hotel in Pasadena. Either of those places would make the Big M fade into history in the wedding plans.

"Oh, they're ready to start," Doug says as the spotlights are dimmed.

I look around. I hadn't noticed how all of the seats around us have become filled with people. I hear the noise start to quiet down as a few final people slide into their seats. When everything is quiet, a female soloist steps forward on the stage and begins to sing "Amazing Grace." In all the church services I have gone to I have heard hundreds of hymns. This one is hands-down my favorite.

"Wow," Doug says softly when the song ends.

I agree, but I don't say anything. I have my notebook in my hand and I just make a notation. "Opening Hymn: Amazing Grace."

I am expecting it to be difficult to take down the notes that I promised Doug, but it's not. The Reverend Johnnie isn't very flashy considering he is speaking to a whole crowd of people. He does tell a few funny jokes. I don't put them down completely because I figure Doug wants the notes to be more about the serious part of what the man is saying. I do jot down a clue, though, in case Doug wants to remember the jokes.

I want to ask Doug if the man is saying the same things that he said when Doug was here before, but I don't. Doug is listening carefully and I don't want to interrupt him.

The man keeps referring to the fourth chapter of

first John. I'm sure Doug doesn't know what this first, second and third business of John is all about. There are other writers like that, too, in the Bible. I make a note in the margin of my outline to tell Doug what I know about how the Bible is set up. I did, after all, go to Sunday school for years so I know how to get around in the Bible. It's really organized very well. Surprisingly well, really. I think a little bit on how the Old and New Testament are divided and then the books and the chapters and the verses.

Now that I've been doing the filing at the Big M I can appreciate a good filing system and that is really what the Bible has going for it. Anyone can come in and find the same information as someone else in only a few seconds if they know how the system works and they have the code for finding it. I call it the code, but it's just the chapter and verse combination.

You know, someone must have added that to the Bible after everything was written. I hadn't really given it much thought before, but I must say the organization in the Bible is brilliant. I'd like to shake the person's hand who decided to add chapters and verses to all of those words. It's absolutely perfect. We use an alphabetical system at the Big M. I wonder if Mr. Z would approve using some sort of code instead of the deceased's name.

I might have mentioned before that I like to distract myself in church and I'm feeling even more nervous here tonight than I usually do in a church service. Maybe it's because there's no roof between me and God so He can see right down at me. That's a little scary.

I'm trying not to listen too much, but I do want to

listen enough to write down the man's key points for Doug. The basic points the reverend is making are these:

Number one, God loves us;

Number two, God showed His love by sending us Jesus; and

Number three, if we love God, we need to make a commitment to Jesus and then love each other.

Well, that pretty much sums it up. No obscure points here. If you've been to church, you've heard it before. I remember that Doug hasn't been to church. Maybe that's why he's sitting here looking so interested in everything the man has to say.

I've noticed that a person can't be alive in this world without somebody going on about loving this or loving that. I've heard people say they love a television show or a haircut or a jelly doughnut. Love isn't really that big of a deal—well, except for when it happens between a man and a woman. That still seems to be important. Look at all the fuss Elaine's wedding is causing and that's simply to mark a man and a woman telling the world that they love each other.

Weddings are good things. But God loving us? Isn't that like saying the government loves us? Or that we love our government. You've seen those Love It or Leave It T-shirts, haven't you? So I would say we are used to loving things that are bigger than a person. That's all that this God loving us or us loving God stuff is.

When I was eight years old, I had a Sunday school teacher—there was no escaping Sunday school when I lived with Aunt Inga—and she asked me if I might not be afraid to love God because my mother had left me. The teacher sounded nice when she said it, as if I already knew my mother wasn't making any plans to have me live with her. This was before I'd given up on living with my mother, though, and I told her my mother hadn't left me, she just needed some time to get a place ready that was big enough for me. The teacher nodded when I said that and didn't say anything more about it to me.

I can't help but wonder what Doug thought about God when he was doing his rotation circle with his aunts. He probably never gave Him any thought at all. Maybe he liked having a new house every few weeks and maybe the aunts all lived close enough together that he could stay in the same school even when he switched houses. Maybe it wasn't totally horrible

Still, the picture of Doug carrying that suitcase of his from house to house is one that has stayed with me since he told me about it. I feel really sorry that he didn't have a place like I did with Aunt Inga where he could at least unpack his T-shirts. I guess it's like that old saying about a man who complains he has no socks until he meets a man who has no shoes.

I am trying to keep my mind on my notes and not think about what the man up front is saying, but even I recognize silence when I hear it. I look around me and everyone is starting to bow their heads. Some people are lifting their arms to the sky and some are folding them together in the way little children do when they pray.

Everything is so quiet, even the air feels somber.

Oh, no. I forgot to warn Doug about this. I think the man is going to ask people to raise their hands or something to say they have decided to love God. Since

Doug doesn't know about church, I could see where he might think this is a simple vote and, if it was, who would want to vote against God? But I know that it is more than that. This is what people do when they want to make a big deal about God in their lives. This is the Big Commitment.

Sure enough, the reverend is asking people to come forward and dedicate their lives to Jesus. I really should have talked to Doug about this. Hopefully, he realizes that the dedication the reverend is talking about is supposed to last for more than just tonight. With that moving-around history of his, Doug might not realize what a long-term, until-you-die commitment the man is talking about.

I feel Doug's leg move against mine and I reach out my hand to put it on his thigh and hold him in place.

"It's not what you think it is," I whisper to him. "You don't want to go forward."

I see an older woman looking at me. I think she heard me.

"But maybe I do want to go forward," Doug whispers back. "I need to do something in my life."

"There's that ice plunge in Sweden," I hiss as I press down with my hand a little harder. "You could do that. That's exciting."

An ice plunge is just about the right amount of excitement, too. You go there. You do it. You take a picture. You come home. That's what an exciting adventure should be. There's a short-term rush, but no real long-term harm. It doesn't change your life.

"I could do them both," Doug says as he starts to rise. I grab for his knee as he stands and, while I don't get my hand around his knee, I do get a good grip on the denim of his jeans in that place that's baggy behind the knee. "You don't know what you're doing by going down there."

"Yes, I do," Doug turns to whisper. "I'm making a commitment."

So, now Doug decides he's okay with the commitment thing. "But you don't like commitments. You've got that suitcase packed. Remember?"

"Let him go, dear," that older woman leans over and whispers to me. "He'll come back to you a better husband."

The surprise of that makes me let go of the denim of Doug's jeans. "Oh, but we're not—he's not…" I look up at Doug for support and all I see is his back as he walks to the end of the aisle so he can go down. "We're not together in that way."

"Oh, well, obviously you care for each other," the woman says as she pats my arm in a comforting way. "You'll see, it will be all right."

"I don't see how," I say as I turn to watch Doug make his way down the outside aisle. He's one green T-shirt in the maze of color.

I feel as if I've lost a friend. I look up at the woman who's been patting my arm and say, "He doesn't even know what it means. He probably thinks it's like when a baby gets dedicated in church. Everybody smiles and takes a picture and that's it."

She smiles down at me. "It'll be fine."

I turn around and see the whole section of my gang neighbors start to make their way to the outer aisle, as well. There's the guy with the black lipstick and the woman with the spikes around her neck and all their friends. Commitment doesn't seem like their style, either. I wonder if they're going down just to start trouble. Doug wouldn't be any match for that guy with the lipstick, or the woman and her spikes. Now I have a whole new set of worries.

I lose track of Doug's green T-shirt. He gets swallowed up in the sea of colored shirts.

"I hope there's someone down there to keep track of everyone," I say. They need a big white board like Mr. Z has at the mortuary. You just can't have people wandering around at a thing like this. "I don't even see a line forming."

"I think they'll pray first," the woman says. She looks like someone's grandmother so I suppose I can trust her to know what she's talking about.

By now, people all around us are talking with each other in low voices. The soloist who sang "Amazing Grace" earlier is now singing "The Old Rugged Cross."

I must admit I am feeling a little abandoned. If I had thought Doug would walk down to the front of this, I would have—well, I guess I would not have come. I don't like being left behind while he walks on to his commitment. It makes me feel the way I felt when my mother left me at Aunt Inga's—as though I was something that wasn't important enough to stay put for or take with her when she moved. Not that I wanted Doug to take me with him when he went down. It's just that—

"He's my ride home," I turn and whisper to the woman. That, at least, anyone could understand as a reasonable concern. They really should have these things organized better.

"I'm sure they won't keep him long," she says.

If I wasn't afraid of getting caught up in the group of people going down to be prayed over, I would get up from my seat and make my way out of the Bowl. I guess I could always call Cassie and ask her to come pick me up. There's not much parking left around the Bowl, but I could meet her at the entrance and she could pick me up without needing to park.

I look up at the woman. For the first time, I notice that she is sitting alone just as I am. "Thanks for everything."

"You're welcome, dear."

I notice now that she has a cane so I ask if she needs help walking down the outer aisle to the exit.

She shakes her head. "I'll be fine. I just need to sit here to let the rest of the people leave so the aisles are clear."

"I'll wait with you," I say. "I'm going to call my friend to pick me up and it will take a little while for her to get here anyway."

Okay, so I know the woman's a stranger and that I'll never see her again. But I don't want her to have to walk down the aisle by herself. It's steep and she could stumble. Besides, I know how it feels to be left until the last and it's always a little sad. She's been kind to me and I want to return the gesture.

"Thank you," the woman says. "I just lost my husband last year and I'm still not used to doing things alone."

"Oh, I'm sorry," I say. "I work at a mortuary and I hear people say that a lot. It must be hard getting used to not having him with you."

"You never do get used to it," the woman says and

then brightens. "But I'm so pleased you work at a mortuary. The staff people at my husband's mortuary were so kind. That's such an important job."

"Yes, I guess it is." I smile.

I'm glad I didn't have time to change after work so I still have my black suit on tonight. I think it helps put people at ease when they talk about their departed loved ones. We talk some more about Harry, the woman's dead husband, and then Alice, that's her name, tells me about her pet birds.

We're silent for a bit, just sitting still under the night sky. Finally I pull out my cell phone and put in a call to Cassie. She says she'll be happy to pick me up at the entrance to the Bowl.

I then call Doug's cell phone and leave him a message that I called Cassie for a ride home. I also tell Doug that I'll leave the notes I took for him with the guy behind the counter at the coffee shop. I suppose that's a little cowardly, but I'm not sure I'm ready to have a friend turn holy on me. All Doug will probably want to do is pray all the time now anyway and I have Aunt Inga for that.

By that time, the aisles have cleared and I help the woman walk down the outer aisle to exit the Bowl. We go slowly and she holds on to my arm so she doesn't have to use her cane. She's planning to take a taxi home so I walk her over to the taxi stand and wait while she gets seated in a cab.

The taxi stand is close to the entrance and I only have to walk a few yards to find the place where Cassie is going to pick me up. People are driving their cars out of the Bowl parking lot and there is a steady stream of them going through the exit. It's a chilly night and I hug the black jacket of my suit around me so I keep warm.

Cassie is there before I know it and I slip into the passenger seat of her car. Cassie has the car pulled over to the side of the road so she puts her blinkers on to enter back into traffic.

"Thanks for coming," I say.

"Where's Doug?" Cassie pulls out into the slow-moving traffic.

"He went down front," I say.

Cassie looks puzzled for a moment and then she gets it. "Down front! But doesn't that mean—"

I nod. "He appears to have no problem making a life-altering commitment to God."

"Wow," Cassie says. We're waiting at a stoplight so she turns to look at me. "I thought he wasn't ready for any commitments."

I shrug. "I'm not sure he knows what he's doing."

"Wow," Cassie says again.

Cassie wasn't raised going to church every Sunday as I was, but she has gone enough times with Aunt Inga and me that she knows one doesn't make a commitment to God and then just forget about it.

"I tried to stop him," I say.

We drive together in silence for a while.

"I met a nice older woman," I say. "Alice Green. She sat near us. All alone now that her husband is gone."

"It's sad to be alone." Cassie turns from Vermont onto Melrose Avenue and then goes west toward her apartment.

There is a moment's pause then Cassie continues.

"I keep wondering if my mother is all alone some-where like that woman. Do you suppose she can't read and that's why she never has registered with any of those agencies?"

"She might not know about them even if she can read," I say. "I wouldn't have known about them if you weren't here to tell me."

"But wouldn't you think she would ask some-one?" Cassie asks. "Like that woman would have asked you for help?"

I know how Cassie feels. I feel the same way. Sometimes it just seems that the people we love aren't willing to go to much bother for us. I force some brightness into my voice. "Well, if she can't read, I'd guess the people around her can't read, either. But someone official will come along and tell her. I'm sure the letters you are writing will prompt someone to go talk to your mother."

In actuality, I'm not sure of that at all. I don't know if anyone in the adoption bureaucracy even cares about Cassie and her mom. The adoption was so long ago and I suppose no one can complain about the way Cassie was treated. She might not have been loved by Jim and Marge, her adoptive parents, but she had her physical needs met. She even has straight teeth today because of the braces they provided for her. And Marge had dinner on the table every night at six o'clock.

I don't know if anyone in a bureaucracy knows how much it would mean to Cassie to see her mother. At least I know what my mother looks like. I know what her voice sounds like. When I was younger, I used to

fall asleep with a picture of my mother in my head.
Cassie was never able to do that. She doesn't know if
her mother is tall or short, dark-haired or blond, pretty
or plain. She could be a bank president or a cleaning
lady.

"Maybe we should try some other way to locate
your mother," I finally say. "Maybe there's a way other
than going through these organizations."

Cassie doesn't answer as she turns her car into the
parking lot of her apartment building. The building she
lives in is an older brick building and there is no under-
ground parking as there is in newer apartment buildings. There are a couple of security lights in the
parking lot, but the residents have learned to look out
for any strange cars that aren't parked in the designated
visitor spaces.

Cassie and I both take a look around the parked cars
before we unlock her car doors. It's about eight-thirty
and, even though that's not so late, we're always
careful when we walk through the parking lot at night.
Parking is one thing that is better in Blythe than here.
Aunt Inga has a garage and a wide carport so she and
I always park close to her house, well within the circle
of light cast by the porch light. But even the public
parking lots in Blythe are not this scary.

The back door to the apartment building is not
locked until eleven o'clock each night so it opens
when Cassie turns the knob. Her apartment is on the
third floor so we climb the wooden stairs. There is a
thin carpet on the hallway, but everyone can still hear
when someone is walking down the hall. The residents were going to complain and send a petition off

to the building owner asking for new, thicker carpet, but then they decided it was good security to know when someone was walking down the hall.

Cassie and I are almost to her door when her across-the-hall neighbor, Mrs. Snyder, opens her own door and whispers at Cassie. Mrs. Snyder moved to the building shortly after Cassie did.

"There was someone at your place," she says in a low voice, with a nervous look down the long hallway. "A man. About ten minutes ago. Knocking on your door."

Cassie frowns and looks at me. "Do you suppose Doug took a cab over here?"

I frown also. "I don't think he would be finished with his commitment stuff at the Bowl yet."

I really don't know what goes on when someone walks forward at one of those rallies, but, given the number of people who did that tonight, it would take twenty minutes just to get everyone organized.

"Are you sure he knocked on my door?" Cassie asks Mrs. Snyder. "Maybe it was Max's door next to me."

The older woman shakes her head. "It wasn't Max's. I could see pretty well through my peephole and he was knocking at your door. He was a mountain of a man."

Cassie looks down the hall even though it is obvious no one is in the hall except the three of us. "It must have been someone who got the numbers wrong. I'm sure by now he's found the place he wanted."

"I suppose so," Mrs. Snyder says as she starts to close her door. "I just worry about the two of you living alone like you do with no man to take care of you."

"I have a shovel," Cassie says.

"That little shovel of yours wouldn't hurt a fly," Mrs. Snyder says. "It's half plastic. But don't worry. I'm a light sleeper and I keep my eye to the peephole if someone comes around."

"I appreciate that," Cassie says.

I am grateful, too, so I smile at Mrs. Snyder. Some people might not like a neighbor scrutinizing everyone who knocks at their door, but I feel safer knowing Mrs. Snyder does just that. At least she would be able to give the police a description if someone broke into Cassie's place.

I didn't ever worry about anyone breaking into Aunt Inga's house when I was in Blythe. I miss that sense of security. When I decided to move to Hollywood, everyone in Blythe told me to be careful. And Hollywood does have a reputation for strangeness. But, I'm learning it also has people like Alice Green, who I met tonight, and Mrs. Snyder, who always looks out for us.

Cassie opens her door and turns the light on. She has some of her bags of potting soil on a piece of plastic on the floor so I assume tonight has been a plant night for her. The yellow light from the overhead bulb gives a warm look to the room. The heater has been on and it is cozy inside.

Cassie doesn't have a lot of furniture yet, but she is adding something every week and I see a new magazine stand sitting beside her sofa. She got the sofa at a used furniture shop and it is well-worn, but it does have a foldout bed and I have slept on that as well as on the air mattress that Cassie has. I haven't decided which one is more comfortable yet, but it feels luxurious to have the choice of two places to sleep. Cassie, herself, has a twin bed in the small bedroom.

I put my notebook down on the table and remember the notes I took tonight. I turn to Cassie. "Could you take something over to the coffee shop tomorrow when you go to work? I told Doug I'd leave his notes there with his name on them."

Cassie has walked over to her kitchenette, but she turns. "Don't you want to talk to him? Returning the notes would make a good reason to call."

"I think I'll pass," I say as I tear out the pages for Doug and fold them over. "I don't really know what to say. I'm not sure congratulations are appropriate. Or sympathy. It's all just a little awkward, you know?"

I dig in my purse for a pen and then sit at the table so I can write Doug's name on his notes.

Cassie has walked over to the stove and nods as she lifts the teakettle off the burner. She turns the water on and starts to fill the kettle.

"Cocoa?" I ask as I set Doug's notes on the counter beside the door.

Cassie and I have a long tradition of ending difficult days with cups of cocoa topped with handfuls of miniature marshmallows. We've had some of our best sad times with cocoa.

"I stopped and got macaroons today, too," Cassie says as she nods toward the top of the refrigerator. Sure enough, there is a pink bakery box with a black sticker on it that means it comes from our favorite Jewish delicatessen. They make the best macaroons, moist and chewy. Perfect cocoa food.

I am reaching up into the cupboard to get a couple of small plates to go with the mugs when there is a knock at our door.

Cassie, who is opening a packet of cocoa mix, stops in midtear. She looks at me. Neither one of us knows anyone who would be dropping by for a visit, especially not at this time on a Tuesday night.

We don't say anything in the hopes that whoever is knocking will go away if we don't answer. It doesn't work. The first knock is followed by a second knock. The second knock has a little bit of a desperate sound to it.

It's good to know Mrs. Snyder is probably still up and looking out her peephole about now. Cassie's peephole is so high that neither one of us can see out of it unless we pull a stool over to stand on. If we do that, we'll make so much noise that the knocker will know we're here. When the peepholes were put in the doors, a tall basketball player lived in this unit. Cassie asked the landlord for a new peephole, but he said if she wanted a different one, she'd have to put one in herself.

"Who's there?" Cassie finally says, while stepping over to pick up the shovel she has leaning against the counter. Mrs. Snyder is right, the shovel is mostly plastic. It would be like defending yourself with a toy broom.

"Is that you, Cassie?" a man's voice answers on the other side. The man is obviously trying to keep his voice low so it is hard to hear him. I wonder if he has a mask over his face.

"Don't answer. He could have gotten your name from your mail," I whisper to Cassie when she looks as if she's going to step forward and open the door. The mailboxes are at the front of the building and they are locked, but you never know who can pick a lock these days.

"Julie, let me in," the man's voice isn't so soft anymore. "I can hear you two in there talking."

The man's voice is sounding very familiar to both of us.

Cassie goes to the door and opens it. "Jerry?"

There stands my cousin Jerry, looking rumpled and red-eyed. With his dark hair a little longer than usual and his smile a little more forced than I remember, he is over six feet tall and more muscular than I remember. I guess I will always picture him as a gangly boy, but it is obvious that he has developed muscles that were not as evident in his tuxedo as they are now in the brown T-shirt he's wearing. He must have started going to a gym recently. No wonder Mrs. Snyder said he was a mountain of a man.

"I thought Aunt Inga said you ran away from home." I cross my arms so he knows I mean business. "You have everyone worried."

"I didn't run away. I left a note saying I was leaving for a few days," Jerry says as he stands in the hallway with a duffel bag over one shoulder. "I don't know why people in our family can't just leave well enough alone."

Those thoughts sound too close to my own for comfort. What kind of a world would it be if Jerry and I agreed?

"But you've never left before," I say just to give myself a minute or two to get used to seeing Jerry in a new light. "I'm sure your mother is worried."

Jerry and his four brothers are the sons of my aunt Gladys. None of the boys live in her house anymore, but they all have small apartments around Blythe. Jerry has lived in a small apartment behind the garage where he works ever since he moved out of Aunt Gladys's house five or six years ago. Jerry is in the middle of the brother lineup, with two brothers older and two younger.

Jerry sighs. "I don't know what the big deal is. So I want to spend a few days someplace other than Blythe. People are entitled to see the world a little."

"I can understand that, but what are you doing *here?*" I can't help but ask. It hasn't escaped my notice that Jerry hasn't looked me in the eye once since Cassie opened the door. I have a feeling something more is going on here than that Jerry has decided to broaden his travel horizons. He hasn't insulted me once while he's been standing there and that isn't like Jerry.

"I don't know anybody else who doesn't live in Blythe," Jerry says with a shrug that moves the duffel bag and the brown T-shirt beneath it. "Okay? I'm desperate."

"Everyone thought you ran off to be with the wedding planner," I say.

Bingo. Jerry's face flushes and he looks me in the eye for the first time. "People need to mind their own business. She seemed very nice when I fixed her car that day it was stalled in Aunt Ruth's driveway."

"Did you do something to her car so you could meet her?" I ask.

"Of course not." Jerry is indignant. "I could have just gone inside Aunt Ruth's place for a glass of water if I was that desperate to meet Mona. Besides, I'd never mess with her car." Jerry's eyes look a little glazed. "Man, you should see that car. It's a 1966 Thunderbird convertible in a light baby blue—completely restored right down to the hubcaps. Mona had a little problem with the starter, but I charged up the battery for her and that got her going. That's all."

I'm beginning to think maybe Jerry is smitten with the car and not with Mona.

"Someone takes really good care of that car because of the shine on it," Jerry says. "All the chrome is buffed out. You can tell when someone is really into their car—and I thought a good-looking woman like that and her mechanic, well, who knows what could happen."

"Jerry, she's a criminal," I say as my heart softens toward him a little. Jerry teased me all the time when we were kids, but he does sound a little pathetic now. Imagine weaving fantasies about a criminal. Even I haven't done that.

"But she needs a new part. Parts for those old cars aren't easy to find. And they're expensive. When I told her what the problem was with her car, she told me she couldn't afford to buy a new starter—so I offered to have one of my buddies look in the junkyard to see if he could find one for free. He got it to me yesterday," Jerry says.

Then he looks at me as if he's making an important point. "Now, how do you figure a woman who can't afford a hundred-dollar part for her car is a criminal?"

"Please, the facts speak for themselves," I say. "Besides, she can probably afford the part now that she has Aunt Ruth's nineteen thousand dollars."

Jerry doesn't respond to me and we all just stand there.

"And she probably had a hundred dollars before,"

I add. "She just didn't figure there was any reason to spend it when some guy would probably come by and get a starter for her for free."

There's some more silence.

Finally, Jerry clears this throat. "Look, I just need a place to stay for a few days while I figure things out. I can't go back to Blythe right now and I'm hoping I can stay here. I can't pay much, but I'll pay what I can and I'll do chores."

Cassie looks at me and I nod my okay. I guess family ties do mean something. Still, I'm going to keep my eye on him.

"I could use some help with my plants," Cassie says as she gestures for Jerry to come inside. "If I had someone to help me lift, I could bring some of the bigger plants home."

"I have my pickup truck out back in your parking lot," Jerry says. "I was here and left for a bit and then came back so I parked it."

"In one of the spaces marked Visitor?" Cassie asks. Jerry nods.

"That's good then," Cassie says as she steps around Jerry and walks across the hall to Mrs. Synder's door.

Before Cassie even gets a chance to knock, Mrs. Snyder answers the door with a towel around her head and her robe on.

"It's all right. He's Julie's cousin," Cassie says.

"Good," Mrs. Snyder says as she squints up at Jerry. "You need a man around."

"He's not staying for long," I step out in the hall and say just so Mrs. Snyder doesn't give up her peephole defense. "Just a few days."

"A week," Jerry agrees. "Ten days max."

I wait for Mrs. Snyder to close her door and then I look Jerry square in the eyes. "You're just trying to avoid all the wedding stuff, aren't you?"

I should have known. "Aunt Inga said your brothers are making origami flowers for the reception tables and you're just goofing off."

"I was out looking for orange candles," Jerry says defensively. "Do you know how hard they are to find?"

"I see them all over in party stores," Cassie says as she walks back into her apartment.

"We don't have any party stores in Blythe," Jerry says as he follows Cassie into the apartment.

"Well, you're in Hollywood now. All people do here is party. I'll call around tomorrow and find you some orange taper candles," I offer as I also walk back inside the apartment and then close the door.

"You won't regret letting me stay," Jerry says as he steps over and puts his duffel bag down close to the window.

That's all he knows. I'm already starting to regret it.

Then Jerry continues, "Besides, I noticed your door squeaks. I can fix that."

Well, maybe he will be useful.

"Can you put in a new peephole, too?" Cassie asks hopefully as she turns the dead bolt on the door and then looks over at Jerry. "The landlord said I could add one if I wanted. One that's more my height."

"It'd be my pleasure," Jerry says as he walks back to where Cassie is standing and smiles down at her in this come-hither way he must have picked up from the movies. "We need to keep you safe."

Just as I'm thinking "Oh, pl-eee-aa-se," I see Cassie's face get all pink and I have the shock of my life. You know, I think Cassie might like my cousin Jerry. As in *like* like. Of course, if she did, she would have said something years ago, wouldn't she?

I know the answer to my question before it even pops into my mind. No, Cassie would not have told me if she liked Jerry. After listening to me talk about him, she would have sworn he was my mortal enemy. Cassie would have felt disloyal to say she liked him, even in a generic-friend sort of a way. She would never have admitted to being attracted to him.

But how could I not have noticed? Cassie and I have been best friends since we were five years old. I should have known she liked my cousin without her saying anything. Of course, maybe she's only started to like him recently. She just saw him at Elaine's party. Maybe she developed a sudden liking for him then. It might even be a passing interest in him. She might have noticed that he's gotten more muscles lately and decided he wasn't so bad after all.

I'm not sure how I feel about this Cassie and Jerry possibility. I try to be happy for Cassie, but then I think about it being Jerry. He used to tease us unmercifully when we were young. Cassie and I couldn't have a pretend wedding without Jerry showing up and wanting to throw rice at someone.

Now that I think about it, though, maybe the fact that he showed up when Cassie and I wanted to play wedding meant something even back then. I hope not. I would feel that I'd been so blind for so many years.

I put my air mattress in the bedroom with Cassie

and Jerry decides to take the Hide-A-Bed after offering to sleep on the floor several times if we think flipping out the Hide-A-Bed is too much trouble. I can see he's trying to be a considerate guest. He even helps us make our cocoa. He doesn't even complain about it being woman's work or anything.

For the first time in my life I'm wondering if Jerry has turned out to be a regular human being. After all, if Cassie likes Jerry, he must have some finer points. I can even see how a woman who is not related might think Jerry is a little cute now that he has that muscle thing going.

Oh, dear. I don't know when my life became so flip-flopped.

"It'll be nice having Jerry here," I say as I settle into my air mattress bed on the floor of the bedroom. Jerry is out in the living room where he can't hear me. Cassie is sitting on the side of her bed putting some lotion on her hands. She always puts this special honey lotion on her hands before she goes to sleep. It's funny that I know something like that about her and I didn't know she had a crush on my cousin.

Cassie looks at me. "If he gives you any trouble, he'll have to leave."

"He won't," I say. And if he does, it's time I learned to be a little more tolerant anyway.

"It'll be nice to have someone around to lift things," Cassie adds as she puts her hand on the lamp switch and turns it off.

"Uh-huh," I agree.

I hear Cassie sigh as she pulls her covers up to her neck.

"Good night," she says.

"Good night," I reply. "And sweet dreams."

I go to sleep trying to remember the last time I liked a guy, I mean really liked him. I had that twinge of attraction toward Doug before the rally started tonight, but that might have just been the spotlight on his hair and my sympathy about that suitcase he carried around as a kid. Besides, now that he's, you know, committed to God, I don't think we would have any hope of a future even if we had something going on. If Doug becomes all holy, I'm not sure he'd be allowed to have a girlfriend anyway so it's just as well my attraction was only a passing twinge. Ah, well, there will be someone else, someday. I hope. Before I die.

Chapter Seven

I wake up to the sound of Cassie giggling in the kitchen. It's a Wednesday. Nobody giggles in the kitchen on a Wednesday morning. Besides, it's half-dark out. I lift my wrist so I can see the illuminated hands on my watch. Its six-thirty, which is half an hour earlier than Cassie and I usually get up.

That's when I remember Jerry. I groan and put my pillow over my head. Jerry's here, out on the Hide-A-Bed, just past the bedroom door. Actually, it sounds as though he's walking around instead of still being in the Hide-A-Bed. I wish I was hearing the sounds of a phone conversation that would tell me Jerry was calling home, but he is laughing, too. It's not likely he'd be doing that if he was talking to any of the aunts at this time of the morning.

I take the pillow off my head and, instead, try to go back to sleep.

I keep thinking, though, that one of us is going to have to call the aunts this morning and tell them that

Jerry is here. He might have left a note, but it is obvious that it didn't say enough to ease everyone's worry. I can't stand the thought of any of the aunts lying awake worrying about Jerry's miserable self. Of course, Jerry should be the one to call, but if I've learned anything lately it's that what should be isn't always what actually happens.

I lie in bed for a little while longer. The giggles have mostly ended, but now I hear the steady murmur of voices. I'm not sure which makes me more nervous, the giggles or the regular conversation. I still can't believe that Cassie is interested in my cousin Jerry.

All of a sudden, I'm wide-awake. Now that I know that Cassie is interested in Jerry, I wonder if he is interested in her—in a caring way, that is. If Jerry was out chasing after that wedding planner, he is probably ready for one of those rebound situations where a guy leads a woman on just to get revenge against all the women who have ever spurned him before he met her.

I'm thinking Jerry might have a good-sized list of women who have said "no thank you" to him over the years even if he is looking better than he used to. I bet he's lifting weights. Anyway, he could very well be plotting some revenge. I know that's what Jerry did when we were kids. If you crossed him, he bided his time, but he always got you back.

All I can say is that Jerry better not hurt Cassie's feelings.

If anyone in the world knows how sensitive Cassie's feelings are when it comes to love, it is me. Because her mother gave her away, Cassie always seems to take any rejection hard. Of course, no one likes rejection. But Cassie's heart breaks awfully easy.

I get up out of bed even though the alarm hasn't rung yet. I wrap one of my blankets around me and go out into the living room in my flannel red-heart pajamas.

"Is everything okay out here?" I try to say the words in an offhand way as I run my fingers through my hair and clear my throat. I think about yawning so I look even more casual, but no one is exactly looking at me suspiciously so I don't bother.

Cassie and Jerry are sitting at the table with coffee cups in their hands. The lights are all on and everything looks orderly. The kitchen, living room and dining room are all the same room in Cassie's apartment. The table is along the left wall, in front of the tiny kitchen.

"Oh, hi," Cassie says as she looks up at me. She's got a yellow sweatshirt and jeans on. That's probably what she's planning to wear to work. The staff doesn't wear suits in the floral shop, but they do wear long green aprons that cover up a lot of denim. "We were just talking about what plants will need to be brought back from the shop today."

"Yeah, I got my pickup," Jerry adds. "It can haul anything you've got."

He's wearing the same brown T-shirt and jeans that he had on last night. I'm guessing he slept in them, which makes me wonder if he thinks the wedding planner would have been impressed with his wardrobe choices. He would have done better to keep the rental tuxedo he wore to Elaine's party. For a minute, I wonder if that's what he's got in that duffel bag he brought in last night.

"There's a large ficus tree that I thought we could move," Cassie mentions and then takes a sip of her coffee.

"Great," I say, feeling more than a little foolish. They have been talking about houseplants. Not exactly the language of love. Maybe I am imagining any romantic interest.

I look at them a little closer. Cassie has her makeup on and Jerry has his hair already combed. Cassie doesn't like makeup and usually doesn't put any on until she's ready to leave the apartment. I'm not sure Jerry even combs his hair before he leaves his apartment. I think he keeps his comb in his pickup truck and gives his hair a swipe while he's in traffic. I look at both of them again. They look oblivious, but I know something is happening, even if neither one of them knows it yet.

"I've wanted to move that ficus plant, but I haven't been able to because I didn't have someone strong enough to help me lift it," Cassie adds with a small smile for my cousin.

Jerry beams.

I clear my throat. "Jerry needs to call his mother before he goes lifting anything. Or, at least one of the aunts. They all tend to worry about the boys. It's like Jerry has three mothers. All worrying over him."

There, I figure that will slow down any budding romance until reason can take hold. Cassie knows the aunts and there's nothing like reminding her that, if she's involved with Jerry, she has to face all the aunts, including Aunt Ruth. No one has married one of the cousins yet so it remains to be seen how much grief the aunts will give a new bride with all of their opinions about the need for ironed collars and proper cooking. My guess is that it could be considerable grief, though.

"Don't worry. I'm going to call in half an hour or so and leave a message on Aunt Ruth's phone," Jerry says. "I didn't want to call before eight."

"She'll be up by then and answering her phone," I say, so Jerry doesn't think he's putting anything over on me. I wouldn't put it past him to call a wrong number and leave a message on some stranger's telephone just to make me think he'd called Aunt Ruth.

"Aunt Ruth doesn't answer her phone anymore," Jerry says as he lifts his coffee cup and holds it while he finishes his thought. "I just don't want to wake her up with the ringing before eight."

The aunts consider it a sin to be in bed after eight o'clock in the morning unless they're in the hospital. Of course, no one knows how close they each sleep to the eight o'clock deadline.

"Aunt Ruth answers her phone," I say. "After eight anyway."

"Well, of course, she answers when it's you calling." Jerry takes a gulp of coffee. "Have you ever noticed how you're always in the middle of your message when she picks up? Well, she might pick up for you, but she doesn't pick up for anybody else. Not anymore."

"Really?" This pleases me. It probably shouldn't, but it does. "I had no idea Aunt Ruth would take my calls when she doesn't take any others."

Jerry snorts. "Take your calls? That's not the half of it. Since Aunt Inga convinced her that you might have the backup plan for all her problems, you should hear her go on and on about how sweet you are to try to help by offering the small wedding chapel where you work. Of course she'll pick up on your calls. She doesn't think your chapel will be fancy enough, but she doesn't want to cut off any of her options, either."

"Oh."

"I'm sure Aunt Ruth cares more about Julie than about some wedding chapel," Cassie says indignantly.

"Sure," Jerry says cautiously.

I've got to say right here and now that Jerry is not accustomed to being nice or considerate. I think he might be biting his tongue so he doesn't say anything sarcastic to Cassie and me.

"I'm sure she does," Jerry says more firmly and this time he works up a smile.

"Don't strain yourself," I say to Jerry. "I know Aunt Ruth is worried about having a place for Elaine's wedding. But I agree with her. I'm not sure the place I work is the best place to have the ceremony. And not because it's not good enough. There's nothing little about the place."

Jerry shrugs. "I'm only passing the word along."

"Besides, if she thinks the place isn't up to her standards, why does she even want to keep it on her list of possibilities?" I know I should leave well enough alone. Since I don't want Aunt Ruth to come near the place where I work, I should be glad she thinks the Big M is too small. The truth is, though, that I have always been sensitive to words like short, and half—and now small. I have a lot of pride in the Big M. It rises up to the sky like a great cathedral. Aunt Ruth has no idea what she's calling small.

"But, it would be okay if she backed out of even thinking about having the wedding at the place where Julie works," Cassie adds quickly. "Julie would completely understand."

"Of course," I say. "I wouldn't want you to think otherwise."

Believe me, I wouldn't want Jerry to think otherwise.

"And if you happen to talk to Aunt Ruth," I say, "it would be okay if you mentioned that I said there's lots of other beautiful places to have weddings. Places that aren't as small."

Jerry doesn't look happy. "Small was her word. Don't be mad at me."

"I'm not mad." I smile.

"Of course, she's not mad," Cassie adds quickly and then looks at me. "Do you want some coffee? I made the special kind."

So that's what I smell. Freshly ground French roast with vanilla. This is a special morning. Most of the time we make do with a tea bag.

"I'd love some coffee," I say as I stand there looking like a refugee. Unfortunately, Cassie only has two chairs for the table and she's sitting in one. Jerry is in the other. "I could just pull up a…"

I look around the room. There's the sofa and the new magazine rack and Jerry's duffel bag. Oh, and the wooden crate that we use for a coffee table, but it has plants on it.

"Please, sit here," Jerry says as he stands. He gives me another smile.

I look at Jerry. All this politeness must be killing him. I grin. "Thank you. Would you mind bringing me a cup now that you're up?"

Jerry's smile turns a little grim. "Why don't I just put the coffee in it, too, as long as I'm walking around?"

"Terrific," I say.

Jerry brings me my cup of coffee and he barely spills any of it.

"I think it's eight o'clock," I say as he sets the coffee down.

"Oh, yes, the phone is right over there," Cassie says as she points to her cordless phone.

"Tell Aunt Ruth hello for me," I say. I know that's playing with fire, but I do it anyway. I've decided I like having Jerry here more than I ever thought I would. "And, maybe you can get the newspaper before you make your call. It's right outside the door."

Jerry's smile is a grimace by now. He doesn't even answer as he opens the door and uses his foot to push the *Los Angeles Times* into the room. "What is this, five dead trees worth of bad news? You could print the Blythe phone book with less paper than this."

"Precisely," I say.

Jerry grunts and grabs the cordless phone before sitting on the sofa. He punches in a series of numbers which I assume are Aunt Ruth's.

"Hi, Aunt Ruth." He looks at me and whispers, "answer machine," before continuing. "This is Jerry. I'm sorry if everyone's been worried, but I've been out of town. I'm fine. I'm here staying with Cassie and

Julie…" There's a pause. Then Jerry looks at me and holds out the phone. "Aunt Ruth wants to talk to you."

"Tell her I'm having breakfast," I whisper to Jerry. I'm not ready to talk to Aunt Ruth. "I thought you said she'd have her answer machine on."

Jerry gets up and brings the phone over to me. He lays it down on the table in front of me. I have to pick it up.

"Hello, Aunt Ruth," I say in my best voice.

"You're not getting sick, are you?" Aunt Ruth asks. "Your voice sounds a little nasally."

"No, I'm fine, Aunt Ruth."

"Well, I want to thank you for offering your little chapel as a place for Elaine's wedding."

"It's not little," I say. "The chapel is very large."

"Fortunately, we probably won't need it," Aunt Ruth continues on as if she hasn't heard me. "I still have a call in to one of the large hotels in Palm Springs. I think they may reconsider and let us have the wedding there, after all. There's nothing like those big hotels to do justice to a wedding. This one looks out over a golf course."

"Oh, that's good news." She has no idea how good.

"Of course, Inga worries so much. She told me to ask you to keep your place in reserve, just in case, even though I'm quite sure we won't need it. I think I have a real rapport with the manager at this hotel in Palm Springs. I'm even thinking of taking golf lessons there."

If Aunt Inga is worried Aunt Ruth won't find a hotel for the wedding, I'm worried, too.

"There are more places than hotels," I stammer and then I close my eyes. "Maybe a garden somewhere. Or the ocean."

"Goodness, we couldn't have the wedding at the

ocean," Aunt Ruth protests. "No one wants to get sand on a three-thousand-dollar wedding dress. Besides, we want to show Gary's family that we have some sense of what's appropriate for a wedding between two families of our social standing. If we were at the ocean, someone might come barefoot or something. That would never do."

"Well, there are other places that aren't on the beach. I can do some calling around today. I'm sure we'll find the perfect place for Elaine's wedding."

"Of course, we will." Aunt Ruth takes a breath to slow herself down. "In the meantime, I promised Inga we'd get ready just in case worse comes to worse and we have to use your little chapel. So when can we come down to measure the chapel? We will need to know the exact distance between the pews and the distance from the pews to the pulpit. We still need to order the flowers. Doesn't your friend, Cassie, work in a florist shop near there?"

I pause. "Yes."

"We'd want some exotic flowers. If we have to go with a small place, I want it to, at least, look expensive. Do you think Cassie's shop could get some rare flowers for us? I know it's short notice, but I was hoping…" Aunt Ruth's voice trails off a little.

"You'd have to talk to Cassie about flowers, especially if it turns out that they need to go to Palm Springs," I say and then clear my throat. "And about measuring. I'm not sure that there would be—"

"Oh, well, Jerry's there," Aunt Ruth says as though something is finally working out right. "Why didn't I think of that? He can get the measurements I need.

That will keep Inga happy. There's no reason for Elaine or me to go crawling around on the floor of some simple little chapel making sure the carpet rug will fit between the pews, especially when we probably won't even have the wedding there."

"It's not simple. It's beautiful."

"I'm sure it is, dear," Aunt Ruth says in a voice that indicates she's not sure of that at all. "There's probably not room to lay the carpet rug anyway."

"Carpet rug?"

"Well, of course, a bride needs a white carpet so she can walk down the aisle. That's almost as important as the walls and the ceiling."

"Of course." I nod. "And, don't worry—I'll only look for new places that have an aisle."

"Let me talk to Jerry," Aunt Ruth says. She's sounding more like herself now that she has someone to boss around. "I'll tell him what needs to be measured."

"Back to you," I say to Jerry as I hand the phone back to him.

I let Jerry talk to Aunt Ruth while I go into the bedroom and get dressed for work. Actually, it's turning out to be a good thing that Jerry is here. He can hold the aunts off with all of his measuring tasks while I try to find a different place for Elaine's wedding.

"Do you have a tape measure?" Jerry asks when I come out of the bedroom in my black suit.

"I think Cassie has a yardstick," I say. She uses it to keep track of how tall her potted plants are growing. "It's over beside the refrigerator."

Cassie has apparently already left for work. I look at the counter next to the door and see she's taken the papers for Doug. That's good. Cassie always does what she says she will. Other people could take lessons from her.

I look at Jerry. "I thought you said you were going to help Cassie today. Shouldn't you go to work with her?"

Jerry is pulling the yardstick out from beside the refrigerator. I forgot the thing is broken off at the two-foot mark.

"What good is this?" Jerry asks.

"It works fine for measuring plant growth," I say. "Maybe when Cassie brings a larger plant back she'll need to get a longer ruler. Remember you were going to help her move that ficus back here."

"I can only do one thing at a time," Jerry snaps back at me. "And Aunt Ruth is going hysterical."

"She sounded okay to me on the phone."

"Well, of course, she's not going to yell at you on the phone. You're her backup plan. With me, it was measure this and measure that. What am I? I can only do one thing at a time. I kept trying to tell her that I didn't have a tape to do that with, but she said the wedding chapel would have one."

"Oh." Of course, the Big M has an impressive assortment of measuring devices. Tape measures. Yardsticks. Foot-long rulers. We've got them all. I have just realized now, though, that for Jerry to measure anything at the Big M, he has to actually come down to the place. Once he sees the Big M in business, he will know what's going on.

"You do have a tape measure where you work, don't you?" Jerry asks me. "I'm not spending twenty bucks going out to buy some measuring tape just to please Aunt Ruth."

I try to smile and look natural. The Jerry of old used to be able to smell fear in the same way a dog could. I need to look as though there's nothing to hide.

"Oh, sure, we have plenty of measuring devices," I say and pause. "Before we go there, though, I'm wondering if it wouldn't be better for you to move plants today and do the measuring tomorrow."

"And have Aunt Ruth breathing down my neck for another day? No way."

I'd forgotten I am wearing my black suit. A black suit gives a person a dignity that others just naturally follow. I stand up straight. "I'm afraid today won't be a convenient day for you to measure in the chapel."

"Some movie star getting married?" Jerry asks as he puts the broken yardstick on the table and turns to me. "That would be great. It might make Aunt Ruth stand up and take notice of your chapel. Who is it?"

"The names of people using the chapel are confidential," I say. Which is true. I think. I know it's true with hospitals and death should be as private as any illness.

"Oh," Jerry says. "Well, I guess I'll just have to meet you when you leave work. Cassie can show me where it is. She gave me directions to her shop and it looks pretty easy."

"I don't know when I'll get off tonight," I say a little desperately. "And, I'm going to be looking for other places to have Elaine's wedding so I might work late."

I can get a lot of calls made on my lunch hour and Miss Billings might have some suggestions.

"Besides," I continue. "You'll have a long day with moving those plants. You'll be tired. Maybe you should just take it easy tonight. You could even stop someplace and take Cassie to dinner."

A deep flush crawls up Jerry's face. "Do you think she would go? Out with me, I mean?"

I shrug. "I don't see why not."

Actually, I can see several reasons why not, but I'm not going to go into them here. It's mostly just things Jerry did in the past that destroyed any hope I had of him turning into a caring human being. I guess, though, we can't judge everyone by what they did when they were ten years old.

"Yeah, I suppose you're right," Jerry says. He doesn't sound too happy about it. "She wouldn't want to upset you so she'd say yes even if going out with me was the last thing she wanted to do."

"I don't think it would be the last thing she'd want to do," I say cautiously. I don't want to encourage Jerry just in case he isn't genuinely interested in Cassie. "I thought you were interested in Mona, that wedding planner, anyway."

"Well, that's going nowhere."

Wait a minute. It just occurred to me. "But you must have some idea where she is. You would not have taken off from your job unless you thought you knew where the wedding planner would be."

"I was already taking time off from my job to help with the wedding," Jerry says. "Boy, I can tell you I'd rather rebuild an old engine that has its bolts all rusted shut than run around helping with this wedding. All that candle business. It drives a person crazy."

"Someone has to do it."

"Yeah, well," Jerry looks uncomfortable. "I guess I should be getting down to the floral shop and start lifting things for Cassie."

I look at the clock.

"Yeah, well, I need to get to work, too," I say as I pick up my purse and loop it over my shoulder.

I notice Jerry carries his duffel bag with him when he leaves the apartment with me. I wonder if he's worried about whether or not we'll let him in tonight. He offers to drop me off at my job on his way to the floral shop, but I decline.

"So is the place you work a pit, or what?" Jerry says as he opens the door to his pickup truck. "You seem very anxious to keep me away from there."

So, Cousin Jerry had picked up a few brain cells lately.

"It looks like a European cathedral," I say.

Jerry grunts as he climbs into his cab. "Then what's the big problem?"

"There's not a big problem."

"Yeah, and the moon ain't made of cottage cheese."

"We all know it's not," I say. That cottage cheese and the moon remark was one of those annoying things Jerry used to say when we were growing up. He said he heard some detective on television say that, but I never heard it. I doubt you have either.

I think Jerry was just making things up in his head, because, back then, he wanted to be a detective when he grew up. Personally, I always thought it was all just an excuse so he could spy on people with those things in his Greatest Detectives of the World Kit and feel justified in doing so. I was jealous when he got that detective kit for Christmas one year. All I ever got were frilly little dolls.

I would tell Jerry again that the moon isn't made of any kind of cheese, but he's already got his door closed and he's starting his pickup truck. So, I just shake my head, and turn in the other direction to walk to the bus stop. I'm hoping Miss Billings will have a minute to talk when I get to the Big M. She knows more about Hollywood than anyone I know and I can count on her to have some suggestions for places where people can hold a wedding.

Miss Billings is with a client when I get to work. Usually, she leaves the clients to the customer representatives, but she takes any special clients that are less than three feet tall. She must have been waiting for me because I don't even have a chance to start the filing before she comes into the break room to find me.

"Oh, good, you're here." Miss Billings looks ready to burst. "I told my little friend, Breanna, that you would sit with her for a while and tell her the Cinderella story."

"Cinderella?"

"All little girls love that story," Miss Billings says as she impatiently gestures for me to follow her. "You remember it, don't you?"

"Sure. Wicked stepmother. Jealous stepsisters. Pumpkin at twelve and don't forget your shoe." I follow Miss Billings out into the lobby area and then into one of the consultation rooms.

"Ah," I say almost involuntarily.

"This is Breanna," Miss Billings says brightly with a nod at the little girl curled up on the couch.

The little girl doesn't smile at either Miss Billings or me. She does, however, acknowledge us with a fierce scowl. Her face is red and I'd guess she's either been crying or throwing a temper tantrum, or both.

"Miss Julie is going to tell you a story now," Miss Billings says to the girl as she starts to back out of the room.

Then she turns to me and whispers in an aside as she passes me on her way to the door. "She doesn't want a lamb. Or a lollipop. Or a hug."

I notice one of Miss Billing's stuffed lambs lying on the floor with its ear torn off and take another look at the deepening scowl on Breanna's face.

"Wait," I whisper as I turn to catch Miss Billings before she leaves the room. "Does she want a story?"

"I hope so."

With that, Miss Billings shuts the door. Why do I feel that final click of the door closing is like the clank of a dungeon cell being locked? Of course, there's nothing to fear from a little girl, is there?

"You do want a story, don't you?" I turn to the girl and force myself to smile.

She stares at the closed door and doesn't answer me.

"I can tell a really good story," I add as I go to the sofa and sit on the end opposite of where Breanna is curled up. I'm not sure she's going to bolt for the door, but I don't want to be in her way if she does. "A story about beautiful princesses and—"

"I hate princesses," Breanna says still staring at the door.

"Oh, well, me, too," I say. "But this one is okay

because she doesn't know she's going to be a princess."

"Is she slow?" Breanna asks. She turns to actually look at me. "I know a boy on our street and my mother says he's slow."

Now isn't the time for me to give Breanna a lesson on politically correct terms for specially challenged children. Unless I miss my guess she hates me less than she did when I walked in the room and I don't want to damage that fragile beginning.

"No, Cinderella doesn't know she's a princess because she hasn't met the prince yet."

"I know." Breanna gives a deep sigh. "She lost her shoe. Nothing nice ever happens to me when I lose a shoe."

I move a little closer down the sofa. "Nothing nice ever happens to me when I lose something, either."

"I lost my daddy," Breanna says as she leans toward me a little.

"I'm so sorry that happened." I move close enough to Breanna to put my arm around her.

To my surprise, Breanna snuggles into my arms.

"I tried to find him, but he wasn't in his room," she says. "My mom said he went to heaven, but I don't know where that is."

"My daddy's in heaven, too," I say.

Breanna sits enough forward so that she can turn and look at my face. "Do you know where that is?"

"No, sweetheart," I say. "I don't."

I hold Breanna while her mother finishes making the arrangements with Mr. Z for her husband's funeral. I wonder who held me when my mother made the arrangements for my father's service. Then I wonder why God can't tell people where heaven really is. Does it need to be such a big secret? If little girls only knew it was the left star to the right past the Little Dipper, it would make them feel better.

I've come to appreciate how comforting it is to know where things are. Maybe it's because I've become more aware of good filing systems lately with all of the filing that I do. There's nothing like a good filing system to let you know where everything is.

In any event, I do think God could do a better job of making things more orderly. It wouldn't hurt Him to say Breanna's father is number A-89 gazillion plus or minus ten in heaven and he is located forty degrees left of the moon. Does He have any idea how comforting that would be to the bereaved? I know it would be comforting to me.

I look up at the ceiling while I hold Breanna. Someday when I look up there, I would like to see my father's face looking down at me. My real father's face. Maybe, like Breanna, I still believe that if I only knew where to look I could find my dad.

Chapter Eight

It is almost lunchtime before I have a chance to ask Miss Billings if she knows of other locations for my cousin's wedding. She is sitting at her desk and peeling some golden star stickers off of their backing for a special request made by a customer.

"It's the older couple, the Berkstroms," she says as I sit in the chair next to her desk and take one of the sticker sheets to help her. "They want these stickers on the programs for their son's memorial. They said he'd always liked stickers like these when he was in school and that he'd been a good boy so he deserves them."

I remembered seeing the forms for their son, Joey Berkstrom.

Joey was "slow" to use Breanna's word. He'd lived with his parents all of his thirty-eight years, but he had enjoyed his days at a special school. From all I read about him, he might have been slow at some things, but he wasn't slow when it came to loving other people. He loved with his arms wide-open. Mr. Z is planning to use the double room for Joey's final viewing because so many people are expected to come and say goodbye to him.

I like peeling the stars off their backing and pasting them on the programs Miss Billings has on her desk. "I wish I'd known him."

"They say everybody loved him," Miss Billings says.

Miss Billings and I stick stars on programs and are quiet for a while.

At moments like this at the Big M, I have to admit that I don't understand death. I had never thought about it much before, which might be strange since my father died on me when I was little. But, to be honest, my mother left a bigger hole in my childhood. And, she wasn't dead, she was just in Las Vegas. Not all absences are equal, I guess. In some ways death is easier than just having a parent decide to leave you the way my mother did me and Cassie's mother did her.

Maybe it's because, even though we don't know much about death, we do know the basic rules and one of those rules is that dead is dead and people don't have much choice about it once it happens. Living is so much more complicated. I feel as if my time at the Big M is helping me learn a little more about it all, though.

"Do you know if Mr. Z talked to his brother in Florida?" I ask. I'm not the only one learning things at the Big M. "Are they going to get together for Thanksgiving?"

Miss Billings nods. "Haven't you noticed that he got himself a new shirt?"

I looked up from the programs. "I haven't seen him today."

"He's wearing a Hawaiian shirt under his suit jacket. I told him it's Florida, not Hawaii, but to him they both seem like foreign countries. Fortunately, this is the Hollywood mortuary so people expect a little bit of the unusual. The Berkstroms seemed to take it in stride. But, then, they were used to Joey."

"At least Mr. Z sounds like he's happy," I say. I can't quite picture him wearing anything but a white shirt. "Is he still wearing his black tie?"

Miss Billings nods. "He looks like a man who's torn between enjoying himself and tending to business."

I grin just picturing him. Way to go, Mr. Z. Then I remember that I need some information.

"I'm wondering if you know of a backup place I could look at for my cousin's wedding, just in case something happens and Mr. Z wants to keep his place open," I say.

"What could happen?"

I shrug. "He and his brother could have another fight before he leaves."

Miss Billings shook her head. "That won't happen. His brother could say white is black and Mr. Z would just nod his head and agree. He doesn't want another fight."

"I hate to see Mr. Z close the Big M for my cousin's wedding. Her mother is still looking for a location in Palm Springs and she might get it. Or, my cousin could get cold feet at the last minute and cancel the wedding."

Miss Billings shrugs. "At this point, Mr. Z would leave it closed anyway. I don't think anything will stop him from going to Florida to see his brother. Even if there had been no mention of a wedding, Mr. Z would still close the Big M when he's gone."

"But if, for some reason, my cousin couldn't use the Big M for her wedding, what would some other places be?"

Miss Billings thinks a minute. "Well, there's Griffith Park. And there's the big Chinese restaurant by Universal Studios. What's their name? Spring Garden, that's it. A friend of mine got married there. It was her fourth time getting married. Imagine that? But it was nice. They have an outdoor garden for the ceremony and people move inside for dinner. The walls have pictures of cherry blossoms on them and all the fixtures are brass. It looks wonderful when the lights are dim. Besides, they have great egg rolls."

"That might work," I say. What's not to like about dim light and egg rolls?

"And they had fortune cookies made special for the wedding with the bride and groom's name inside," Miss Billings says.

"Elaine might like that." I'm feeling pretty good about now. I know for a fact that Elaine likes fortune cookies. She always opens three or four until she finds a fortune that she likes—which I call cheating but which she calls taking charge of her life. I sometimes wonder if Elaine will end up like Aunt Ruth, always telling everyone what to do.

Miss Billings and I spend a few more minutes putting Joey's programs in neat stacks before I leave to go outside so I can get good reception on my cell phone.

Before I call Information to get the number for the restaurant, I notice that I have a message waiting. I'd

turned my phone off this morning because Mr. Z
doesn't like cell phones ringing inside the Big M. I
don't always remember to turn it off, but I try to.

I think Mr. Z is right. It's a mark of respect for the
dead that we're a little quieter around them. Not that they
care since they're not listening or anything. I've noticed,
though, that people tend to whisper around the caskets
and tiptoe into the viewing rooms. We tend to treat the
dead as if they're just taking a nap and I've wondered if
maybe the quiet is for us. It doesn't make the departed
ones seem so far away if we think they're just asleep.

The message on my cell phone is from Cassie and
she's inviting me to meet her and Jerry after work at
the coffee shop. I hesitate for a minute because I'm
wondering if Doug will be there at the same time. I'm
not sure I'm ready to face him. But, even as I think
about it, I decide that the last place Doug will be is at
the coffee shop. He probably doesn't even drink coffee
now that he's taken those religious vows.

Okay, so that sounds a little bitter on my part. I'm
sure Doug does still drink coffee even though he's
probably not hanging out anywhere now that he's got
more serious things to think about. He's probably on
his knees someplace praying. A lot of fun that is. I
can't help but wish things were back the way they
were before we went to that rally.

You know how sometimes you don't figure something out until it's too late? That happens to me. It took
me a while to realize Doug and I could have become
friends. Of course, we had all that weirdness at
Elaine's party so I can't say it was obvious at first that
we could do the friendship thing.

Once I found out he was raised by his aunts like me, though, I felt a lot of pieces come together. I could so totally understand why he was a jerk at Elaine's party. I think it's kind of like my toppling. As a kid, I was so afraid I wouldn't please people—like my mother, no big surprise there—that I ended up doing stupid things. I figure Doug has the pleasing problem multiplied on him. The insecurity makes you do the opposite of what the normal, well-adjusted thing would be. He and I could have started a support group for people raised by their relatives.

In any event, Doug is probably off living his new life somewhere and doing just fine with his new circle of religious friends. I doubt very much that he's hanging out at the coffee shop anymore.

I call Cassie and leave her a message that I will be at the coffee shop around five-thirty.

Then I call the restaurant and talk to the manager. He tells me that they have the garden free the Friday evening after Thanksgiving and that they can accommodate a party of two hundred people if we are willing to be seated in the outdoor pagoda and lawn area. They'd give us the empress dinner which has six entrées and all of the egg rolls and pot stickers we wanted for eight thousand dollars. That includes the setup of the chairs and use of the special wedding arch. If we wanted something simpler—aka cheaper—they could give us the egg rolls, pot stickers and various fruit in a buffet style in the lawn area for five thousand dollars. I told him I would call him back after I had talked to my aunt.

I took another minute and called Aunt Ruth. She

didn't pick up during my message, which surprised me because she is always home in the afternoons and, well, Jerry had said she always picked up for me.

Anyway, I left a message that I had another option for Elaine's wedding that sounded great. It was in a Chinese garden that had exotic flowers already so she wouldn't need to worry about ordering more. Plus, the restaurant could provide the food so everything would be set. The price was reasonable and Elaine's dress would look good in the night lights. That all didn't seem like enough so I added that the beads on Elaine's dress would glimmer in an outdoor setting.

I spend the rest of the afternoon looking happier than a person should look in a mortuary. But, what with Mr. Z in his Hawaiian shirt and Miss Billings walking around unaware she has a gold star stuck to her forehead, no one seems to notice my unnatural cheer.

After I check out of the Big M for the day, I take the Metro bus over to the coffee shop. Now, Los Angeles is the land of gourmet coffee shops with our Starbucks and our Peet's and our Seattle's Best. The coffee shop next to Cassie's floral shop was there long before coffee went gourmet. It does its best to keep up, however, and offers lattes, cappuccinos and, when Asad is working the counter, an espresso stronger than any I've ever tasted anywhere. They also have all those bottles of coffee flavors. To tell you the truth, though, the best thing on their menu is a blended orange tea that has just a whiff of nutmeg.

I step inside the coffee shop. There are large windows on all three sides of the shop and light floods the place all day long. There are a couple of women I don't know sitting at a table in one corner and a man reading a newspaper along the back wall. There is classical music playing softly in the background and discarded newspapers sitting at several empty tables.

From behind the counter, Asad waves at me. "Julie, welcome. I delivered your notes to Doug when he came over at lunch."

"Thanks," I say although I'm hard-pressed to drum up any enthusiasm for Doug or my notes.

Asad looks at me as he pulls down a cup from the shelf above his head. Regular clients here all have their own mugs and mine is the white one with Seattle's space needle traced in gold on the front of it.

"They are love notes, no?" Asad asks. "My English not so good, but I see the love word many times."

I wince and then walk toward the counter. "It's not that kind of love."

Asad looks surprised. "But the notes say love, love, love—all over is love."

Asad is happily married and thinks everyone else should be, as well.

"That's love of God."

"Ah," Asad says as he fills my cup with hot water. "It's good to love God, too. That is the blessed life."

Asad puts the cup of hot water on the counter and pulls out the small wooden box that holds the tea bags. "Here's your tea."

I always pick the orange tea, but I like to flip through the rows of tea bags anyway just in case a new flavor has been added. Besides, I like the confusion of smells from the tea.

Asad reaches to the shelf behind him for a wrapped cinnamon biscotti and he puts it on the counter. I always order cinnamon biscotti with my orange tea. Someday I will sit and ponder whether that means I'm in a rut. Today, though, the predictability feels good.

I unwrap the tea bag and set it in my cup of hot water.

Then I pay and take my cup of tea and biscotti to a side table. I take off my suit jacket and hang it on the back of my chair. I wore a short-sleeved pink blouse under the black jacket I wear at the Big M and it feels good to be a little informal now. I didn't realize until I lost my job at the bank that one of the pleasures of work was getting casual after work. If you were simply not working all day, you would miss that moment.

I look out the window behind me because I can see the side of the floral shop where Cassie works. I see Jerry's pickup behind the store so I know they're both there, especially because a huge ficus plant and several smaller ficus plants are loaded into the back of his pickup already.

I like to dunk the biscotti in the orange tea and so I do that. While I'm chewing, I see the florist shop door open and out come Jerry and Cassie. I see a few dirt marks on Cassie's yellow sweatshirt so I'm guessing they just recently moved the ficus plants. The two of them are laughing about something and I see that Jerry still has his duffel bag in his hands. I don't even get a chance to take another sip of tea before Jerry opens the door and they both walk in.

I take a good look because I think Jerry has grown taller than I remember.

"Are you wearing some kind of boots?" I say to

Jerry when he comes closer. I can see his jeans and they go all the way down to his shoes. The shoes don't look as though they have a higher than normal heel.

"No, why, you got something you want stomped?" Jerry says in his usual cocky manner as he carries his duffel over and dumps it on the seat of one of the hard-back chairs that goes with my table. "Keep an eye on this, will you?"

I look at that duffel bag. "Isn't that the bag you got for Christmas when you were ten?"

"I wanted a motorcycle," he says as if it was somehow my fault.

"Hey, don't look at me. I didn't even get you anything that year."

"Yes, you did. You got me a package of red cowboy handkerchiefs."

"Aunt Inga got you those. She just put my name on the package."

Cassie follows Jerry over and puts her purse on one of the chairs, as well. "You can still see the motorcycle insignia on that duffel bag if you look close. I'm sure everyone thought a bag would be safer than a motorcycle. Besides—" she looks up at Jerry "—you were only ten."

"Christmas was never the same after that," Jerry says, but he's smiling now as if he's making a joke of it. Of course, he's smiling at Cassie and I'm still not sure if I think that's a good idea.

"I haven't seen that duffel bag for years," I say to stop the smiling if I can. "It must bring back memories."

"He's kept it in his closet all those years," Cassie says as though Jerry is very clever to have done that.

Doesn't she know that millions of people keep old
Christmas presents in their closets? There's nothing
special about it. It's called being a pack rat. Most
people don't consider it a sign of genius.

Jerry and Cassie walk over to the counter to order
something to drink. I take another look at that duffel
bag and shake my head. Jerry used to carry all of his
stuff around in that bag when he was a kid.

I wonder what's in it now. The late-afternoon sun
is coming through the window and falling right on that
fabric duffel bag. I would guess Jerry is just carrying
around his tuxedo so that he'll be ready in case he
actually does find the wedding planner and she wants
to go out on a date with him or something. Talk about
delusional. As I look at the bag, I can tell that there is
more than clothes inside. In fact, it's obvious that there
are some large solid objects in the bag, because I can
see their outline in the sunshine. There's a square
something and a round something and—I look again.
I can't be seeing things right.

"Jerry," I say in what I hope is a normal tone of
voice. "Could you come here please?"

Jerry looks over at me as suspiciously as though I
had sworn at him, but he comes. He's carrying a black
mug filled with something hot. I can't believe Asad
gave him his own mug already. I had to wait two weeks
to get my white space needle cup.

"What's up?" Jerry says as he sets his cup of coffee
on the table and straddles one of the chairs.

I speak slowly. "I know when you left Blythe to
come here, people probably told you that it is a scary
place—"

Jerry shrugs. "No one knew I was coming. Remember?"

I lower my voice and point to his duffel bag. "Then why did you bring a gun?"

There it is, for all the world to see, the outline of a gun on the side of Jerry's duffel bag.

"Oh, that," Jerry says and I swear he's blushing. "That's nothing."

"Nothing?" Okay, my voice is rising a little.

Cassie is here now and she sets her cup of coffee on the table. "What's wrong?"

I look up at her and whisper, "Jerry has a gun."

"What?" Cassie sits down. "You mean the kind with bullets?"

"There are no bullets," Jerry says. "And it's not a real gun."

I'm not that gullible and I would hope Jerry knows that by now. I stare at him. "I can see it."

It doesn't escape my notice that Cassie sees it, too. She has a little frown on her face that is deepening. "Jerry?"

Jerry sighs. "Look, it's really nothing, but—"

Jerry reaches over to lift his duffel bag on to the table. "I can tell it'll just freak you two out if you don't see."

Jerry unzips the duffel bag. "Look all you want. Pull it all out."

Now that the bag is open like that I'm not so sure. "I'm not going to be putting my hands into your dirty socks if I reach in there, am I?"

Jerry shakes his head. "The socks are in a zippered bag at the bottom of the duffel."

I'm still not eager to go in blind, so I peel the side of the duffel down enough so I can see. There's enough

black plastic down there to start a new landfill somewhere. As I look at it closely, I identify a pair of
binoculars, a plastic pencil box with Tracing stamped
on it, a pair of black gloves, and the top of a box—

"That's your Greatest Detectives of the World kit!"

"I forgot it had that toy gun in it," Jerry says. "That's
why I moved it to the side. So no one would see it
when I open the duffel."

"Well, they can see its outline anyway now. I'd put
the toy gun down in that zipped bag with your socks,"
I say. "Couldn't you have emptied the duffel before
you grabbed it?"

Okay, so I'm a little slow. I can tell by the sheepish
look on Jerry's face that I've missed something.
"Don't tell me you were using that kit, were you?"

"Well, it has directions for things," Jerry says defensively. "And those binoculars work great. And the
instructions have some good ideas for finding people
that don't want to be found."

"You can find people with that?" Cassie asks.

I need to put this in perspective for Cassie before
she gets her hopes up that Jerry could help her find her
mother. "It's a toy kit. He's never really found anyone."

"Maybe I can find the wedding planner. Maybe she
hasn't left the country like everyone thinks," he says.
"My kit said to think of what your suspect values and I
thought of that 1966 Thunderbird convertible. The way
that car was buffed out, someone loves it. She wouldn't
leave her car no matter what so all I have to do is find
the car and I'll find her if she's anywhere around."

"Well, I doubt you need the kit for that," I say.
"Besides, a true detective has a client."

"I have Elaine," Jerry said stubbornly. "She's my client."

"Well, you're not going to find the wedding planner sitting around Cassie's place."

Jerry's face flushes and he's quiet for a minute, which isn't like him. He likes to argue with me.

"Jerry, what did you do?" I ask cautiously. This is the guy who thought it made sense to keep the lizards he'd found on his walk home from school in the back closet at Aunt Ruth's place. Right now, I can see he knows he's messed up and that makes me nervous since he never did repent for the lizards. "Jerry?"

"I may have left Cassie's number for Mona to call."

"You may have *what?*" I start and then stop because I am speechless.

"The detective kit says to use any history you have with the person. I thought it made sense so I left a note on Mona's apartment door saying I have the starter for her car and that she could call me—only I didn't want to leave a Blythe number. I figured she wouldn't call anyone in Blythe, because she'd sense a trap."

"Way to go, Sherlock. Of course she'd sense a trap, only a fool would—" I begin and then I look at Cassie's face. She's white now. I take a deep breath and try for a little less panic. "Well, she won't call you anyway, will she?" See how helpful it is to stop and think before you panic. I feel so much better. "She knows you're related to Aunt Ruth."

My comfort gauge keeps going up when I think of the Aunt Ruth connection. The wedding planner might be a thief, but no one has ever accused her of being stupid. If Aunt Ruth even suspected where Mona was, the police would be all over it and, since Mona has worked for Aunt Ruth, Mona knows Aunt Ruth Gets Things Done even if it means badgering officials in the process. Mona might love that Thunderbird of hers, but she probably values her freedom a little bit more.

Jerry looks truly miserable. And a little green around the mouth.

"I sort of didn't tell her I knew Aunt Ruth that day in the driveway," Jerry says with a grimace. "No one else was around and I figured why ruin my chances with her. By then Mona had seen how Aunt Ruth can be. I figured I wouldn't have that many chances to rescue a woman like Mona, and rescuing her seemed like my best shot at a date—you know, if I decided I wanted a date. Which, as it turns out, I didn't."

I'm thinking "yeah, right, who didn't want a date?" but I don't want to give Jerry the satisfaction of an answer, so I'm quiet.

Jerry is not looking at me anyway. His eyes are all for Cassie. She's not saying anything, either, so he continues and his voice sounds a little more desperate. "I never was interested in dating her, not really. It was just something to do at the time. And I wouldn't go out with her now if—well, anyway, that day I figured if I fixed her car, she'd have to go out with me at least once." Jerry took a deep breath and I reluctantly nod in hopes it will hurry him along. Believe me, Jerry doesn't need to explain to me why he'd have to do a favor for a woman to get her attention.

"So I told Mona I live in Los Angeles," Jerry confesses in a rush. "It's not that much of a lie. I could be living in L.A. if I really wanted to be here. Besides, I couldn't tell her I live in Blythe. I figure a woman like Mona wouldn't give the time of day to a guy who lives in Blythe. I was going to say I lived in Palm Springs, but that's where she lives and I figured that was too close. She might think she should know me."

Jerry's voice trails off. "So I told her Los Angeles."

There's a long moment of silence. I'm pondering how much Aunt Ruth has rubbed off on all of us cousins. It's amazing any of us are honest about where we live.

"And you gave her my number?" Cassie doesn't get sidetracked like me and she gets right to the heart of the matter. "The 323 one? My real number?"

"To a criminal?" I ask because I think that point needs to be clear and because I feel a little guilty about letting my mind wander to Aunt Ruth's lies about where she lives. I'm beginning to wonder if we have a genetic defect in our family that leads everyone to pretend to be living where we are not. But that's not our biggest problem so I focus on Jerry again. "What were you thinking?"

Cassie has this stunned look on her face. She doesn't even give out her real phone number to normal people. Sometimes she gives out her cell number, but that can't be traced back to her address.

Jerry looks even more uncomfortable. "I guess I didn't think it all through until last night. That's why I came here just in case, well, you know something were to happen and you would need protection."

I can't even look at Cassie. I'm hoping Jerry isn't thinking he's rescuing us by saving us from his own foolishness.

"Besides, what's Mona going to do?" Jerry says.

He's talking a little fast. "Steal the car part that I'm giving her for free anyway? Mona probably didn't even get the note—who goes back to their apartment to get notes off their porch when the police are looking for them?"

"Crazy people, that's who," I say. "You've got to go back and get that note."

Jerry looks even more miserable. "I already tried. I went back last night when I realized a phone number could be matched to an address."

"And?"

"I think a dog got the note. It wasn't there on the porch anymore and I looked all over the yard and under the porch."

"Why would a dog take the note?"

Jerry shrugs. "I sort of used the bag I got my hamburgers in at that place by the freeway. I got fries, too, and they really make the bag smell."

"You're sure this Mona doesn't know you're related to Aunt Ruth?" I say to Jerry. Maybe a dog took the note and maybe one didn't. One thing that would stop the wedding planner from calling Jerry anywhere, though, is Aunt Ruth. "What if Mona followed you back to your apartment that day? She could have asked about you at the garage where you work."

I figure this Mona didn't become a thief without learning to find out things like that before she went around calling people. After all, how many guys who live in Los Angeles drive around the streets of Blythe looking for stalled cars?

"She doesn't know where I live," Jerry says. "And,

even if she figured out about the garage, no one there knows I'm related to Aunt Ruth."

Well, this is a side of Jerry I never knew existed. "I can't believe you'd keep that a secret. Aunt Ruth is family. At least, *your* family. You don't keep secrets about something like that."

Jerry snorts and looks at me. "I'm not the only one with secrets Miss-Don't-Come-to-My-Work. Makes me wonder what you really do at the place. What is it—that this fancy assistant job you have puts you in charge of the brooms and not the brides?"

I can tell Jerry is relieved to stop talking about the note he left for the wedding planner and, truthfully, so am I.

"Aren't you the funny one," I say.

"No, wait," Jerry says. He's on a roll now that he thinks he's off the hook for the note. "Don't tell me it's one of those international services where you hook up foreign brides with guys they've never met? Aren't those places illegal?"

"Is this how you do your detective work? Badgering people to death?" I say and wonder what guilty feelings made me pick a sentence with the word *death* in it.

"At least I'm trying to do something," Jerry says.

"Yes, you are," I say.

Jerry looks a little surprised that I've stopped arguing with him, but my mind is too busy at the moment to worry about fending him off. It has suddenly occurred to me that I might end up like Jerry if I keep lying about things. Or Aunt Ruth with all her lying about where she lives. Add me in there and we could be a family, or at least a half family, of liars. Believe me, that's not a happy thought.

"I work at a mortuary," I say real fast.

Cassie's eyes pop open even wider than they had at Jerry's confession.

Jerry's jaw sags. "What?"

I take a deep breath. "The reason I don't want you to visit me where I work is because I work at a mortuary."

"With dead people?"

I nod. "All around."

"Wow," Jerry says. "That's—wow."

"I'm not ashamed to work there," I say in a rush now that I've opened up the subject for discussion.

"So Elaine's backup plan for getting married is to get married in a mortuary?" Jerry asks. His eyes are still wide.

"No, I'm hoping Elaine's backup plan will be this nice Chinese garden," I say patiently. "I talked to the manager today and they have the right date open. I just need to talk to Aunt Ruth. I left her a message and I'm sure she'll call back anytime now."

"Wow, a mortuary," Jerry says again. "With caskets and everything?"

I nod.

"Cool," he says as he leans back in his chair. "That's all right."

After all of this, Jerry grins at me and, I must admit, I grin back. It's nice to know I can tell the truth to one person in my family.

"Oh. You can't tell anyone yet, though," I say to Jerry.

Jerry laughs. "Don't worry. I wouldn't touch that news with a ten-foot pole."

The three of us sit and finish drinking our tea and coffee as the sun starts to set. We all kind of mull over the note Jerry left on Mona's door and decide it is probably harmless enough.

"If someone does call asking for Jerry, though," he says. "Just say it's the wrong number."

Well, that would seem as if it would work.

As it turns out, Jerry has asked Cassie out to dinner—good for him—and she is still going even though I doubt she's thought through all of the note problems—good for her, I think. The plan is for them to stop at some restaurant on their way home with the ficus plants. My guess is it will be a casual place. Maybe that soup and salad place Cassie likes. I feel a little nostalgic as they get up to leave the coffee shop and I notice that Jerry has his hand on Cassie's elbow just like a gentleman should. He might be a little reckless by leaving notes around, but the aunts would be proud of his manners.

It's too bad that a hand on one's elbow doesn't mean much anymore. I sigh, looking down at my empty teacup and think of Doug. I kind of liked the way I felt about him better before I knew he'd faced his problems in life, too. Back then I could just write him off as a jerk. Now, I have these ambivalent feelings. I hate it when that happens. I want to know if I like a person or not. I'm not much on gray. I shake my head. I wonder what I will tell the aunts when I show up at Elaine's wedding without a date.

Oh, look. There's a gold star floating down. It must have been in my hair or stuck on my blouse under the black suit. Anyway, it's kind of nice to see it float down and land in my empty teacup. Not that it makes up for not having a man to take me to dinner.

But then I smile, thinking of Joey. I bet he would have liked to watch that star fall into my cup. I start to brush off my shoulders just in case there's another star waiting to fall, but then I stop. Maybe I should give up trying to figure out when everything is going to happen. I'll let the star fall when it wants. It's good to have a surprise or two in life.

Chapter Nine

I take the Metro bus back to Cassie's place and get off a stop earlier than I need to so that I can pick up some groceries to make my dinner. After I walk the aisles in the store for a few minutes, I see a red rose that is set apart, a little behind the other flowers in the buckets next to the produce section. It's the only one in the half-price bucket.

I don't know why I pick up the long-stemmed rose and put it in my checkout basket. Maybe I just can't stand it that one stem is left behind all alone with a half-worth sign on it. I'm sure it's been passed over a dozen times already today. Even with the water tube on its stem, the rose has started to droop. Still, a full-bodied rose like that is made for romance and I haven't seen much of that lately.

Well, unless you count Jerry and Cassie. Maybe I'll put the rose in a vase and leave it on the table for the two of them. Sort of a very subtle blessing on their budding relationship, even though I doubt either one of them is ready to admit such a thing even exists yet.

I shake my head just thinking about the two of them. How did things ever come to this? My best childhood friend and my most bothersome male cousin on a date together. Between the two of them, they know all my secrets. It should alarm me to think of them sitting together and talking without me there to defend myself.

Instead, I smile thinking about it. Hopefully, they have so many other things to talk about that they both forget that they even know me. Life certainly has its unexpected moments when it comes to romance.

Maybe something like that will happen for me one day. I've always thought I'd meet the love-of-my-life when I least expected it. Like maybe I'd be in a coffee shop and he'd order the exact type of latte I ordered and we'd start talking about what we liked and one thing would lead to another until he asked me out on the date to end all dates. Or maybe I'd just be stepping out of a beauty salon with my short auburn hair swept back the way it can be and he would be so struck with my titian beauty he would have to stop right there on the street and invite me out to this fabulous dinner.

Don't laugh. It could happen. Granted, it wasn't happening in Blythe.

When I left Blythe, there were two coffee shops of the kind I see in Hollywood—one on the north side of town and one on the south side. There were also a handful of beauty salons. One of the reasons I knew I had to leave Blythe was because there were so few places where I might actually meet The One. I just couldn't imagine him even being in Blythe.

Well, it was also the fact there were no good jobs to be found. I'm not one of those women who thinks she has to have a man or she will die unfulfilled. I have more sense than that. But if I am not going to meet a man, I at least want a job that has enough excitement to it so that I can tell I'm alive. My bank teller job sure didn't do it for me, but I think the job at the Big M has possibilities.

Besides, I like it in Hollywood. I've been meaning to knock on the manager's door in this building and ask him to let me know when the next apartment becomes available. I paid Cassie for part of the rent when I got my first paycheck from the Big M last week. I haven't decided yet whether or not I will keep working at the Big M long term, but it pays more than I've ever made on a job and, since I like it there, I plan to stay.

For one thing, I learn stuff at the Big M that I might not learn other places. Even ordinary things like the different smells roses can have.

The rose I bought is leaning against my suit jacket as I climb the stairs. This is a classical red rose with a deep traditional smell to it, but other roses, particularly yellow ones, can have such a light floral scent that one barely notices them. And orange roses, at least the ones at the Big M, can have a slightly fruity scent. Now, that's all something I can use as a wedding planner, don't you think? I can suggest special fragrance themes for a wedding. I didn't know any of the stuff about roses before I started working at the Big M.

I wave to Mrs. Snyder as I set my grocery bags

down on the hallway floor so I can get my keys out of
my purse to open the apartment door. I know you're
supposed to have your keys in your hands when you
come in at night, but it's hard to do that when you're
also carrying groceries. Besides, it's not quite dark out
even though the lights in the hallway have probably
been on for some time.

"Welcome home, dear," Mrs. Snyder says after
opening her door a bit. I see a strip of fuzzy purple
bathrobe, one lively blue eye and half a nose in the
crack of the doorway.

"Thanks," I say as I smile over my shoulder at her.
"How's it going?"

"I'm watching a movie on television," Mrs. Snyder
whispers. "Rock Hudson."

I nod. "Sounds good."

After I step inside the apartment, I reach down and
pull the grocery bags in behind me. My eye automatically goes to Cassie's answer machine and I am relieved
that the red light isn't blinking so, at least for now, no
one has called about that starter for Mona's car. After
I finish eyeing the answer machine, I close and lock the
door, turn on the light and lift the bags onto the small
kitchen counter. A head of lettuce and a couple of
tomatoes share one bag with a box mix for rice pilaf.
A rotisserie chicken has its own foil bag inside a plastic
bag. I just lay the rose on the table for now.

My cell phone rings just after I put some water on
to heat to make the rice pilaf. I'm glad I have one of
those fancy sound tones so it doesn't sound like the
regular phone ringing. I wouldn't want to answer
Cassie's phone and find out Mona was calling.

"Julie?"

Uh-oh. I recognize that voice. "Hi, Doug."

I try to keep the surprise out of my voice. I didn't really think I'd hear from Doug again. Not after I tried to keep him from walking down the aisle at the rally. I wonder for a minute if I should apologize for trying to hold him back. After all, there's the whole freedom of religion thing and Doug is big on civilization and apologies.

I open my mouth, but I don't get a chance to say anything.

"You've got to help me," Doug says in a frantic low whisper.

I still remember how pale he looked at Elaine's engagement party. Maybe he's anemic or something. You might not know it, but unhealthy people die at an alarming rate. "You're not sick, are you?"

"No, I just never realized what I was getting into," he says. I can picture the intense look in his eyes about now. He sounds the way he sounded when he was talking to Aunt Ruth.

Doug is resisting some commitment and he can't blame this one on me. I stop myself from announcing to him that I told him so, but it does feel good to have my common sense applauded. Nothing good ever comes from making hasty commitments. He should know that.

"Look, can I come over and get your help with this stuff from the rally?" Doug says, his voice still strained enough that I know he's not feeling calm.

"Of course." I look at the pan in my hand. "I'm just fixing dinner. There's plenty for two if you want."

"Great, I'm starving," Doug says.

After Doug hangs up, I look at the roasted chicken lying in the foil pan on the counter. It's plump and good-sized, so hopefully it is enough even if Doug is starving. I put the pilaf seasoning in the water so that it can simmer for five minutes before I put the rest of the contents of the box in with it. Then I take some plates down from the cupboard and put them on the table.

Cassie has a vase that works for a single rose and I put the rose in that and set it in the middle of the table. I also bring out a couple of nice napkins; they're paper napkins, but those nice paper napkins that advertise that they feel like cloth. I almost feel as though this is a party and I'm humming away. Maybe I haven't lost my almost friend before we really had time to become solid friends, if you know what I mean. Maybe he'll come back to my side of things.

Just so you know, I'm not thinking romantic here. I'm thinking how nice it would be to have Doug for a friend. I've thought about the time Doug and I spent flirting with each other at Elaine's party—that was before the meltdown, of course—and, you know, we had more fun together than I've had in ages.

And, now, look at this turn of events. I've got to hand it to Doug. I've heard of people who've walked down the aisle at a church service and then backed out of the agreement, but I've never known anyone personally who did it. I've got to respect Doug for having that kind of courage. I just hope that going back on his commitment won't be a problem later on his deathbed or anything. Suddenly, I stop humming. I'm feeling a little uneasy. I'm not sure I should help someone break their commitment to God.

Wow. I just stand a minute with the pilaf spoon in my hand. This could be major. As I've said before, I don't disbelieve in God. I'm carefully sitting in the neutral zone. But if I help someone desert their post, I don't know. That's not so neutral any more. God might not be too happy about that. I've never gone up against God before. Mine is mostly an ignore thing.

While I finish cooking the rice pilaf, I think about what to say to Doug. I'm beginning to feel that I should give him both sides of the story. That way, if and when Doug chooses to undo his commitment, it won't be because I convinced him to do so. Even God has to respect fairness like that, don't you think?

Of course, I will assure Doug that there is no shame in changing one's mind about a commitment—that some commitments shouldn't be made unless a person is very, very sure. There are those gym memberships for one thing. You know, the ones where a person is pressured into buying a whole year and then they want to quit after four excruciating days on those sweaty machines, but they can't get any of their money back? Or the times when a guy tells the barber to shave all the hair off his head. Some commitments should have a cooling-off period before they go into effect. In fact, there is something legal along those lines, isn't there?

I'm pretty sure you can return a car you just bought within seventy-two hours after you sign the papers. If a person can return a car, they should be able to say nay to a religious commitment they made. That's what I'll tell Doug. It will make him feel good that he's got the full weight of the law on his side.

I have some time left so I take a few seconds to fluff

up my hair and put on a light coat of lipstick before Doug knocks at the door. I give a quick nervous glance up to the ceiling hoping my real father might get the hint that this is not a good time for him to be watching over me. A girl needs some privacy. I suppose dead people don't need any privacy, but then they don't do anything but sing hymns anyway so what's the use of privacy for them. But a girl who wants to spend time with a male friend, even if she's not ready to date him, definitely needs privacy.

I open the door. "Hi, I—"

Doug grunts as he steps inside. "I just read your notes and I had to come over."

He looks as though he didn't sleep at all last night.

"Really?" Imagine, me taking good enough notes so that Doug could understand how serious the commitment was that he'd been asked to make. "And my notes were enough to make you change your mind?"

"I need your help," Doug says.

Doug has his tan jacket zipped up all the way and a black backpack slung over his shoulder. He seems nervous; I don't think he's listened to anything I've said so far so I decide I need to be very clear. "You know, you can just decide to ignore your commitment. You didn't sign any legal papers. You don't need anyone's help."

Doug looks confused. "You said in your notes you could teach me about the Bible."

"Me?"

"Of course, you," Doug says as he swings the backpack around so it's in his hands. "You wrote it on the top page of the notes you took."

"Oh." Now I know what he's talking about. "You mean when I said I could show you how to *find* things in the Bible? The books, the chapters, the verses."

This is kid's stuff. If you've been in Sunday school as much as I have been, you have all these things memorized. There's even a little song that includes the books of the Bible. It's a little singsongy so that once you get it in your head, you can't get it out no matter how hard you try. Believe me, I say that from experience.

Doug nods. "I don't even know what a verse is." Even though he's got his backpack in his hands, his shoulders are slumped and he looks defeated. "I thought it was something to do with poetry so I asked the person next to me if we'd be quoting from any French poems about God because I know some French and I thought it might be useful for pronunciation."

"It's a natural mistake," I say sympathetically.

"The guy laughed."

"I don't think they're supposed to laugh at you," I say. Now I'm indignant. That's not how Christians are supposed to act.

"It was just another guy who walked down to the front so he probably didn't know what he was supposed to do, either."

"Oh." We're quiet a minute. And then because I have to be sure, I ask, "So you don't want to take back your commitment?"

"Of course not," Doug says. He straightens his shoulders and he doesn't look defeated any longer. "I'm not a quitter."

Okay, so he has his pride. "You don't need to be a quitter, you could just say it was a mistake and that you've remembered you need to take a trip to Sweden and take one of those ice plunges."

There, I've pulled out the big guns. Who can resist a trip to Sweden? I feel like Vanna White with my big smile. "It's probably even winter there now. Remember Sweden. Nice and cold?"

"I'm not sure I could stand all that cold," Doug says without even thinking about it. "Besides, I don't want to quit. I just don't want to look stupid and have anyone laugh at me again."

"Ah."

"When I went down front at the rally, people were talking about this in the Bible and that in the Bible and I didn't know where any of it was located. Well, of course, you know that by now. I thought the Bible was written in poems. How ignorant can I be?"

"For the record, some of it is in poems. But I'm sure no one expected you to know all of that," I say.

Doug looks up in surprise. "*I* expected it. If I'm going to talk about what's in the Bible, I should be able to sit down with the book and find where it says that."

"Well, it's not that hard," I reassure him. To tell the truth, I'm kind of relieved he's not bailing on God. This certainly keeps my record cleaner with God. I'm back to the neutral zone.

"So, you'll show me?" Doug asks.

I am silent for a minute. The only sound is the clock ticking away. I'm not sure I'm the right person to be doing this.

"I guess I can give you a quick lesson after we eat," I finally say. I have never been one to hoard knowledge. Of course, I've never had someone come to me and ask for this particular knowledge before, either. Books of the Bible is not exactly party conversation—well, unless you're Doug.

"I brought my Bible," Doug says as he unzips his backpack and pulls out a huge black book.

"Did they give you that at the rally?" I ask. That's one impressive book. It is three inches thick. The guy and girl at the rally with the spike necklace and lipstick could do some serious damage with a couple of books like that.

Doug shakes his head. "They just gave me a flyer at the rally. I went to the bookstore and got the biggest Bible I could find. I didn't want to get any kind of a condensed version."

I nod and look at the book. It has King James Version and Extra Large Print stamped on the cover. It probably has reference material, too. "Well, that should have it all."

Doug carefully sets his Bible on the corner of the table next to the wall. It sits there the whole time we eat and I keep eyeing it, wondering if I'll remember everything I know about it when I start talking. The King James Version isn't the most friendly version of the Bible. People just don't talk that way anymore. But the books and verses are all in the same order so Doug can use it to begin to learn how to find things.

"You know, sometimes people think that belonging to a church is like belonging to a family," I say. I want to be sure Doug understands what he's getting into before we start talking about the King James. "But it's not always like that. I mean, I know that someone like us who has family issues might think it's the solution, but—"

Doug smiles. "It's okay. I'm doing this despite my past, not because of it."

I kind of study him to see if he's been brainwashed or anything. His eyes look clear so I think he's okay. His eyes are green, by the way. A nice mossy color. "I just wondered because of the suitcase thing."

"I wondered about that, too."

He doesn't say anymore, but I thought if he had wondered about his commitment problems he would have slowed this train down some. "There's nothing that says you can't take some time to evaluate your decision. Maybe you jumped in too fast?"

Doug shrugged. "So I make a decision too soon here. What's the worst that can happen?"

I don't answer Doug on account of the fact that I don't generally use those kinds of words. But if he doesn't know what kind of trouble he can get himself into—for eternity, yet—I'm not going to be the one to tell him.

"I guess it's too late anyway," I say and go back to eating.

Doug waits a bit and then answers me some more. "It's different with God. It doesn't seem like He's going to ask me to pack my suitcase and move down the line in a month or two."

I shrug. I guess Doug is making his own misguided decision here and, one thing I know for sure, is that we're all entitled to make our own mistakes in life.

Finally, we've finished eating and have washed the plates and neatly stacked them in the dish drainer. I don't remember until then that we didn't say grace before we ate. Aunt Inga always says grace before a meal. I guess Doug doesn't know the rules as well as

Aunt Inga, because he didn't make any mention of grace.

"Ready?" Doug says as he folds the dish towel and hangs it on the hook that Cassie has for it.

I nod as we walk back toward the table. "You might want to take some notes."

I have moved the vase onto the counter again so the table is completely clear except for that big Bible. Doug pulls a notepad and pen from his backpack and sits down in one of the chairs. I sit in the other.

I clear my throat waiting for inspiration to come to me. Where do I start? "One thing you need to know is that everyone says a grace before they eat so if they give you anything to eat, wait for everyone to be served and then bow your head. Someone will say grace."

"Thanks. I didn't think of that."

"Unless, of course, it's communion," I look at Doug and see blankness in his eyes. "That's when they pass around little bits of crackers and some really little cups of grape juice. You bow your head before you eat that but no one says grace, well at least not like at a meal. Someone will probably pray, but they won't do it like its grace."

"When does that happen?" Doug looks anxious. "Do I have to bring crackers?"

"No, the church has the stuff for it and there's not a set time when it happens. You'll know when it's going to happen because someone will say something."

Doug nods and looks grateful. I'm encouraged. I can do this. "The next thing to know is that the Bible is a big book."

Doug nods and starts to write that down in his notes.

"This is just the introduction—this and the grace stuff," I say. "You don't need to take notes on this part."

"Okay," Doug says and he sits back to listen.

I tell Doug that the Bible is really just a big series of books written by various people.

"Really?" Doug seems a little skeptical. "I thought it was all the word of God. I didn't know about other writers."

"These were people writing what God told them to write," I say. I figure we should move on here as I don't really know all of the theological things to say about this. "Well, actually, it was mostly men who wrote down things and you have their names in the Bible."

I open the Bible to the Table of Contents and show him the names.

"Isn't that plagiarism?" Doug asks with a frown. "If they copied God, they shouldn't have their names on it. They could be sued."

"I don't think people sued over that kind of thing back then," I say. "Besides, God didn't exactly write it down, either."

"You mean it was some psychic thing—I'm not into voodoo hoodoo?"

"It's not psychic." I don't think. I know I'm not too sure and a teacher needs to have confidence. Doug looks at me with his skepticism showing so I say, "I never claimed to be able to explain anything. All I said is I could show you how to find things."

Doug seems okay with that. I show him some more of the names in the Table of Contents and I talk about the importance of organization. I may not know anything about the God part of any religion, but I can talk organization like a pro. I give Doug my deluxe pep talk on keeping things in a logical order and I'm thinking that, if it doesn't work out for me at the Big M, maybe I could become an organization consultant, you know, one of those people who claim they can help you organize your life or, if not that, at least your closet. I never realized there was any similarity between cleaning out closets and talking about the Bible, but I guess there is.

I must be talking a lot about the different ways to organize things because Doug is starting to look at me a little funny.

"You don't believe what the Bible says, do you?" Doug finally asks. "I mean, I know you don't. I just didn't know you knew so much about the Bible and still didn't believe."

"I don't choose to believe or to disbelieve," I say in what I hope is a properly philosophical voice. There's nothing wrong with being neutral. "Some of the smartest people who ever lived were neutral. I can't think of any at the moment, but I will. And, there's Switzerland, of course. That's a country, but they're famous for being neutral."

"I thought I was the one with the cold feet," he says as he keeps looking at my face. "I can understand after what's happened with your mother that you might have a problem with commitment. Maybe I could help."

With most people, I would deny I had had a problem with my mother, but Doug knows how it is with me. Still, even though he knows how it is with me and my mother, he hasn't always read me right so he might be wrong now.

"Why are you so into commitments suddenly?" I say. "When you thought I was all over you trying to get you to make a commitment, you were scared to death. Now you think *I'm* the one who's afraid of commitments. It wasn't me turning to jelly at Aunt Ruth's feet."

Doug smiles. "I guess we are a pair, aren't we?"

I had never noticed that Doug's eyes get warm and crinkly when he smiles.

I cannot help but smile back. "You know, you didn't need to worry. I never thought you meant anything at that party except that you were being nice to me. We'd agreed you were going to act like my boyfriend, but that didn't mean I was confused and thought you really were—well, you know—*attracted* to me or anything."

"Oh, you wouldn't have been confused if you thought that."

Okay, now I can't breathe.

Doug clears his throat. "What I mean to say is that, of course, I'm attracted to you. I'm not dead. You're beautiful."

Okay, again. I need to put this in perspective. "Some people think my hair is too red. And I trip up a lot. Nerves."

"A nervous redhead. Sounds about perfect." Doug grins and then he grows serious. "I thought you knew it was my feelings I was scared of, not yours."

"How would I know that? Besides, you left."

Doug is looking at me. "I always leave. That's what I do."

"Of course."

"I'm going to change, though." He's not smiling anymore. "That's part of the reason I went to that rally. Something about God has been getting under my skin ever since that first rally. I would have gone down to the front then, but I thought there was no point because I never stay with anything."

I nod.

"When we went there again, though, I realized I can make a commitment and keep it. It's impossible to move to a place where God isn't going to be. And He can't kick me out. So He's here no matter what. That's what made me think I can do this. Besides, I want to do this."

"That's good," I clear my throat. I'm glad that Doug has had these new insights on commitment. That's good for him. I'd hate to think of him going through his life with his suitcase packed, never making a commitment to anything because he thought it wouldn't last. I'm not sure it means much for me, though. Not about Doug; I mean about God. I can't just walk up to God and tell Him I've decided to make a commitment after I've bad-mouthed Him for years. I doubt He's wasting any time waiting for me to walk down the aisle at any rally.

I look up at the clock. It's eight o'clock. "I think we should get going with the lesson."

Doug takes the hint. "Okay. I'm listening."

It's been a long time since I've flipped through the pages of the Bible and looked for some of the old, familiar verses that I memorized all those years ago in Sunday school. And, of course, having now worked in the files of a big institution myself, I have a much better appreciation for the organization of the Bible. I wonder who thought of using the writer's names and calling the sections books. They could have organized the whole thing by topics like Genesis and Exodus or by their intended audience like Hebrews. I wonder why they chose author's names for most of the books.

Doug gets the sense of the organization before long and he and I are looking up this verse and that verse. Mostly we're just looking up the verses he has in the homework they gave him from the rally. Can you believe they gave him homework? He's to have it ready for the follow-up meeting next Monday night. I'm surprised they actually have follow-up meetings, too. Doug says there are eight weeks of them.

At some point during the discussion, I take the rose from the counter next to the sink and bring it back to the table. I set the rose next to the wall. Talking back and forth with Doug like this makes me think that the religious thing he has going isn't so big that we can't be friends. I'm glad about that. Doug's a little intense—and probably anemic—but, now that I know he's not thinking I'm going to trap him in some fake boyfriend scam, I kind of like him.

I notice Doug is looking at me a little intently and I hope he can't read minds or anything.

"So, are you ever going to tell me why you're not ready to make a commitment to all this?" Doug finally says as he gestures to the Bible. "If I had known a tenth of what you know, I would have walked forward at a rally years ago."

"There's no big mystery," I say, trying to keep my tone casual. I want to talk about me and God even less than I want to talk about me and Doug. "Say, I forgot to tell you what all these red letters mean."

Doug lets me distract him from his question. I am glad. How do you explain to someone why you don't want to believe in God? A lot of people already believe in God so it's not that it's freakish. It's just, well, I'm not sure I can rely on God to actually care about me.

I'm just not one of those people. In all these years, God has never bothered to answer my prayer that my mother would take me to live with her. It doesn't seem as if it was too much to ask. If someone else had prayed that, God would have been all over it. I'm afraid that God will always see me as halfway important, kind of like the half cousin and half niece thing that happens with Elaine and her mother. I don't like being a half.

I am telling Doug the story of Joseph and his coat of many colors when Cassie and Jerry come home. I have been acting out the story with my hands as well as telling the story so Doug and I are too engrossed to hear the key turn in the lock.

"Hey, Doug," Jerry says as he walks in the door and sees us. "What's up, man?"

"Doug," Cassie's voice echoes in a pleased greeting.

"Hey, it's great to see you guys," Doug says as he looks up at them.

Jerry and Cassie sound a little too friendly, if you know what I mean. And they're looking at Doug funny, as though they're waiting for him to turn around in his chair so they can see whether or not there are little wings growing on his shoulder blades. I don't think either one of them has known someone who has gone down the aisle at a religious rally.

"So, what am I? The invisible person?" I say just to break the tension. "Does Doug get all the hellos?"

"Of course, not," Cassie says, "But we just saw you."

I smile to show I'm teasing. "We can finish up here if you want. Then we could play a game or something. Maybe Bunko."

A game should show them that Doug is still a normal person.

"So, what are you doing?" Jerry, the great detective, says as he walks a little closer to the table. As I have said all along, the only reason Jerry wanted to be a detective was because he wanted to be a snoop.

"Not much," I say as I fold my arms over the open book on the table.

At the same time, Doug says, "Cassie's teaching me the Bible."

"What?" Jerry's face turns a little white. He must have thought this big book was a dictionary. Or a medical reference book. Even Cassie looks shocked. I think they would have been less appalled if it had been a medical book and Doug had told them I was teaching him how to be a surgeon.

"Just the organization of the Bible," I say to clarify. Really, they have no reason to look so shocked. "You know the filing system of it all. The books. The chapters. The verses."

"You know that?" Jerry turns to look at me with utter astonishment on his face. "About the *Bible?*"

"Of course," I tell him. "I've gone to church with Aunt Inga since the day I started living with her. What did you think I was doing all that time?"

"I don't know. Throwing spitballs at other kids,

maybe," Jerry says and he's serious. "I sure never thought you were listening."

"I've never thrown a spitball in church in my life," I say. It's true, but I shouldn't have to defend myself to him. "Besides, it was hard not to listen—sometimes things were loud. And I had to go to Sunday school, too."

"Quick, tell me what John 3:16 says," Jerry challenges me.

"I'm not going to dignify that with an answer," I say and cross my arms. "You're treating me like I'm a trained seal."

I notice that Jerry gives Doug a look that assumes Doug is with him on this. Have you ever noticed how guys do that? It's sort of a male bonding thing that happens when they tease a female.

Just then there is a rapid knocking at the door. I look at Cassie. She looks at me. Neither one of us is expecting any company beyond what is already in the apartment with us. We don't even know that many people here in Hollywood.

"Who's there?" Cassie says softly as she walks closer to the door and picks up her plastic shovel from its place by the counter.

Jerry snorts when he sees the shovel. "What's that?"

"Hush," I whisper.

"Julie, is that you?" the voice on the other side of the door asks.

Jerry, Cassie and I all look at each other. We recognize that voice. We might not believe it, but we recognize it.

Cassie opens the door. "Elaine?"

Everyone inside the apartment just looks at Elaine.

She's a sight. I've never seen her like this. Elaine never leaves home without flawless makeup and a matching outfit. She makes sure her hair is styled, not just combed. This Elaine look-alike has streaks of mascara on one cheek and her hair looks as if it hasn't been combed in a week. It even looks less blond than usual, as though maybe she forgot to put on some kind of mousse to add highlights. She does have lipstick on, but it's only on the upper lip and it gives her a ghoulish look. Plus, she's got a ketchup spot on the white T-shirt she's wearing with her jeans and it doesn't look as if she even tried to wipe the ketchup off.

"Elaine?" I ask just to be sure. "What's happened?"

"Did you have a car accident?" Jerry asks.

I step a little closer to be sure the ketchup isn't blood.

I guess that is enough sympathy for Elaine to decide she is welcome. She walks into the apartment, dragging a huge garment bag behind her.

"I don't know what to do," Elaine wails as if this would make us understand what was happening. And then she hiccups and starts to cry. "I can't just leave my wedding dress behind. My mother helped me pick it out. And, who are they to say I can't take it on a cruise? That's not fair."

"No, of course not," I find myself saying, although for the life of me I don't know what she's talking about. No one is planning a cruise that I know about and Elaine should be able to take her wedding dress anywhere she wants to take it. "Who said you can't take it on a cruise?"

Elaine's lip is trembling with indignation. "Gary's parents. They want to pay for a cruise wedding, but they want me to get a different dress. Something with no lace that will pack better."

"Well, that makes sense," I say. I have to bite my tongue to keep my joy from erupting in a huge yell of triumph. This would certainly solve all my problems. Why didn't I think of that? Elaine would love to get married on a cruise ship. Aunt Ruth and Uncle Howard would love it, too. I mean, who wouldn't absolutely love it? I may live to see my grandchildren, after all.

"The only reason they don't like my dress is because Mom and I picked it out," Elaine says. "They don't like anything that we planned. They don't even like my hair."

We all just look at Elaine's hair. I don't think now is the time to ask her about mousse, not with everyone staring at her. She doesn't seem to notice, though. She probably can't see us with the tears in her eyes.

"Your hair's good," Doug says, a little feebly. I can tell he is trying to be sincere. "And healthy. Like it's been outdoors in the fresh air. That's good."

Elaine turns to Doug as though she needs to explain her problem to him. "They want me to wear a straight dress with no lace. No lace at all. Gary's mother said the dress I have looks common because of all the lace."

Elaine stops to take a little sobbing breath.

"Oh, I'm sure she didn't mean it like that," Cassie says.

As I said, Cassie is the eternal mother and I know she must be wanting to go to Elaine and give her a hug. So far, though, Cassie is holding back.

"The shop where we got the dress said I could have as much lace as I wanted," Elaine says haltingly.

"Wouldn't they have said something if my dress was going to look common?"

"I'm sure it won't look the least bit common," Cassie says softly as she takes a step toward Elaine and puts a hand on her shoulder.

I'm willing to second that opinion, but Cassie makes it sound like a good thing so I let her go with it.

"It's got two thousand beads hand sewn on it," Elaine says. "And with all the lace, I thought it would be elegant."

"Oh," I say. I remember the two thousand beads. I see the garment bag that is trailing behind Elaine. I wonder how fragile those beads are. "Maybe we should lay the dress down on the sofa."

Elaine just clutches the bag closer to her and looks as though she's going to cry harder. "This dress makes me look beautiful. Everyone said so. The woman at the shop. Her assistant. They all said the dress was perfect for me. It is meant for me."

Now, I know they must tell every bride that about her dress, especially when the dress is as expensive as this one must be, but I'm not going to share that insight with Elaine.

"I'm sure there's a way to take your dress on a cruise," Cassie says as she finishes the pat on Elaine's shoulders. "There are some pretty big suitcases out there."

"It's got a seven-foot train," Elaine says.

"Wow," I say.

Doug looks surprised. "I didn't know they made them that long. Don't they have to fit in the aisle?"

Jerry grunts. "Women."

Elaine looks at us and I guess she can see the looks on our faces. "It's the fashion. They're called cathedral trains. The women at the shop said I could have it that long if I wanted—as long as I had a carpet to walk down so it didn't drag on the floor. I was going to have rose petals sprinkled on it." Her lip begins to quiver again. "Why has everything gone so wrong? Gary and I were supposed to get married in that beautiful church in Palm Springs. You should have seen that aisle. It was extra long. That's why I got a long train. And now we have to choose between that little chapel where you work," Elaine says as she looks at me as if it's all my fault, "which probably doesn't have any aisle to it at all, or some cruise of the Mexican Riveria."

"Well, the Mexican Riveria is always nice at this time of the year," I say. I'm not going to tell Elaine that the center aisle at the Big M is perfectly long enough for her bridal train and I'll let the "little chapel" remark pass right on by. I have more important things to say. "And a cruise ship would have a super long aisle. They'd probably let you walk all around the deck if you wanted. You could have a huge train and all the rose petals you wanted."

"I wouldn't mind a cruise," Jerry says.

Elaine starts to cry in earnest. "Gary's parents are staying at his place until the wedding and they're planning the cruise."

Jerry and Cassie both look at me.

"And that's a problem because…" I gently ask Elaine.

She looks at me as though I've lost my senses. "It will be their wedding. The wedding they want."

"Ah." I nod. "Of course. And you're worried it won't be the wedding you want?"

Elaine stops wailing long enough to nod.

I give Elaine what comfort I can. "Lots of people make compromises on their weddings."

"Really?" Elaine stops crying.

I can't help but think how good I would be as a wedding planner. See how I just comforted the bride-to-be and helped her adjust her attitude?

"Besides, a cruise wedding would be very nice," I continue on smoothly. "Just think how beautiful the pictures will be with the ocean in the background. Maybe you'll get married as the sun goes down. That would be cool. And your mother won't have to worry about organizing all that food—"

Elaine begins to cry again. "She won't have to worry about anything."

"See there. That's what we want. Everything will be done for her. I'm sure she's in favor of the cruise idea." I have to restrain myself. I'm getting ready to go into the happy dance. My problems are almost over. No wedding chapel anywhere could compete with a cruise. I bet the ship even has a swimming pool. And a wedding only takes thirty minutes or so. All of us cousins would have the rest of the time to work on our tans. Hello, sunshine, here we come.

Elaine takes a deep shuddering breath. "I haven't told Mom about the cruise."

"Oh, well, that's not a problem. Just tell her as soon as you can. I can guarantee she'll be relieved. She's been worrying about measuring the chapel at where I work and everything. She'll be so glad when you tell her. I bet she even buys a new dress to wear."

Elaine shakes her head. "She won't need a new dress."

"I know you're thinking she's already spent all that money on your wedding," I say, "but, trust me, your mom will be happy to spend a little more to see you happy and smiling on your big day. So just go ahead and tell her so she can relax."

Elaine stops crying and crunches up her face. "I don't know how to tell her. Gary's parents don't want her to come."

Jerry goes pale. "Not come?"

"To the *wedding?*" I add for clarification. "They don't want her to come to your wedding?"

Elaine nods. "They want to give us the cruise wedding as a gift, but they say there's only room for Gary and me. And them, of course. And Lynda, their daughter. And maybe Gary's uncle if he wants to come. The cruise ship is almost sold out."

"But there will be cancellations," I say. "They can't be serious about you getting married without your parents there."

"Gary's mom says we only need a couple of people for witnesses."

"Well, that's true, but…"

Cassie and I exchange a look. Neither one of us can believe Elaine has the story right.

"Gary's mom says lots of couples don't have either set of parents with them when they take a wedding cruise, so we should consider ourselves lucky that they will be able to come with us," Elaine says. "At least, we'll have one set of parents."

Elaine looks about as far from lucky as a person can look and still be breathing.

"I don't even want to be around your mother

when you tell her she can't come to your wedding," Jerry says.

Even I know that's much worse than getting the wrong punch cups at the hotel in Palm Springs. This is big-time serious. Aunt Ruth has planned for Elaine's wedding for years.

"That's why I needed to come here," Elaine says. "I feel so guilty being around Mom right now."

None of us even question Elaine on this. I know I'd be getting out of Blythe, too, if I had that kind of news waiting for Aunt Ruth.

"I was hoping maybe I wouldn't have to tell her for a while," Elaine says. "If all of you can keep a secret."

I can't look at Cassie or Jerry or even Doug. The words coming from Elaine's mouth are words that could have come from my mouth a day or so ago. What is it with our family and secrets? We may not be a fully matched family with all of the same grandparents, but we sure seem to share the same habit of hiding the truth when we see trouble coming our way.

"You're sure you understood Gary's mom?" I say gently. I know that there is a lot of stress in planning a wedding just as there is stress in planning a funeral, but I simply can't believe anyone would expect to keep Aunt Ruth away from Elaine's wedding. The mother of the bride always has to be there.

"Gary's mom and I talked on the phone for an hour this afternoon," Elaine says. "I know what she said. I just can't imagine telling my mom."

"I can understand why you'd want a place to stay then," Cassie says with a nod. "You're certainly welcome to spend the night here."

I add my nod. Elaine isn't looking as relieved as I thought she would.

"Actually, I was hoping someone would help me tell Mom about the cruise," Elaine says then.

There is dead silence in the room.

"Oh, no," Jerry says as he steps away from Elaine.

"We'll give you moral support, of course," I add as I force myself not to take a step away. For once, I'm kind of glad I'm only half cousins with Elaine. Jerry has more duty here than I do.

But Elaine must not see it that way. She's looking at me instead of Jerry and I've got to admit it's making me nervous.

"I was hoping you could tell her," Elaine finally says. She's still got her gaze pinned on me. "You're so good with bad news."

"Oh, no," I say. And, trust me, I'm not *that* good with bad news. Granted, with all my fumbling, I'm called upon to say enough difficult things, but practice doesn't always make perfect. "I couldn't."

Cassie pats Elaine on the shoulder. "You'll be able to do it yourself. You just need a good night's sleep and you'll do fine. We'll help you think of what to say."

Remembering how upset Aunt Ruth can get makes me think of something else. I turn to Elaine. "Does your mom know you're going to spend the night here?"

"I left a note."

"I wish we had more sleeping space," Cassie adds. She's looking around with her hostess expression as though she's expecting to see another room spring into being. It doesn't happen. "There's really only the floor left."

I tell myself I need to give Cassie a larger percent of the rent now that all of my relatives have decided to come and stay with us. Cassie may be closer to me than my half family, but there are limits and I think we've reached them.

Doug helps Jerry carry in the ficus plants from the pickup and then he leaves.

"He's okay," Jerry says after Doug leaves. "You wouldn't know he got dunked."

"He didn't get baptized, he made a commitment," I say.

I look at Jerry's grinning face and I wonder why I bother.

"I knew you know stuff like that. I'm still waiting for John 3:16," he says.

I give him a look as I take the seat cushions off the sofa. "Here, you can strap these together to make a pillow bed for Elaine."

Elaine drapes her bagged wedding dress over the table. I can see the pattern of the lace through the plastic at the bottom and I wonder how such a dress could inspire so many tears.

"I think I'm too upset to sleep," Elaine says.

I still have the air mattress. Cassie has the bed. And Jerry has the Hide-A-Bed in the living room

"It'll all work out," I say, even though I know it might not.

Cassie and I would usually talk a few minutes as we got ready for bed, but Elaine is here and I'm afraid if we all start talking that she'll start crying and we'll be up all night. I do manage to ask Cassie if she had a good time at dinner and she smiles so I'm assuming that's a good report. She asks if I had a good dinner with Doug and I can't think of a code for the jumble of feelings that question brings up so I just shrug. I'll tell her more about it tomorrow.

The lights are all off and I'm looking at the outline of the window in Cassie's bedroom. Earlier, I put the air mattress in front of it so I could look out and see the stars. Of course, there's so much street light that I don't see any. Still, I think of Joey and his gold stars.

Then I hear a sniffle. Then another one.

"Elaine?" I ask a little reluctantly.

I hear a full-blown sob now from the direction of Elaine's pillow bed. "I can't get married without any of my family there."

"A wedding is just a day. It's the marriage that counts," I say. "Your family will be part of that."

For a moment, there's silence again and I think I've made my point.

"I still don't think it's right that Gary's mom is taking over the wedding. She's not my mom," Elaine says.

"What does Gary say?"

"He's busy studying. He's got some papers to finish before the wedding."

I get an uneasy feeling. "Elaine, when was the last time you saw Gary?"

Elaine gives a subdued sob. "The party."

"The engagement party?" I ask. "That's almost two weeks ago!"

"He's been studying for our future," Elaine says indignantly. "When you marry a doctor, you have to expect things like this."

"He's a dentist," I say.

"I know." Elaine begins to wail in earnest. "But he's almost a doctor."

"Well, I'm sure he'd want you to get some sleep," I say. "So try not to worry about things. We'll figure out what to do in the morning."

Okay, so now I can't sleep wondering about what kind of a man Elaine is marrying. Isn't it just a little abnormal for a woman's fiancé to not see her while the wedding plans are on? Especially when his mother seems so involved? I mean, it's only a two-hour drive for him to get to Aunt Ruth's house. Even if his parents are staying with him, surely there would be a Sunday afternoon when he could go say hi to Elaine even if he had to take his parents with him. I don't have the heart to ask Elaine if she's talked to Gary on the phone since the engagement party.

I know everyone loves in their own way, but Gary seems as if he loves Elaine from the opposite side of the world. Either that or he's afraid of his own mother and is letting Elaine take the brunt of his mother's opinions, none of which are probably easy to live with. I don't think much of that kind of love. A man should stand with his bride not with his mother, at least some of the time. But then, I don't know a lot about love.

I think of Jerry trying to get me to recite the "For God so loved the world" verse. He thinks I don't know the verse, but I do. I remembered so many of them tonight talking to Doug. I can't help but think that Elaine would be better off relying on God's love instead of this Gary's love.

Elaine could do worse than to look to her Bible. Of course, she won't hear that opinion from me. I'm neutral in this one, too.

Chapter Ten

I had no idea it would be so hard to fix breakfast with three ficus trees crowding my back and a good-sized begonia sitting on top of the refrigerator next to me.

"I think they're too large to move out to the fire escape," Cassie says as she frowns at the plants. "I didn't think of that."

Cassie is wearing an aqua-blue sweatshirt this morning.

"I can move them up against this wall," Jerry says as he yawns. He's wearing a different brown T-shirt this morning. Apparently, man of fashion that he is, he has two. He's already straightened up his blankets and is pushing the mattress part of the Hide-A-Bed back under so we can all sit on the sofa. Cassie and Elaine go over and sit there now. They both look tired and the day has just begun.

Cassie looks around and says a little numbly, "I'll have to think about what to do with the plants, I guess."

Neither Cassie nor I got any sleep last night. When

Elaine wasn't crying, she was talking in her sleep. She wasn't saying anything we could make out, but there was a lot of whimpering. The funny thing is that I started to have more compassion for Elaine as the night wore on and not less. In all her fussing, she was just a little girl who wanted somebody to rescue her. I can relate; I used to feel the same way.

"I'm going to tell Gary's mother I won't do the cruise," Elaine announces for the tenth time this morning. She's got some frilly ivory blouse thing happening today and her makeup is within the lines so I guess she's better. When I first glimpsed the lace it reminded me of the wedding dress, which has been moved to Cassie's bed so we can use the table for the breakfast of cooked oatmeal that I am fixing everyone. It's Thursday and I think we might need some fortification to cope with the rest of the week. Oatmeal should be good for that.

"Just because you're afraid to tell your mom about the cruise, that's no reason to refuse the cruise completely," I say. "Maybe you can negotiate with Gary's mom."

"Me?" Elaine says and looks around her. Her eye stops at Jerry.

"Don't look at me. I have some measuring to do for Aunt Ruth," Jerry says. He's not looking at Elaine when he answers her, but she doesn't seem to notice. "Cruise or no cruise, Aunt Ruth gave me her orders."

"Speaking of Aunt Ruth—" I forget about Jerry and try to catch Elaine's eye "—shouldn't you call your mother? I'm sure she'll be worried about you."

"She knows where I am," Elaine says with a stubborn lift of her chin. "If she wants to see me, she can come here."

Okay, well, that's not a good plan for oh so many reasons.

I look to Cassie for help.

Cassie turns to Elaine. "Don't you need to be back in Blythe yourself to keep making plans for the wedding?"

"Why bother? Everything is falling apart," Elaine says and I see tears starting to form in her eyes.

I'm not sure any of us can take more crying. Besides, it will make her mascara run again. I rush in with a question of my own. "Don't you have some sort of a bachelorette party coming up with your brides-maids? That should be fun."

"I don't have any bridesmaids left." Elaine begins to wail.

Okay, so much for her feeling better. Cassie starts to walk toward the box of tissues she keeps beside the sofa, but then she turns and brings back a towel from the bathroom. She hands it to Elaine without her usual pat on the shoulder.

"I thought you had all the bridesmaids lined up," I say. "Aunt Inga said you asked the Bowman twins and Allison Murry."

All three of these girls are from Blythe and Elaine has known them all her life. Well, Cassie and I knew them, too. And Jerry. There were no strangers in school when we were growing up in Blythe. The twins and Allison always seemed as empty-headed as Elaine and I was never comfortable around them. Not that I was a rocket scientist. I just couldn't stand to talk about clothes and boys all day. Okay, so maybe it was because I didn't have much to talk about in either of those categories. Still, those conversations used to give me headaches like the one I'm getting now.

"They all quit," says Elaine. Her mascara is starting to run and I'm wondering what kind she uses. Probably something organic. I didn't think they made any mascara that ran like that anymore.

"All three of them quit?"

"Well—" Elaine stops to take a breath "—Gary's sister is still going to be in the wedding."

Gary's sister lives in Boston and she didn't come to the engagement party so I'm sure she's not planning to come to any bachelorette party.

"I can't believe the others would bail on you like that," Cassie says. "Just because it's not going to be a fancy wedding in Palm Springs, that's no reason for them to pull out."

Aunt Ruth isn't the only one in Blythe who thinks Palm Springs is as close to Mecca as any of us can ever hope to get. When we were in high school, it was the place to go if you wanted to have a serious date. Even now, the expensive weddings take place there.

Jerry grunts as if he's heard this all before. "They're not backing out because of Palm Springs. It's those orange dresses. They finally had sense enough to try them on in front of some mirrors. Everyone says they look like pumpkins. The maid of honor is the only one who is wearing brown."

Elaine sniffles. "Allison said she refuses to walk down the aisle looking like some vegetable out of the produce section."

"I don't think pumpkin is a vegetable," Cassie says.

"The orange is not pumpkin anyway," Elaine says

as she dabs at her eyes. "The store says it's their Fall Sunset color. Sunsets are beautiful." Elaine takes a breath, but can't manage to hold in her feelings. "My wedding is ruined."

I hate to bring up the obvious, but I guess it's time. "If you have a cruise wedding, you won't need the bridesmaids anyway. And, if you did have brides-maids, who wouldn't go? I mean it's a cruise."

Even though I am turned away from everyone now because I'm momentarily adding raisins to the oat-meal, I become aware that the silence behind my back is going on a little long after my speech so I turn around. Elaine is looking at me with a calculating look in her eyes.

"You and Cassie could be my bridesmaids," Elaine says in a rush when she sees I'm looking at her. "I don't think there would be any money involved, but I'm sure Mom would pay for the cruise—"

"Of course, there wouldn't be any money involved," Cassie says indignantly. "No one accepts money to be a bridesmaid. It should be an honor. Of course, there's no more room on the cruise, remember?"

I hope Elaine doesn't interpret Cassie's response about it being an honor as a yes.

I turn back to the stove and lift the pan of oatmeal off the burner. "Regardless of where you get married, if you still have that same color, we're in trouble. I thought you said it wouldn't go with my hair."

I know it's too late to get new bridesmaid dresses of any color so the orange pumpkins are it.

"You can put a darkening mousse in your hair for the day," Elaine says.

"I like my hair—I'm not going to hide its color," I say as I set the pan of oatmeal on a trivet in the middle of the table.

"Of course, nobody in my family will know my wedding is ruined because they won't be there," Elaine says.

"I can't believe Gary's mother isn't open to compromise about who is going. Besides, your parents can certainly afford to pay for their own cabin. Maybe Gary's mother just meant they were only going to pay for their side of the family to go. That makes sense."

"Nothing makes sense," Elaine says as she stands up and walks toward Cassie's bedroom.

"It'll be okay," Cassie says.

"How would you feel if this was your wedding?" Elaine asks as she opens the door and stands in the doorway. "It's supposed to be the most wonderful day of my life and it's turning out awful."

Now that Elaine has stopped crying, none of us know what to say to her so we are silent as she closes the door. Part of me thinks she's right. She's going to have a hard time keeping all of the parents happy on this one.

There aren't many gray mornings in Hollywood, but this is one of them and the gloom comes through the window and settles on the three of us as we sit at the table. Jerry has taken the plants off the wooden box that serves as a coffee table and has upended it to make himself a stool so he can sit at the table with Cassie and me.

"You need a couple of folding chairs," Jerry says. "I'll keep my eyes open for some used ones."

Cassie nods, but gives a worried look toward the closed bedroom door.

"She just needs some time alone," I say quietly. I'm not sure that's true, but the rest of us need some quiet time without her. We eat our oatmeal with raisins in peace for a minute.

"She's going to have to tell Aunt Ruth pretty soon," Jerry says.

I nod. I always thought people in our family were trying to spare each other's feelings, but now I'm seeing that all this sidestepping of the truth has only stopped us from being close. Elaine should be sharing her troubles with Aunt Ruth. It might make them closer. I know I feel a lot closer to Jerry now that there are fewer secrets between us.

I think I'm becoming warped. Somehow the me I always knew isn't the me I am these days. I think it's because of those Bible verses from my childhood that have come back to haunt me. I have started to wonder what my relationships would be like now if I had become a Christian back then in Sunday school. I'm not wondering what my life would be like, because it might be close to the same as it is now. At least the un-attached, rolling-around part.

But I might be closer to people, especially the cousins and the aunts. Maybe I would even have been able to be on Elaine's side sometimes growing up instead of always picking the opposite side just to show that I was my own person. Maybe even if she kept calling me her half cousin, I could just have accepted her as family. If I had done that, maybe there would have been no reason for her to keep calling me a half cousin. Forgiveness and truth should be the backbone of any family, even a mismatched one like ours.

I think it might be because of lack of sleep, but I decide right then and there that, if I'm hoping everyone in the family will be more truthful, I need to do my part.

"I'm going to tell Aunt Ruth about the Big M," I announce.

"What?" Cassie says.

"Are you nuts?" Jerry, always the diplomat, adds.

"What's the Big M?" Elaine asks from the doorway of the bedroom. She's combed her hair and stopped crying.

Well, this isn't quite how I'd pictured it, I think to myself. I hadn't meant to tell Elaine. I mean Elaine is stressed out enough over the wedding; she doesn't need to know that the chapel that is the backup place for her wedding is a mortuary.

There's a minute of shuffling silence.

"It's a new kind of milk Julie found," Cassie finally says. "You know, the Big M. Big Milk. Lots of vitamins. She's planning to buy some at the store later."

"Good," Elaine says with a shrug. "You can't get too many vitamins."

"Nope, you can't get too many vitamins," I agree.

There is another minute of silence as Elaine walks over to the sofa and sits down.

"Oh, here," Jerry says as he stands up from his stool with his empty bowl in his hand. "Sit here and have some oatmeal. There are lots of vitamins in that. It even has raisins."

I think to myself that Jerry has been using manners he probably didn't even know he had. He doesn't seem to be minding it, though, so I have reason to hope that he's turning into a thoughtful kind of a guy.

Elaine has barely sat down at the table when my cell phone rings. My purse is beside the sofa so I walk over to it and pull out my cell phone. I think it might be Doug, but I see from my number display that it is Aunt Ruth.

"Oh." I pick the phone up without answering it and walk it over to Elaine. "Sorry, but this is your mother. I'm sure she wants to talk to you."

Okay, so I know that is the cowardly thing to do. I do plan to tell Aunt Ruth about the Big M soon, but I don't want to do it at seven-thirty in the morning with Elaine listening. No one, at least in our family, is at their best before midmorning.

Elaine talks on the phone for about ten seconds and then holds out the phone to me. "It's really Aunt Inga. She's just calling from my mom's place."

"Oh," I say as I reach for the phone. "Hi, Aunt Inga."

"Oh, Julie," Aunt Inga says with her voice gushing loud enough I wonder if everyone in the room can hear her. I look at Cassie and can tell from the smile on her face that she hears the gush. "I couldn't wait to talk to you."

"Did you call about Elaine? She's still a little upset, but she's doing fine."

"Well, of course, she's doing fine," Aunt Inga says. "It's a wonderful day."

Even for Aunt Inga this is a little happy for this early in the morning. "Have you had breakfast? Maybe a little protein would—"

"I called your mother," Aunt Inga announces, which stops me in midworry.

"What?"

"I called your mother in Las Vegas," Aunt Inga says proudly. "I remembered how she could always make a room look pretty. I thought maybe she'd help us decorate the chapel."

I blink and look over at Cassie. She looks as shocked as I feel.

"You asked my mother to help?" I finally manage to say. "What did Aunt Ruth say?"

"Your aunt Ruth is lying down with a wet towel on her forehead. The hotel with the golf course told her they had no openings for the wedding. They even refused to give her golf lessons."

"Oh. But there might be another hotel they can use," I say.

"Your mother was so excited that I asked for her help," Aunt Inga continues just as though I hadn't hinted that we need to keep looking. "It will be a real family affair. I even told her all about the place where you work and how your boss is letting us use it for Elaine's wedding so he must think the world of you."

"Oh, well, he just—"

"Once your mother is done with that chapel of yours, it will look ten times better than the church in Palm Springs." Aunt Inga rushes to the end. "Isn't that wonderful? It's been a long time since the whole family worked together on something."

I cannot even speak. Our family has never worked together.

"But what does Aunt Ruth say?"

"She's not saying anything right now. But she'll see the chapel is for the best. I never did believe in having a wedding in a hotel anyway. A marriage should begin in a place where God is respected."

"God is respected in nature," I say. "He created the ocean."

"Ruth refuses to consider the beach."

"But maybe a ship," I say. "There's no sand on a big ship."

"Who has a big ship?" Aunt Inga asks. "No the chapel will work just fine, but we have a million things to get ready. Make sure Jerry takes those measurements today for us. I've gotten all of the phone numbers for the guests gathered up and Ruth and I are going to have to call everyone on Saturday to tell them where the ceremony will be."

I move my jaw. Now is the time to speak. I swallow. Nothing comes out so I try again.

"Maybe—" I manage to squeak, but it is too late. Aunt Inga has already said goodbye and hung up.

Wow. I look around the room. No one has moved since the phone conversation began. Jerry has his mouth hanging open. Cassie is looking dazed. Even Elaine has stopped moving.

"Did Aunt Inga say she'd called your *mother?*" Jerry finally finds his voice and asks. "The one in Las Vegas?"

I nod. "She's going to decorate the chapel. For the wedding."

"My wedding," Elaine says. She's found movement in her face again because I can see a frown happening. "I don't want a wedding chapel that looks like a casino."

"I'm sure it won't look like a casino," Cassie says.

"My mother's coming," I repeat myself.

"I'm going to go talk to my mother about this," Elaine says. "I mean even if I have to have a small wedding, I at least want it to be dignified. I'm marrying a doctor, after all."

This time I don't even bother to correct Elaine. If she wants to pretend Gary is a doctor rather than a dentist, who am I to force her to see the truth? For one thing, I have bigger lies of my own to worry about.

Elaine marches into the bedroom. I look at Jerry and then at Cassie. We're all thinking the same thing.

"I better get down to measuring everything," Jerry says to me.

I nod. "You can go ahead and measure, but I don't think we should give up on the Chinese restaurant. You know, they have these cute little fortune cookies, too. They can make them special with the names of the bride and groom."

Cassie looks at me with pity in her eyes, as if she knows that we're way past the Chinese restaurant plan.

Elaine walks back into the main room from the bedroom. She barely says goodbye as she drags the bag holding her wedding dress past us.

When Elaine is gone, Cassie looks at me. "Well, I should get going. I open up the shop this morning."

I nod.

"Maybe we could all have dinner together tonight," Jerry says to Cassie.

Jerry nods toward me to include me in the invitation.

I am touched, but… "No, I don't want to be the third wheel."

They both look a little pleased that I had noticed they have something going on that would make someone else a third wheel.

"We could ask Doug," Jerry says. "I kind of like him."

I nod. "Okay."

I am back to hoping Doug will go to Elaine's wedding with me and, if he does, it wouldn't hurt us to practice some. Not that I mean practice to look like something we're not. I've learned my lesson doing that. No, I mean to practice being what we are—two friends on a very casual date with no expectations of anything or commitments to anything.

"I'll call Doug a little later and we'll come up with a plan," Jerry says.

I never thought I'd ever go on a double date with any of my cousins. Not that it's exactly a date since it's Doug, but still it's close enough to make me wonder what my life is coming to.

"Is this place you work a pit?" Jerry asks me. "I mean, is it obvious that it's a funeral home?"

I shake my head. "It's beautiful. I thought it looked like a bridal chapel when I first saw it."

"It does look like it could be a bridal chapel," Cassie adds.

"That's good," Jerry says. "It might just be the best place to have that wedding after all."

Cassie and I both nod even though I'm still holding out for the cruise ship.

"I do intend to tell Aunt Ruth and Aunt Inga about the Big M," I say into the silence that follows. "I'll leave it up to them to decide what to tell the guests, but I need to tell them both before they make their calls on Saturday."

"The Big M looks so good that, at least, the pictures will turn out great," Cassie says. "You know how the aunts love their pictures. All those scrapbooks."

Jerry nods. "I wonder how much it is to rent a video camera. Maybe if Elaine had pictures she'd eventually forget about—"

"Being married in a mortuary," I say.

Now, I've got to admit that normal-looking pictures would help make the whole thing better, but this generation would have to die off before those pictures would ever be viewed without someone bringing up the fact that they were taken in the mortuary where poor cousin Julie worked when she was so delusional she thought she was working in a wedding chapel.

Jerry and Cassie both look as grim as I feel. Even the sort of happy feeling of knowing my mother is coming is tempered with the knowledge that, when everyone finds out that my fancy wedding chapel is a mortuary, it could be enough of a problem to stop everyone in the family from talking to me

"I don't know why Elaine can't elope," I say.

No one even bothers to answer that one. We all know there is no two-hundred-person audience in an elopement. There are not that many presents, either.

But then, maybe I am selling Elaine short. With all of her tearfulness about not having her parents on the cruise with her, I would say she understands one thing. If Aunt Ruth isn't at Elaine's wedding, no one will ever hear the end of it. That, more than the presents, may be why she doesn't want a wedding that has no guests.

Jerry decides to drive Cassie to her floral shop and then stop at a store near there and ask about video camera rentals. I get on the bus to go to the Big M.

When I get to the Big M, I walk over to Miss Billings's desk. She isn't there, however, and I notice her coming out of one of the viewing rooms. She's dabbing a handkerchief at her eyes.

"Is something wrong?" I say as I take a step forward.

"I went to pay my respects," Miss Billings says with a nod at the viewing room that she had just left.

At the Big M, we become so accustomed to funerals that we tend to forget that others on the staff might actually be here sometimes as a mourner as well as a worker. As I've said before, all kinds of people die.

"I'm so sorry," I said. "Did you know the person well?"

Miss Billings shook her head. "I didn't know him at all, but no one else was coming to the viewing and he went to all the trouble when he made his arrangements to have the most beautiful guest book for people to sign and all those flowers. I thought—well, it's a shame to have no one there to even sign the book, so I went in to be with him for a while and signed my name. I was the only one so far."

"Have all his family died already?" I say. "And no friends?"

We often have small mourning parties, but usually everyone has at least one or two people who want to come and say goodbye. Miss Billings is the one who people call to arrange the final viewings so she usually knows most of the people who are coming to the small viewings. If she says no one is planning to come, then she knows.

"His family is in town for the reading of the will and they sent a big plant, but they're not coming over here," Miss Billings says.

"That's not nice," I say.

Miss Billings shrugs. "Mr. Longe wasn't a nice man. Made a lot of money in the housing market, but didn't bother to make any friends along the way. I expect if enemies were invited, we'd have a few come just to be sure he's dead. I think he foreclosed on a lot of people."

"Well, then he doesn't deserve to have anyone come to his funeral," I say.

Miss Billings nods. "You're probably right. Still, it's sad."

The day outside is gray and that makes the lobby of the Big M look more subdued than usual. Miss Billings is wearing her black suit just as I am and, for the first time, I find the suits to be a little depressing. Mr. Z should lighten up on the gray days and have a navy suit made or something. Maybe I should get a few scarves, the kind my grandmother used to wear, and add a little flair to my black suit on days like this.

I walk into the chapel every chance I get, hoping for new ideas on how to make it the chapel of Elaine's dreams. I know it's odd for me to start wanting her wedding to go well, but I do. Maybe seeing how upset she's been has given me a little compassion for her.

Jerry calls me on my cell phone just before lunch and I meet him in front of the Big M. I want him to get the full picture of the Big M so I tell him to park in front of the building.

"It's impressive," he says as he steps out of his pickup and looks over at the chapel. He sounds a little surprised.

There is a nice green lawn in front of the building and a walkway right up to the chapel. From the front of the building, you don't see the new addition that Mr. Z added when he made the place a mortuary. There are a few tall trees on each side of the walkway and some dark green shrubs that line the base of the chapel.

I nod. "I think it looks like one of those European cathedrals. You know the old, old ones."

"I hope it doesn't have paved stones inside for floor. Those would make measuring difficult," Jerry says as he shuts the door on his pickup.

"No, it's wood floor with a carpet runner between the aisles."

We start up the walk to the front door of the chapel.

"I found a place to rent a video camera," Jerry says.

"Good."

The first thing I do is take Jerry to Miss Billing's desk to meet her. She's pleased to meet him, she says, and just the thought of an upcoming wedding in the Big M brightens up her eyes.

"I always love a bride," Miss Billings says. "Is the bride coming over to see the chapel?"

Jerry looks at me.

"Not yet," I say as I lead him away from Miss Billing's desk before he can tell her all of the troubles we're having. Not that our troubles are a secret, I just want her to be able to keep her fantasies.

I think I'll remember for a long time the expression on Jerry's face when he steps past the chapel doors for the first time. He is amazed at the inside of the chapel.

"I don't see how Elaine could find any fault with this," Jerry says as he looks around.

I don't remind him that Elaine has a lot of experience finding fault with everything. I should know. Hopefully, though, on her big day, she will ease up and just enjoy the time. It seems to me that everyone is worrying so much about the wedding that no one seems to be asking what kind of a marriage Elaine is getting into. Her fiancé seems completely uninvolved in the wedding preparations. Even Jerry is here measuring things. And the fact that Elaine hasn't told her fiancé that she is having problems with his mother makes me worry.

I know Elaine and I have had our differences, but lately I have come to care more about her and I don't want her to jump into a bad marriage just because so many other problems are going on that she doesn't have time to focus on the questions she should be asking herself.

Ah, who knows. I'm not Dear Abby. Maybe Elaine knows her Gary very well and maybe they sit and talk on the phone for hours. Or, maybe there's some good reason that they aren't seeing much of each other lately. Maybe Gary really is just hitting the books really hard so he'll be able to totally focus on his wedding when it happens.

Chapter Eleven

We have two final viewings and a funeral service this afternoon so I am busy directing people. Jerry has ducked in and out of the chapel several times and I've seen him conferring with Miss Billings. He has a talent for measuring. He's been using some graph paper. I think it's from his Greatest Detectives kit, but I haven't said anything to him about it since I kind of like the truce we have going.

Finally, I have a free minute and go into the chapel to see how he's coming along. He's making a draftsman's drawing of the entire chapel, including where the sound system is and how long the area is in front beneath the stained glass window.

"We could put some candle stands there." Jerry nods to me and then points to a place beside the pulpit. "I did manage to get some white taper candles and, if the wedding is at night, we can use candles and not worry about flowers. If we get enough of those candles going, it'll look like we've got a blowtorch in here."

Just what every wedding needs—a blowtorch, I say to myself. But I say to Jerry, "Sounds good."

Jerry has a pencil behind his ear and a satisfied look on his face. "I checked out the hearse for Mr. Z, too, since it was idling funny. I put in some new spark plugs. Wouldn't want it to stall on the way to the cemetery. Not that it would. That thing's built like a tank. It'll get you there."

Mr. Z bought that hearse when he started the Big M back in 1980. Since he only drives it to the Hollywood Cemetery and back a few times a week, it doesn't have all that many miles on it. He keeps it parked under a canopy close to the back door of the main viewing room. The staff takes turns washing it, but, so far, it hasn't been my turn.

"Mr. Z said we could use the hearse for the wedding," Jerry says looking proud of himself. "They don't make them like that anymore. It's a classic."

"A classic *hearse*. Don't you think it looks too much like what it is to use it in the wedding?"

"Yeah," Jerry says with a grin. "But it would be great for a little after-the-ceremony humor. You know to loosen people up after they've been sitting in the chapel. We could use some of that soap to paint Just Married on the back window and drive the bridal couple around. I bet we'd get some attention even in Hollywood." Jerry looks at me and shakes his head. "I guess you need to be a guy to appreciate the humor of it. You know, now that they're married, they're dead."

"I get the point," I say. I try to keep my face straight, but I must admit I give Jerry a grin at the end. "Elaine would never agree."

"Gary might, though."

"So do you know this Gary?" I ask now that we're on the subject.

"Not really," Jerry says. "But I figure once he's married to Elaine we'll get to know him better."

"You don't think he's a little odd?" I say after a moment's hesitation. I don't want to gossip about a guy who is almost family, but I'm worried. "It doesn't sound like Elaine has seen him for weeks."

Jerry shrugs. "When Elaine's the way she is with this wedding, the guy probably knows what he's doing by staying away."

"I suppose." Not that that thought makes me happy. But maybe he and Elaine have their own weird agreement and it works for them. Sort of a love from a distance in the bad times and love closer up in the good times. I mean, people marry and still live in separate houses or even separate cities. Who am I to say what works? I'm not even married.

I leave Jerry to his tape measures and go back to the other part of the Big M. I have some filing that I need to do. Working with the files usually calms me down. There is just something so steadying about making order out of all of those forms. The As go at the beginning. The Zs go at the end. Everything has its place and is easy to find. Today, though, the calming thing isn't happening.

I figure I'm on edge about Elaine and maybe it's because I'm avoiding my own stuff. I'll admit that's a bad habit I got into somewhere in my life. It's just that it's easier to see problems coming at another person than to see them coming at yourself. I don't think I am unique in that. Maybe we just watch other people more closely than we do ourselves.

For a while this morning, Elaine almost looked like the toppler and I was the one who was the poised ice princess. Which makes me wonder if all of that toppling stuff that used to happen to me was nothing but a cry for more attention. I still feel that way sometimes. As if there's not enough love in the whole world to make up for the love I didn't get from my mother. Seeing that from where I am now, though, I wonder if I was like Elaine—always so focused on what I didn't have that I couldn't see what was being offered to me.

While I was growing up, I spent so much time lamenting the lack of my mother's love, I'm not sure I properly appreciated the love Aunt Inga gave to me. Oh, I relied on Aunt Inga; it's just that I yearned for my mother. I thought my mother was the ultimate prize, but Aunt Inga was always the one there for me when I scraped my knee. It's kind of like Elaine who is so focused on having this elegant to-die-for wedding that she can't see we're trying to give her a wedding that could be just as nice and is offered with what is, if not full-blown affection, at least increasingly good wishes.

Toward the end of the day, Miss Billings needs my help to sit with the elderly father of a man whose wife has died. I do it willingly and not just because it is my job. I've come to see that simply sitting with people is sometimes the best service we offer at the Big M. Oh, I know, the caskets are impressive and what Miss Billings creates for the final viewing is amazing, but, in the end, the only thing to do with death is to sit with the people who are grieving.

"I don't know what my son will do without his Patricia," the old man, Mr. Frankel, says to me. We are sitting on a sofa in a corner of the lounge. "They've been married since they graduated from high school forty years ago. They've never spent a day apart."

"He's lucky he has you to live with him still," I say. "He won't be so alone."

Mr. Frankel shakes his head. "I'm to go into a home. We've decided. It's too much for him to care for me and work all the time like he does."

"Maybe he could get help from a neighbor, or—"

Mr. Frankel shakes his head again, this time slower. "No, it's time for me to go. I'm ready to leave."

I reach over and take the old man's hand and pat it. I know he's not just talking about leaving his son's house. We sit together and wait for his son to finish making the funeral arrangements.

"I thought I'd die before either of them," the old man says with a sigh and then looks at me. "Why do you suppose that didn't happen? It should have been me to die, not Patricia."

"I don't know why," I say and pat his hand some more. I wish there was more I could do. "I just don't know."

There was a time, not so long ago, when I hated to admit that I didn't know why something happened or didn't happen. Especially when it concerned God. I thought I had God pretty well figured out. I'd decided He liked some people and didn't like others and all of His decisions were based on that liking or not liking thing. The fact that He didn't answer the prayer I prayed over and over again about living with my mother pretty much confirmed what I had suspected. I wasn't one of the ones He liked. I knew He liked Aunt Inga and I suspected He must like Elaine. He probably even liked Aunt Ruth. But me? No. He had no time for me.

Now, since working at the Big M, I sometimes think there are more things I don't know than things that I do when it comes to God. I certainly don't know why God decides who is to die and who is to live. I don't even know if He does decide. Maybe there's just a random wheel of chance somewhere that sometimes spins to a slot named Live and sometimes spins to a slot named Die.

I think of Elaine. I don't even know why God decides who is to marry and who isn't. And when I think of Doug, I have no idea why God lets some people walk down an aisle at a rally and make a crazy commitment that could change their lives while He lets others back away.

I wonder if Mr. Frankel's son will miss his father when he's gone. When Mr. Frankel's son comes back to pick him up, I give the old man a hug and a smile as I say goodbye. After I watch the two men walk out of the Big M I tell Miss Billings I'm going to take a quick break and I go into an empty viewing room so I can call Aunt Inga on my cell phone.

"Aunt Inga?"

"Is that you, Julie?"

I smile. "Yes, it's me."

"Is everything okay?"

"Yeah. I just wanted you to know I love you."

"Oh," Aunt Inga says and I can hear the warm pleasure in her voice. "And I love you, too, dear."

I feel better after I talk to Aunt Inga. She's still crocheting those orange rose petals for Elaine's wedding. I tell her she's probably got enough, but she says she keeps making them because she needs to have something to do with her hands so she doesn't, and these are her words, get ahead of God's planning.

I hadn't thought until then that God might have a *plan* for Elaine's wedding. I'm not quite sure how I feel about that. I mean, if He had a plan, shouldn't He be doing something about these details that are laid square on the shoulders of the rest of us. Even if He'd just handle Aunt Ruth, that would be a big help.

Aunt Inga says she hasn't convinced Aunt Ruth that Elaine's wedding will be okay in my chapel. But then she hasn't convinced her that my mother is going to be a help instead of a hindrance when it comes to decorating the chapel, either.

Before long, Miss Billings is coming into the break room to sign out for the day and to say good-night.

"Be sure and lock everything up when you and Jerry leave," Miss Billings says. "And thanks for inviting me to stay and eat with you. I'm sorry I can't."

Jerry has gotten permission to use the courtyard at the Big M for a candlelight dinner. Well, it's not going to be much of a dinner. Doug is stopping off someplace and getting us all sandwiches. It's really a working dinner. Jerry wants to see how the lighting will work for an evening reception in the courtyard.

Jerry comes out of the chapel with his duffel bag in one hand and a fistful of drawings in the other. He's also got a look of satisfaction on his face that I haven't seen for a long time. I have to admit that he has gone to a lot of work and I want him to know I appreciate it.

"You're doing good," I say.

"Do you think Cassie has noticed?" he asks in a shy voice.

Well, at least that explains his sudden desire to be the hero. I nod. "How could she not notice?"

"Good," he says as he walks over to one of the lounge chairs and sets the duffel bag down.

"Cassie always did like a good wedding," I say just to see if Jerry will flinch.

He looks up from his duffel bag and grins. "I remember. You and her walking down the aisle. Didn't anyone ever tell you that the groom was supposed to be a boy?"

"I was symbolic," I say. "I wore jeans when I was the groom."

"You always wore jeans, even when you were the bride."

That's true. I remember that summer before I started school when Cassie and I played wedding every day. I had two pair of ratty jeans and I lived in them. That was the last time for years that I had my own clothes, ones that weren't Elaine's hand-me-downs. It was such a long time ago.

Jerry has zipped up his duffel bag with the papers inside and stands to face me again.

"Is that why you used to hang out and watch us?" I ask. "Because you wanted to play the groom?"

"I was waiting for cake," Jerry says with a laugh. "I don't know why none of your weddings ever got to the cake part. That's the good part of any wedding."

I groan. "We never gave the cake a thought."

"I know. And I was hungry."

"It's way too late for Cassie and me to have cake. But for Elaine, we'll have to put an order in at a bakery around here."

"And people need rice, too," Jerry says. "We need to throw something. That's half the reason people go to weddings. And, of course, we should talk to someone who does catering. Maybe something easy to eat like shish kebabs and rice."

I'm starting to notice that Jerry is helpful in thinking of things. In the distant future, if I ever open a wedding business, Jerry would make a good partner. "Have you ever thought of going into business for yourself?"

Jerry gets pale and his eyes narrow. "What have you heard?"

"Me? Nothing."

"I do a good job. They'd be fools to lay me off," Jerry continues. He's glowering, but not exactly at me. "Who else is going to lie on their back and change oil pans all day?"

"No one. You do a great job."

"And it's not true that business is drying up in Blythe. Sure Uncle Howard was complaining that his business was off and that one gas station did close and—" Jerry looks at me "—and you got laid off at your job, of course. Sorry about that, by the way. But that doesn't mean other jobs are in jeopardy."

It all falls into place. Jerry isn't on vacation from his job at the car repair place. I should have known he'd never take two weeks off to run around and buy candles. Besides, the owner of that shop isn't noted for being generous. In the past, he didn't even give Jerry two weeks of paid vacation. The man always said one week was enough. "Even if you do get laid off, that doesn't mean you won't find something else."

"Yeah," Jerry says, but he doesn't look me in the eye.

We just sit there together for a moment.

"I really liked that job, too," Jerry says as he moves his duffel bag to the other side of his feet. "I was there seven years if you count the time I worked after school in my senior year."

"Does your mom know?"

Jerry finally looks up at me and then he sighs. "Everyone has been so worried about this wedding. I didn't want to say anything until it was all over."

I nod. "I know what you mean. That's what I told myself about keeping quiet about the Big M. The aunts don't need more stress."

Jerry shakes his head. "My mom says Aunt Ruth has stopped combing her hair. She just goes around with a cold washcloth draped over her head."

"I always thought they were so strong. All of them."

Jerry smiles. "They're Norwegian women. Viking stock. They're tough."

I nod. "That's the way they always seemed—until now."

I rise and Jerry follows. We start to walk to the door that leads out to the courtyard.

"How are you set for money and all?" I ask when we get to the door. I can't believe I'm making this offer. "I'm getting paid on Friday and I could—"

Jerry waves the offer away as he opens the door.

"I got a couple of weeks of severance pay. I'm good for now."

I walk through the open door. "Maybe you could go into business for yourself around here."

"Hollywood doesn't need more mechanics."

"There are other things you can do," I say as Jerry closes the door behind us.

"Maybe," Jerry says as he looks around the courtyard. "Measuring everything here was fun. I don't suppose there's a job in it, though."

"When this is all over, we should talk about jobs," I say.

Jerry nods, but I can see he thinks I'll be telling him to work in the fast-food business so he doesn't seem too excited. That's all right, I decide. We've got time later.

The sun is beginning to set and the light from the west is turning the pale beige stone of the courtyard into a more golden hue. Here and there clumps of ivy are climbing up the walls and there are enough roses along the edge of the paved area to make the air fragrant.

"If we could only keep people out here," Jerry says. "They'd never suspect it is a mortuary inside."

"Oh, but they wouldn't want to miss seeing the chapel."

"I know. It's the hallway between the two places that will give us problems."

Jerry is right. That hallway leads to all the rooms where the Big M does the funeral part of its work. The largest room there is where the caskets are on display. From golden-brushed bronze to solid cherrywood, the caskets at the Big M are a sight to behold.

I was a little freaked out by that room when I was

first at the Big M, but I'm okay with it now. Mr. Z even showed me that most of the caskets have an adjustable bed in them so the final viewing can be better. I don't even have an adjustable bed in my room at Aunt Inga's. It seems odd to think that I'd sleep in better comfort if I were dead than in Blythe.

I don't know if most people know about the bed thing, but I'm sure Elaine would be upset if she wandered in there thinking it was the room where the bride changes into her dress when, instead, it's where the corpse changes into its burial clothes. Well, of course, the corpse doesn't change by itself.

"We'll lock the room that has the caskets," I say. "We'll have that master key that Miss Billings gave us to use tonight so we can lock off any of the rooms."

Miss Billings told me once that all of the rooms at the Big M used to have different keys, but that the jangle of keys from the loaded key chains the staff carried disturbed the mourners so Mr. Z had all the doors fitted onto one master key. He felt it made the staff people look more in charge when they were showing clients around, which was something very comforting to mourners, he always said. The bereaved wanted to know everything was in good hands and that they didn't need to worry.

"And the room with all the files. We'll lock that." No one would freak out about the files, but I feel they are a sacred trust. I wouldn't want a stray guest wandering in there and looking through them.

"Of course," Jerry agrees.

"We'll have to keep the lounge areas open." The lounge areas lead to the restrooms and there is nothing in either of the rooms that would make people think they were in a mortuary instead of a church. At least, not in the women's restrooms.

"Nobody has scratched Lincoln Died Here on the walls of the men's room, have they?"

Jerry shook his head. "It's strictly boring in there."

"Good. And the kitchen that's off the main viewing room—we'll need to have that open for the caterers," I say. The kitchen was there when the Big M was a church and Mr. Z left it the way it was. That's where the staff keep their lunches now when they bring something from home.

Jerry and I are quiet for a moment, thinking of all the things that need to be done and breathing in the scent of the roses.

"I'll ask Miss Billings about caterers tomorrow," I say.

We're quiet some more.

"Do you think we have a chance to pull it off?" Jerry finally asks.

I shrug. "I'm going to tell the aunts that the Big M is a mortuary when we have some of the details figured out. Probably tomorrow will be the day. That gives them a day before they make their calls to people about the new location. I think we can keep the guests from knowing this is a mortuary, but I'll let the aunts make the decision. I guess, if need be, Elaine can always do the cruise."

Jerry nods. "Or maybe that Chinese restaurant."

We hear voices calling our names and realize that Cassie and Doug are here.

"We're in the courtyard," I call out to them as I walk to the opening that goes from the courtyard to the front yard area. I see Cassie and Doug crossing the lawn from where they were by the front door to the Big M.

"I forgot to bring the candles," Jerry says as he leaves his duffel on one of the benches in the court-yard and walks back toward the rear door of the mortuary. "I left them in the chapel."

Cassie and Doug come into the courtyard just as Jerry walks back into the building. I happen to notice that Cassie's eyes go to Jerry the first thing.

Doug is carrying his backpack and he reaches in and pulls out a brown bag that he sets on the wrought iron table next to where we're standing in the court-yard. There are two tables like this one and twenty or so portable round tables in the supply room.

"How was it today?" Cassie asks me.

"Okay, and you?"

"I have some more plants to pick up when Jerry has time," Cassie says.

I nod. "I'm glad Jerry is here. It's good. You know he's changed a lot since we were kids."

There, I've said my bit to show Cassie that it's okay with me if she's interested in Jerry.

"He is nice," Cassie says and gives a smile. "I like him."

"I thought you might," I say with a smile back.

In the meantime, Doug has pulled out four wrapped turkey sandwiches and four oranges from the brown bag and set them on the table. Just then Jerry gets back with a few candles.

The sun is almost gone by the time we light the candles and, I must say, the courtyard is very romantic by candlelight. Jerry has these small metal candle-holders and he places four candles in the center of the table.

One of the candles goes out, however, and he frowns as he examines it and then decides he needs another one. Before he goes back to the chapel to get another one from the pile he has there, he goes to his duffel bag and pulls out a flashlight.

"From my detective kit," Jerry announces with a flourish as he holds the small blue flashlight up. It's plastic and its beam is feeble, but it does give off enough light to see.

"Just what we need," Cassie says as she reaches up and takes the flashlight when Jerry gives it to her.

"You can carry it inside," Jerry says. "If you want to come with me."

Cassie holds the flashlight and the two of them head back through the rear door of the mortuary. They don't even get to the door of the mortuary before Jerry puts his arm around Cassie.

It's funny how them going off like that, arm in arm, suddenly turns this into a serious date instead of a casual date where four people are just getting together to have a sandwich. They might even share a kiss in there. I look over at Doug.

"I didn't know they were going to do that," I say. I'm not sure if he's still afraid I might want a commitment from him or not. "I think they've just discovered they like each other."

"Lucky them," Doug says.

I relax. Doug doesn't sound stressed or anything. I can tell because his voice sounds normal.

"So, how's it going with the homework?" I say because it's something to ask.

"I looked up John 3:16," he says. "You know, after Jerry made such a big deal out of it."

"Jerry likes to tease me."

"Yeah, I got that."

We sit and watch the candle flames for a few minutes.

"I got some waters in my backpack, too," Doug finally says. "I almost brought some bottles of flavored waters."

"No, plain water is good."

We're quiet for a few more minutes.

"Can I ask you something?" Doug says as he lifts his backpack onto the table and opens it up.

"Sure."

"What do you have against God?" Doug pulls out two water bottles and sets them on the table.

"Oh, well." I swallow and look at the rear door of the mortuary, hoping it will open and Jerry and Cassie will step out so this conversation will be derailed. After a second or two, though, when nothing has happened, I decide it is a fair question. "God sort of messed up my life when I was a kid."

Doug has set the water bottles down and is looking at me. "I'm listening."

"You know about my mother leaving me in Blythe when she moved to Las Vegas." I feel a little funny saying that to him when his parents both were killed in a car accident.

"So you think God was mad at you?"

I nod. "Something like that. I just figured He didn't like me much." And for good measure, I add, "Besides, he let my father die when I was little, too. I never even got to know him. It didn't seem like it's fair that I couldn't have either one of my parents."

Doug holds up his hands. "You don't have to convince me. I can see why you would be mad at God."

"Really?" Now that's not the response I expected. "Of course, you know what it feels like."

I'm glad Doug understands. Something is bothering me however. "I notice it didn't stop you, though. You just walked down that aisle."

Doug shrugs as he reaches into his backpack for the other two bottles of water. "We're all different. I might have felt like you did if I had known about God when I was a kid. Maybe not knowing Him gave me very low expectations. I don't think I ever expected Him to do anything for me back then. I bet He was sorry you were mad at Him, though."

I open my bottle of water and take a drink. It never occurred to me to think of this from God's point of view before. All of this working around death is making me crazy. If I'm not careful, I won't have any of my enemies left. I've already caved on Jerry and I'm going soft on Elaine. If I make my peace with God— well, what would my life be like then? I take another drink of water. Wow. I need to think for a minute.

When Cassie and Jerry walk out of the mortuary, they are holding hands. At least both of them have their hands on the flashlight and they are swinging it around as if it's a light saber. I forgot they were both *Star Wars* fans.

"Don't blind us with that thing," I say when they point it at Doug and me. In truth, the beam is so feeble it wouldn't blind anything, but I've grumbled at Jerry all my life. "You'll spoil our force field."

They laugh as they walk closer.

"Oh, I had forgotten how beautiful that shepherd is in the stained glass window," Cassie says as she sits down on one of the chairs around the table. "Jerry turned the back light on so the light would shine through."

I nod. "That's one thing that will be memorable about the wedding. Assuming Aunt Ruth doesn't want to cover it up."

"Why would she—" Jerry begins and then stops.

"Farm animal," I say and he nods.

"But it's a little lamb," Cassie protests.

"Aunt Ruth doesn't like farm animals," I say.

"They smell," Jerry adds.

"Well, of course they smell," Cassie says indignantly. "They're farm animals."

We spend the next few minutes trying to decide what to do if Aunt Ruth absolutely refuses to have Elaine's wedding take place in the presence of a farm animal.

Finally Doug says. "If she's okay with the dead bodies around here, I wouldn't think she'd complain about a stained glass lamb."

That stops us all short. He's right, of course. The rest of us have almost forgotten about the Big M being a mortuary. I wonder if that is wishful thinking or just the natural beauty of the place lulling us into forgetfulness.

Doug passes around the sandwiches and we eat them as we discuss various options for the wedding. Jerry mentions calling hotels in downtown Los Angeles and Cassie mentions the tearoom at the Huntington Gardens, which we decide would be too small.

There's really nothing for it, but for me to tell the aunts about the Big M and leave it to them to decide what to do. Now that Jerry has his measurements, I can give those to Aunt Ruth at the same time I tell her. Maybe if I get her all involved in the numbers of how far everything is from everything, she won't notice when I mention that the place is really a very nice mortuary.

I take another deep breath. I'll have to be sure and mention the roses again.

Chapter Twelve

When I wake up on Friday morning, I am surprised that there are no sounds in the apartment. For the past few mornings, I have woken up either to the sound of someone talking in the living room or someone crying in the bedroom. Today it's nice to just hear the sounds of the cars on the street outside and the clank of the garbage trucks as they empty the trash bins in the parking lot.

I am lying on the air mattress in Cassie's room and she is curled up on her bed sound asleep. The light is just starting to rise and some of that clear morning sun is shining through the glass in the places where the blind does not meet the edge of the window. It makes thin stripes on everything: Cassie's blue fuzzy bathrobe that is hanging on a hook on the open door of her closet; the English flower calendar that she has tacked above her dresser; and the huge ficus plant that she moved to her bedroom last night so there would be space in the living room to fold out the Hide-A-Bed for Jerry.

I try to talk myself into feeling strong today. I need
to talk to the aunts this morning and it's not a task I'm
looking forward to. So, I do some mental pumping
and try to picture myself saying something so
smoothly that neither aunt is upset. It doesn't work—
I can't even think of what I will say, smooth or
unsmooth—so eventually I just get up and give a
quiet knock on the door separating the living room
and the bedroom.

Jerry whispers that I can come in.

The first place I head to is the counter so that I can
start the coffee. We set the pot up last night so really
all I have to do is press a button to turn it on. Then I
head to the bathroom to wash up.

After I come out of the bathroom, all combed and
scrubbed, I slip into the bedroom and change into
some jeans and a sweater, all the while taking care to
not wake Cassie. The alarm isn't set to go off for
another twenty minutes.

When I go back out into the main room, Jerry is just
coming out of the bathroom wearing one of his brown
T-shirts and a clean pair of jeans.

Jerry tells me he's decided he's done all of the measuring that he can at the Big M and he's going to see
if he can find any clues about Cassie's mom today.

I look at the closed bedroom door and speak quietly.
"Does Cassie know you're going to do that?"

He shakes his head as he puts two slices of bread
into the toaster. "I thought I'd see what I can find out
before I say anything to her. There might not be any
way for me to find anything, but I'd like to try. Cassie
said her mom used to live in Los Angeles."

There are a few cups of coffee in the pot so I get some mugs from the cupboard.

Yikes. There's a loud pounding at the door and I almost drop one of the mugs.

"Open up. The police." A male voice calls out.

"What?" I squeak out as I put the mugs on the counter.

"Don't answer that," Cassie whispers from where she stands in the doorway to the bedroom. She's got her robe on, but not her glasses and she is squinting at me. She just got up. "It could be a trick."

"There's a man in here," I call out since we've already made enough noise to tell whoever is on the other side of our door that someone is home and I'm hoping a show of force will prevent any trouble.

"Yes," Jerry adds and he makes his voice even deeper than it is so he sounds like a wrestler.

"It's all right, girls," we hear Mrs. Snyder say. "I checked their IDs for you. They really are the police."

Okay, now that's not right. I step over, unlock the door and open it.

"You shouldn't be out here, either," I scold Mrs. Snyder who is standing there holding a black wallet. I try to avoid looking at the two men who are standing in the hall next to her. They are dressed in police uniforms and Mrs. Snyder is in her fuzzy purple robe with her hair in curlers. "Besides, anyone can get a fake identification card. Police don't go knocking on doors at this time of the morning."

One of the policemen cleared his throat. "We're here to see Jerry."

Now that stops me. "*Our* Jerry?"

"We have someone watching the fire escape," the policeman adds in a voice loud enough to carry inside Cassie's apartment. "There's no way out."

"Is it the plants?" I say. I know Cassie has those plants sitting on the fire escape landing outside her window. Maybe the policemen think she's growing something illegal out there. "They're all just houseplants."

"May we come in?" the policeman who has been doing the talking asks.

I hear the phone ringing inside the apartment so I figure they may as well come in while I answer it. I'll leave the door to the hallway open just in case, though. "Mrs. Snyder has the number for the police, and if she hears anything funny in here, she'll be on the phone."

"That's right," the older woman says, but she makes no move to go back to her own apartment. In fact, she follows the policemen right into this apartment so I'm not sure how much help she would be if these men turned out to be bad guys.

The phone is right by the door so I grab for it. "Hello."

"Julie? Is that you?"

"Aunt Inga," I say, wishing I'd thought for a minute before I answered that phone. Aunt Inga will only worry if she knows we have policemen at our door at this hour of the morning. Things like this don't happen in Blythe.

I can see the policemen looking around Cassie's apartment. They have their hands on their gun holsters as though they might need to be ready for action.

"Aunt Inga, can I call you back?" I say.

"So, which one of you is Jerry?" one of the policemen says as he looks back and forth between Jerry and Cassie.

"It's a man's name," Jerry says as if he's offended the man can't pin him down in an instant. "It comes from Gerald."

"So, it's you," the other policeman says as he eyes Jerry carefully. "We would like to ask you some questions."

I hear Aunt Inga's gasp and realize I haven't hung up yet.

"Who is questioning Jerry?" Aunt Inga asks.

"Just a minute." I put my hand over the speaker on the phone and say to those in the room, "That gun he has is a toy gun. It might look real, but it came inside his Greatest Detectives of the World kit. It's made for little kids to play with."

The policemen look at me as if I'm nuts.

"Oh, so it's a game," Aunt Inga says, sounding more relieved than she should.

I look at my hand. I thought I had covered the phone well enough so Aunt Inga wouldn't hear anything.

"Don't worry about anything," I say into the phone. She probably just heard a word or two of what is happening. "I'll call you later."

"Have a fun time," Aunt Inga says as if everything is right in the world.

I hang up and turn to the policemen. "The gun's plastic. Jerry can show you. For that matter, I can show you."

I look around for Jerry's duffel bag and see it over by the sofa.

The policeman standing closest to Jerry turns to him and says, "We want to know about the note you left at 1802 San Rafael Road in Palm Springs."

"Oh," I say.

"I thought a dog ate that," Jerry says as the policeman holds up a white paper bag carefully flattened inside two flat pieces of plastic. The bag does look as though it's been tossed around so maybe a dog did have it in its mouth at one point.

"So you admit you wrote the note," the policeman says. The policeman turns the bag so we can see the black letters on one side.

"But it doesn't mean anything," I say. The police are obviously not worried about the diet of some mangy dog. I'm beginning to get the picture here and I don't think I like what the police are thinking. Jerry might be a bit dense at times, but he's not a criminal. "He was just trying to impress the woman who was the wedding planner."

"The one who took the money?" the policeman says as if he doesn't believe me.

I shrug. "Well, he's not interested anymore, of course."

"I never was all that interested. I was just being nice," Jerry says. "There's no crime in that."

The policeman talking doesn't look as if he believes Jerry. "We need to take you in for questioning related to the theft."

"Can't he just answer your questions here?" I say. "He didn't do anything, you know. He'd never mess up Elaine's wedding. In fact, he's spending his days trying to make it all go smoothly. You can ask Aunt Ruth. She has him measuring the aisle in the chapel."

The two policemen look at each other and then back at Jerry. "What's your last name?"

"You don't even know his full name?" I ask. "How did you find him?"

"Reverse directory," Cassie says from where she's standing beside the bedroom door. "From the telephone number he left for Mona."

"Ransen," Jerry says. "But my mother's last name is Nilsen. She's Aunt Ruth's sister."

"Ruth?" the policeman prompts.

"Ruth Torrance."

The two policemen look at each other. Finally, one of them looks at Jerry again. "Did you set this whole thing up with the wedding planner? Maybe she wasn't turning sweet enough on you and you thought you'd make it worth her while to pay a little attention to you? After all, you were at your aunt's place. You could have met Mona and given her information on the sly."

Okay, now I'm getting alarmed. "He wouldn't do that. Ask anyone." I look around. "Ask Cassie."

"He wouldn't do it," Cassie says emphatically.

The policeman doesn't look convinced. "Lots of crime happens between family members."

"Not in our family," I say. We've never even talked about stealing from each other. I can't imagine it has entered anyone's mind. We might have our problems, but criminal activity is not one of them. "Call Aunt Ruth if you don't believe us."

I hold the phone out to the policeman. "Her number is on that Post-it note on the cupboard door there."

Okay, so I'm bluffing a little. I don't think he's going to call Aunt Ruth and ask for a reference for Jerry. I'm having a hard time thinking of ways to keep

Jerry out of trouble, though. I know if this had happened a few weeks ago, I wouldn't even blink an eye if Jerry was hauled off to jail. I wouldn't have wanted him to suffer in jail for a long time, but I wouldn't have felt that I would miss him if he were someplace else for a month or so. Now, his troubles are my troubles.

I give a deep sigh. I'm turning so soft I don't recognize myself.

The policeman takes the Post-it note off the cupboard door. "I'll make the call in the hall. Remember, someone's watching all the exits."

"He's not going to escape," I snap at the policeman as he leaves the room.

"Not with someone guarding the fire escape," Jerry says, with a touch of humor.

"You find this funny?" I look at Jerry and demand an answer. Here I am sweating over keeping him out of jail and he's making jokes.

"No," Jerry says but he grins anyway. "I just never knew you'd stand by me like this."

"Well, I shouldn't have to stand by you. You should have the sense to stay out of trouble."

I say the words before I realize I am the one saying them. Me! Miss Toppler! Something's wrong when I am scolding people for getting into trouble. I'm supposed to be the tumbler, not the scolder.

The door to Cassie's apartment opens and the policeman comes back inside. He still has his cell phone in his hand and he looks at Jerry. "Well, Mrs. Torrance vouches for you. She said you didn't know enough about everything to help the wedding planner anyway.

She thought it sounded about right for you to be chasing after the wedding planner with the note, too. So I guess we'll just get a statement here about what you know." The policeman starts to slip his cell phone back in its case attached to his belt and he looks around. "Okay, you're Julie, right?"

"Yes, that's me."

"Your Aunt Ruth wants you to call her. Right away."

I nod. There is no way to escape this one. The only good thing is that I needed to call Aunt Ruth today anyway so maybe I'll be able to mention that the chapel everyone is talking about for Elaine's wedding is part of a mortuary. Maybe she'll be so relieved about Jerry not being in trouble with the law that she won't be upset that the usual clients at the Big M are dead. It's all about perspective.

I grab my cell phone out of my purse and go out into the hall. The policemen are huddled around Jerry and asking him questions so I figure I may as well call Aunt Ruth now. I have to go to work soon and, since she's already up, I may as well get this conversation behind me.

The hallway is cold, but I lean against the wall next to Cassie's door anyway and flip open my cell phone.

"Is Jerry all right?" Aunt Ruth asks when she hears my voice. "I can't imagine the police would think he'd steal a dime from me. He's a good boy."

"Yeah," I say. "They're going to ask him some questions, but that's all."

"Good," Aunt Ruth says. "I told that policeman he was way off base."

"I'm sorry you had to know about this," I add. "I

know you're already under a lot of stress with the wedding."

Aunt Ruth snorts. "Not anymore. When I heard what Gary's mother wanted to do, I said to myself it's time to take action."

"Oh."

"She thinks she can squeeze me out of the wedding when I'm the mother of the bride. Well, I don't think so. That's not right."

I smile. Aunt Ruth is back. "No, it's not."

"Our family might not have the kind of money they do, but we know proper behavior when we see it. We can show them what a wedding should be like. Can you believe they didn't want Howard and me on the cruise? We're Elaine's parents."

"I know," I begin. "But there are many places to have the wedding. For instance—"

"As if there could be a cruise so wonderful that Elaine wouldn't need her mother and father at her wedding." Aunt Ruth speaks without listening to me. "We gave birth to her. We should be at her wedding. What are these people thinking? I mean, it's different if it's the honeymoon. I understand that. I don't expect to go on the honeymoon."

"Well, no," I begin again. "But speaking of places for the wedding—"

"Don't you worry any. I'm so glad we have your help. Your chapel might be simple, but we can make something out of it. Just see if we don't."

Okay, so there doesn't seem to be an easy way to do this.

"Aunt Ruth, you need to listen. I have to tell you

something about the chapel…." I close my eyes. "The chapel is in a mortuary."

I open my eyes. There is silence on the phone line. "Aunt Ruth?"

"We must have had a bad connection. I thought you said the chapel is in a mortuary." Aunt Ruth gives a little laugh. "Who would put a wedding chapel in a mortuary?"

"Because it's not exactly a wedding chapel," I say. "It's the chapel we use for funerals."

There's no response so I finally say. "I'm so sorry I didn't tell everyone right away, but I didn't want to disappoint everyone."

"Funerals?" Aunt Ruth's voice is a little weak. "With dead people?"

Now I know she has the concept. It doesn't make me feel any better.

"You don't need to worry about the dead people. They're all in the viewing rooms. And it's a really beautiful place. The courtyard has roses all around it and the chapel looks like an old European cathedral."

"Oh, dear." Aunt Ruth's voice is almost a whisper.

It's silent for a minute. I can almost see Aunt Ruth's face from here, looking white and all rumpled as if she's going to cry or maybe faint.

"Is Aunt Inga there?" I finally ask. I'm a little worried that I don't hear any scolding words. Shouldn't she be telling me what a mess I've made of things? "Maybe I should call Aunt Inga and ask her to go over to your place."

"Yes. That would be good," Aunt Ruth says. Her voice is monotone.

I really wish she would say something about how foolish I've been. I hang up and stay right where I am so I can make another call. Fortunately, I have Aunt Inga on speed dial.

"Julie?" Aunt Inga says when I tell her I am on the phone. "Is that you?"

"Yes, it's me." I take a deep breath and dive into the hard stuff. "You need to go over to Aunt Ruth's place. I think she's a little upset because I told her that the chapel where I work isn't a wedding chapel, it's a mortuary chapel."

Aunt Inga doesn't make a sound. This isn't how I intended to tell her. I'm just getting a little freaked out about Aunt Ruth sitting there in shock.

"I'm so sorry I didn't tell you sooner," I say. Now I'm a little worried about Aunt Inga. "Say something. Are you all right? I didn't want you to be disappointed in me."

"You're my Julie," Aunt Inga says as though that sums everything up. She sounds disoriented, but not angry. "I'll always be proud of you. Now, let me get my purse and I'll go over to see Ruth."

"Thank you," I say.

I dab at my eyes before I open the door to go back inside Cassie's place. The policeman who had been taking notes on what Jerry was telling them flipped his notebook shut so I assume they're finished.

"Don't leave any more notes for criminals," the other policeman says to Jerry as they both turn to leave. "You call us if you think you have a lead."

"Yes, sir," Jerry says.

The policemen leave and I just look at Jerry. He needs a shave and the T-shirt he has on is definitely the one he wore yesterday. But it's really good to see him still standing here. "Don't do that again."

Cassie has the shades up on the windows in this room and the morning light comes in steadily.

Jerry shifts his legs so he is leaning against the wall next to the bedroom door. He's gets this puzzled look on his face and he looks over at me. "It's kind of nice to have you worrying about me for a change. I used to think you liked it when I got into trouble."

I shrug. "We were kids then. The same rules don't apply now that we are adults."

Did I just say that? I've been playing by the same every-kid-for-herself rules since I was five, at least when it came to my cousins. We wrote those rules in blood and hard feelings. Now, look at me. I don't even know when I decided those rules don't apply any more to Jerry.

I am trying to think of something sane to say that would indicate I haven't gone completely soft in my head when Jerry walks over to me. He stands there a second and then he gives me a quick hug.

"What?" I squeak.

"New rules," he says calmly as he walks over to the kitchen counter.

I, of course, just stand there. It comforts me a little that Cassie is standing there looking about as startled as I am. Only Mrs. Snyder seems to take it all in stride.

"Isn't that nice?" Mrs. Snyder says as she starts back to the door. "Well, now that the excitement is over, I'll head back to my television."

"I should get dressed," Cassie finally says.

"I'll make some more of that oatmeal," Jerry says

as he pulls a pan out of the cupboard. "Do we have more raisins?"

I stand there for another minute. Who can think about raisins? Jerry just hugged me and it wasn't an attempt to put a lizard down the back of my shirt or anything. Wait a bit. I concentrate on my back a second just to be sure nothing slimy is slithering down it, but everything feels normal. I guess we are growing up. Wow. I don't know how I feel about that.

I look over at the counter. He's even going to cook us oatmeal and raisins. It is a new world.

Chapter Thirteen

The aunts called back minutes after "Jerry's incident with the police"—those were Aunt Ruth's words—just to be sure that everything was okay. Jerry and I reassured them that he wasn't going to jail and, no, he didn't need any money for bail. They apparently believed us, because we haven't heard from them since.

Anyway, it is now Saturday morning and I am lying on my back on the air mattress in Cassie's bedroom. I have my head under a blanket so the sunshine won't blind me with its good cheer. I'm awake, but I'm trying to ignore that fact. After all, it's Saturday morning and I had this pleasant dream last night about a wedding on a cruise ship far, far away from here. I couldn't see the bride in my dream, but I didn't need to. Just seeing her twisted up in the long white wedding train attached to her dress was enough to set my mind at rest.

The phone rings and I ease the blanket down an inch trying to see the alarm clock Cassie has on the stand beside her bed. I'm lying on the floor so I have to twist my head some to see that it's one minute past eight. Prime aunt time.

Cassie groans in her sleep and turns over, pulling her covers with her so they will block the light in her eyes.

I hear some kind of muttering come from the living room and then a loud voice. "Julie. Phone for you."

I don't know why Jerry can't decide that those new rules of his apply on Saturday morning. A kind cousin would say I had died in the night and couldn't come to the phone.

"No," I say and it comes out half wail and half protest. "Can't you talk to them?"

I sound pathetic to my ear, but apparently it's not bad enough to move Jerry's cold heart.

"They need you," Jerry says and I swear his voice is growing more cheerful with each word. "Rise and shine. It's past eight o'clock."

"On a *Saturday* morning," I say. "It's the universal day of rest."

"That's Sunday. The Sabbath," Jerry says just as if he's become some kind of Biblical scholar now that he and Doug sat and talked about religious issues last night until midnight.

Cassie and I were there, too, at the coffee shop, but she and I faded a little after eleven when the discussion turned to how dead you needed to be to see heaven. You know, the near-death people who see all those lights. I had never realized there was so much room for discussion in religion. I don't think Jerry had, either, and he's taken with it. It's a whole new field of argument for him.

"Not everyone agrees the Sabbath is Sunday. It could be Saturday," I say.

"Well, it could be Tuesday, too," Jerry says. "But the aunts don't care. They don't let anyone rest on Saturday."

"I know," I mumble as I sit up. I yawn and then make myself stand up beside the air mattress. I stand there a minute, resisting the temptation to fall back down on the mattress in a heap of weary bones.

I'm not about to let Jerry know, but I don't mind so much talking to the aunts. Not that I'm wild about their timing. But I was beginning to wonder if the reason they hadn't called last night as I expected was that I had messed up so bad that they weren't talking to me. If they're calling me at this time in the morning, though, they are okay with me. The aunts never call strangers until after nine o'clock in the morning no matter what day of the week it is. The eight o'clock rule only applies to family.

I pull my robe off a hook on the wall and put it on over my pajamas before gently opening the door. I look back at Cassie. She's still managing to sleep. Or, at least, she's pretending to sleep so she doesn't have to say good morning to me.

Jerry hands me the phone the minute I step into the living area and close the bedroom door. He's opened the blinds in this room so the sunlight is even more merciless.

"Hi," I say into the phone. I try to put enough energy into my voice so that whichever aunt is calling won't know she got me up out of bed. I might complain to Jerry, but I don't want a lecture from any of the aunts on how late I must have stayed up the night before if I wasn't awake until now.

"Julie? Is that you?"

"Hi, Aunt Inga." I stumble over to one of the chairs at Cassie's table and sit down.

"We're getting everything arranged," Aunt Inga says with a surge of excitement in her voice. I bet she's not sitting down anywhere. "Your mom is meeting Aunt Ruth and me in Hollywood today so we can start to buy all the things we'll need for Elaine's wedding. I just wanted you to know that we've reserved some rooms at a hotel near Cassie's place. Elaine found it on the computer."

"Wow." That wakes me up completely. It's a good thing I have the solid chair beneath me, too. "You're going to be here? Today? My mom, too?"

I look over to Jerry and he arches his eyebrow at me in a question.

"Today? Here?" Jerry asks me in a frantic whisper.

I nod again, this time more emphatically.

Aunt Inga has been talking. "We have work to do. We need to get started."

Jerry is standing beside the kitchen counter and he reaches down to pull a saucepan out of the bottom cupboard. I wonder briefly if he is going to bang something with it. I wouldn't blame him. I'm just curious.

I turn a little in the chair so I'm not watching Jerry. I need to focus. "So that must mean everyone's okay with using the chapel at the Big M. Did someone tell Elaine about—you know—the funeral stuff?"

"Of course!" Aunt Inga sounds indignant that I think she'd keep a secret like that. "And there's no need for people to be so squeamish about funeral homes. I can't believe you didn't want to tell us you worked in one. We're not a family who thinks we're too good to work with dead people. I mean, well, you know what I mean. Everyone dies. They can't help it."

"Yes, but no one wants someone dead at their wedding," I say without thinking because I can't stand not knowing what Jerry is going to do with that pan. Then I realize what I've said. "Not that anyone will die at Elaine's wedding. Or be dead. I promise. The last funeral at the Big M is Tuesday morning. Then it's pretty well shut down through Thanksgiving weekend."

I specifically asked Mr. Z about that and he made some joke about death taking a holiday. I think it's an old movie or something so I smiled at him, but waited for him to clearly say that there would be no dead people left at the Big M over that weekend.

"Good. That gives us time to get everything ready," Aunt Inga says. "We're going to make the phone calls before we leave Blythe this morning so we won't get there until this afternoon. That's one reason I'm calling. We need the address for the place where you work so we can tell people where it is."

I close my eyes. Somehow I was hoping it wouldn't really come to this. Even though Jerry has measured every stone in the Big M chapel by now, I still thought a miracle would happen and the wedding would take place somewhere else. But once all of the guests are told to come to the Big M, it won't matter if the wedding does take place somewhere else. All of the people will still be at the Big M wondering what I, Julie White, have done to mess things up this time.

There's no help for it so I open my eyes. "The entrance to the parking lot is a couple of blocks past Vine on Hollywood going west. The street address is 6314 Hollywood Boulevard and there's usually some more parking off of Cosmo Street, too."

"I'm writing it all down," Aunt Inga says. "That was 63-what Hollywood Boulevard?"

I see Jerry pull the oatmeal box down from a shelf so I relax. He's just doing the domestic thing. No banging there.

"It's 6314 Hollywood Boulevard."

"Got it," Aunt Inga says and there's triumph in her voice. Aunt Inga knows how to celebrate her success with little things as well as big things in life.

"You sound good," I can't help but say. "How is Aunt Ruth doing?"

"She'll do fine. Especially when your mother comes to help. Aunt Ruth couldn't stand it if your mother showed her up in the coping department."

Now I know why I should have stayed in bed. I was worried about me and my mom making a scene. I didn't think about my mom and Aunt Ruth. "Do you think there will be trouble with the two of them?"

My mother and Aunt Ruth probably haven't exchanged ten words with each other since my mother left Blythe eighteen years ago. That's not even one word a year. My mother and I have passed a lot more words around and my feelings toward her are still a little raw. I don't give Aunt Inga any time to answer my question because I'm not sure I want to hear the answer. "You're sure Elaine isn't going to change her mind at the last minute and decide to get married on that cruise?"

"I'm not sure of anything," Aunt Inga says. "Except for the fact that we are a family and families figure these things out."

Aunt Inga, to her credit, always thinks of our family as a whole. It was mostly Aunt Ruth and Elaine who were always so insistent on their half this and half that, as if they had some inherent fascination with fractions. Believe me, neither one of them like math. They just didn't really want to claim any close kinship with my mom and me.

"Elaine would be dragging home a small trunk if she was planning to do that cruise," I say just in case Elaine was making preparations that Aunt Inga didn't know about. "One thing I know for sure and that's that she's going to get married in that dress she got from Paris. And she's going to have her train behind her. No matter where she says 'I do,' she'll be in that dress of hers."

Aunt Inga chuckles. "She's bringing that dress with her when we drive to Hollywood this afternoon so I think she's still planning to get married in your chapel."

"Good," I say, but I have to swallow to get the word out. "Maybe Jerry can remeasure how long the aisle is just to be sure there's enough room for that train."

I know there's enough room, I just don't want Elaine to settle for using the chapel at the Big M if she secretly wants to do the cruise.

"Well, I have a lot to do before we can come," Aunt Inga says. "We'll call on Elaine's cell phone when we get into Hollywood."

"I'll see you then," I say as we both hang up. Well,

I don't quite hang up. I have to walk over to the kitchen counter to do that and I think I'll just sit here a minute.

"That bad?" Jerry says from where he's standing by the stove. He's stirring the oatmeal and has the raisin box on the counter beside him.

"It's my worst nightmare come true."

Jerry laughs at that. "Good one."

I give him a weak smile in return. "Yeah, right."

I debate on going back to bed, but decide there is no point. The lazy, all-is-well feeling that I had lying in my bed earlier is destroyed for now.

"Did you make coffee?" I say even though I know I would smell it if Jerry had made any.

He takes the hint like a good cousin and reaches over to turn on the switch that will make the coffee start to brew. One of the things I have learned from living with Cassie is to set the coffeepot up the night before. It does make the mornings go better. I wonder if that's why she's always such an optimist. She knows she has her coffee ready to go.

Ah, yes, I can hear the water starting to sizzle in the pot. There is hope.

I could sit here all day, but I have to prepare for the arrival of the aunts. And Elaine, of course. Aunt Inga didn't mention Uncle Howard so I wonder if he will come. It'll be like having a family reunion. We always have deviled eggs at our family reunions. I look up at Jerry. He knows more about cooking than I ever suspected.

"Do you think we'll need to feed the aunts?" I ask.

"They're going to be here for dinner?" Jerry asks.

I almost smile. That thought took all of the good

cheer right out of him. He's not the only one who can
ruin a good morning.

"They wouldn't want us to fix them dinner, would
they?" Jerry asks, clearly appalled. "I only know how
to cook breakfast. I can't see Aunt Ruth having
oatmeal for dinner. The aunts never visited me when
I lived in Blythe."

"You still live in Blythe," I say just to remind him.
"Besides, there's nothing wrong with oatmeal. I'm sure
they ate it for dinner sometimes when they were kids."

My grandfather never had much money, not when
he was married to either one of the grandmothers. And
my grandmother couldn't cook so she might have
made oatmeal for dinner. She'd, of course, serve it
wearing one of those scarves of hers, though, and have
everyone pretend they were eating in a French restaurant so they might not have minded so much.

"Oatmeal like this?" Jerry looks uncertain as he
picks the pan up off the stove.

"Well, it's healthy food," I say before I decide to let
him off the hook. "Maybe we should just find a restaurant where we can all sit down to eat, though."

"I have to wash my socks today," Jerry says as he
walks the oatmeal over to the table and sets it on a trivet.
"And my T-shirts. Is there a Laundromat around?"

I nod. "I have to do a load of wash, too."

Jerry sits down even though neither one of us have
bowls or spoons. Since he's clearly in overload, I stand
and walk over to the cupboard to get what we need.

I can tell that getting ready for the aunts is going to
take the better part of the day. Which, when I think
about it, is okay. If I'm worrying about getting ready

to pass the aunt inspection, I won't be worrying about seeing my mother again.

I set the bowls down on the table and sit back down. It's not been that long ago that I saw my mother in Las Vegas, but this will be the first time my mother has come to my place instead of Aunt Inga's place. Okay, rest easy. I'm not doing a Jerry here. I know it's not really my place; it belongs to Cassie. But it's my first independent place and my mother is coming. I feel the urge to dust something.

It's the middle of the afternoon before the urge to clean everything in sight subsides. I am sitting in Cassie's living area and I am wearing a dress. On a Saturday. I don't feel so bad, however, because I look over at the sofa and Jerry is sitting there in a new T-shirt. He got so nervous, he drove to the mall and bought another one. It's brown, of course, but it has a black rim around the neck. The only one here who isn't nuts is Cassie. She's sitting on the floor by her coffee table and pinching some yellow leaves off some plant. She told me the leaves needed to be pinched off instead of cut off because the plant would do better that way.

There's no accounting for plants. I'd rather have a leaf cut off, nice and surgically clean, rather than have someone squeeze the life out of me.

There's a ring on the phone and I swear Jerry and I both sigh in relief. We weren't looking forward to everyone coming earlier, but now we're caught up in the agony of waiting and thinking anything would be better than just sitting here, even having the aunts actually arrive.

"Hello," Jerry says into the phone. He picked it up, because he is sitting closest to it.

Jerry gives me a nod so I know it is the aunts.

"Yeah, they gave us a key," Jerry says as he puts his hand over the mouthpiece of the phone. "They want to meet us at the Big M and see the chapel first thing."

"Oh, well," I say. "I guess that's fine."

There's a weekend guard at the Big M and Mr. Z had told him all about the wedding plans so I'm sure there's no problem if we go look in the chapel area. It's just that I wasn't prepared for everyone to see the Big M yet.

I should have spent some time this morning bracing myself for the viewing. I doubt it will go smoothly. Elaine will want to do something foolish like put orange glitter on the brass candle sconces in the entry hall and I will spout off something about how she has no appreciation for tradition. Then she will say it's her wedding day and she wants everything perfect and I will say if she wanted perfection she should have taken the cruise. And then—I stop myself. I don't need to have arguments in my head with Elaine. This is an aunt day. I need to think of ways to avoid arguments.

I smile.

"What's that for?" Jerry looks at me suspiciously. "You planning something?"

"No," I say. "I'm planning to be nice."

Jerry grunts as if he doesn't believe me.

The first thing anyone will want to see when they step out of the cars at the Big M is probably the restrooms. I relax a little. If Elaine wants to do something strange like put orange soap in there, it would be okay.

Jerry, Cassie, and I meet everyone at the Big M.

Aunt Inga drove her car down and my mother apparently went to Blythe yesterday so she could drive over with Aunt Inga. Aunt Ruth, Elaine and Uncle Howard arrive first and, even with only the three of them, I can tell it was a crowded ride. Elaine was in the backseat and she brought her dress. The garment bag was on the seat next to her and I saw the box for the train in the trunk when Elaine opened it to get her purse.

"You put your purse in the trunk?" I say and then I remember to be nice. "That's a good idea actually."

Everyone else is standing around stretching from the long drive so they aren't paying any attention to me and Elaine.

"It's supposed to control impulse spending," Elaine says with a little pride in her voice. "I'm practicing to be a responsible wife. Gary insists we have a budget. The purse in the trunk was his idea."

"Ooo-kay, then," I say. "You must have covered finances in premarital counseling."

"We don't need premarital counseling," Elaine says smugly. "Gary has good instincts about what to do in most situations."

I nod as though I understand her. "So, I guess he's figured out how to handle his parents when they want to do things like stop your mother from being at your wedding?"

"We're still working on his parents," she says, only now she seems more human because there's a hint of worry in her eyes. "Gary says we should be patient. They're not used to being in-laws and having to share us with another set of parents."

Elaine glances over at her mother and father who

are standing beside Aunt Inga's car and looking at the sidewalk leading up to the Big M.

"I never realized how important my parents are to me until Gary's parents started wanting to be my parents, too," Elaine says. "I already have parents."

You know, I think this is the first time Elaine has confided a problem to me. It obviously makes her as uncomfortable as it does me.

"I hope your aisle is long enough for my dress," Elaine says before we can actually talk about her problem. "The place doesn't look that big."

"It's big enough," I say as I start to lead the way down the sidewalk toward the Big M. It's fine by me if she doesn't want to talk about the problems with her soon-to-be in-laws. I don't know what I would say about everything right now anyway except *Run, Elaine, Run*.

I ring the buzzer when I get to the front door of the Big M. I have a key, but I don't want the guard inside to wonder what is happening so I wait for him to come to the door. There are often funerals on Saturdays, but there aren't any today so Mr. Z rearranged the staff schedule to be sure no one, except the guard, had to work this weekend.

We stop at the restrooms and I wait for everyone to assemble before I lead the way again. I am glad I put on a dress today. Aunt Inga is wearing an old cotton dress that she's worn many times before, but Aunt Ruth has on a tailored suit with lapels and everything. She's even got a fuchsia scarf pinned around her neck that matches the lipstick on her face. My mother is wearing a white blouse and designer jeans, but she's got high heels on her feet so she looks like a model.

Aunt Ruth is the first one to walk into the chapel at the Big M. She looks down the long center aisle with its deep burgundy carpet, but she doesn't walk down it. Instead, she walks along the back of the pews and goes down the left side aisle. Her shoe heels make a clicking sound on the wood, because there is no carpet on the outside aisles.

I am watching Aunt Ruth so I don't see someone come up next to me.

"She's calculating how many people can sit on each side," my mother says. "The bride's side. The groom's side. She wants to be sure her side wins."

I turn to look at my mother. I should have gone over to her and given her a hug while we were outside standing beside the cars, but I didn't do it the second I saw her and then Elaine started talking about her in-law troubles and it seemed it would look like an afterthought to go hug my mother when she'd already been standing outside Aunt Inga's car for five minutes. I can't remember the last time I gave my mother a hug anyway. Sometimes we hug before I leave Las Vegas, but usually we're too self-conscious to hug at first sight. It's something we have to kind of work up to.

"There's no way Gary's side will have more people than Elaine's," I say to her so she knows I'm at least following her conversation. "I think Aunt Ruth invited everyone who knows Elaine."

"She's proud of her daughter," my mother says and she puts her hand on my shoulder.

I kind of expect my mother to say she is proud of me, too, so I don't say anything to ruin the moment in case the moment is coming. But nothing happens, except that my mother takes her hand off my shoulder and points to the stained glass window. "That's beautiful."

I forgot that the stained glass window glows like this when the late-afternoon sun hits it on a slant. It's almost impossible to ignore the window when that happens and I had hoped Aunt Ruth and Elaine would have enough time to notice things like the soft sheen of the carved wood on the inside columns at the front of the church before they saw the sheep.

"The stained glass window won't be so obvious in the wedding," I say before Aunt Ruth can demand it be covered. "It's just late afternoon that it looks like this with the sun pouring through."

Aunt Ruth nods from where she's standing at the front of the church.

"It's nice," Aunt Ruth finally says.

I can see we are all going to try really hard to be positive. That will either save us or doom us. I'm not sure which.

"Lambs are clean animals, aren't they?" Elaine says as she walks down the center aisle to where her mother is standing. "And, at least, they don't bark or anything so no one will make a rude sound during the ceremony like they might if it was a cow or something."

"Oh, no, lambs are definitely better than cows," Aunt Ruth agrees.

"And the lamb is with Jesus," Elaine says. "Gary's parents can't object to Jesus."

Actually, from what I saw of them at Elaine's engagement party, I wouldn't be too sure about that. They looked as if they could object to anyone.

"The organ has built-in pipes," I add as I point to

where the pipes are located on each side of the altar.
They are tucked behind the wood columns. "The
sound they make is great."

"Organ music is good," Uncle Howard says as he
walks up the aisle to join his wife and daughter.

I was surprised to see Uncle Howard step out of the
car here earlier even though I had heard he'd stopped
hiding in the bedroom. When he reaches Aunt Ruth
and Elaine, he puts an arm around each of them. That's
sweet and not usual for him. Maybe these troubles
have been good for all of them if they appreciate each
other more.

I look over at Jerry. He is standing in a little half
booth to the side in the back of the chapel.

"Do you want to test the sound out?" Jerry asks as
he speaks into a microphone. It's obviously a rhetori-
cal question because he continues without looking up.
"Testing One. Two. Three."

"The singer we hire can stand there," Elaine says
as she turns around to look at Jerry.

"Usually the soloist is in the front of the church," I
say and then remember my vow to be pleasant. "But
a break from tradition can be good."

I notice all of the aunts and Elaine looking at me.

"We were hoping you might know someone who
sings," Elaine finally says. "I haven't lined anyone up
yet and you mentioned you did have people who sang
solos here."

"They're funeral songs," I say. "You know, the old
hymns. You'll want something light and romantic for
your wedding. I thought you had someone for music."

Elaine shrugs. "I did, but they were going to do

some of the Beatles' songs. Gary's parents thought that wouldn't be dignified for a wedding."

"I'm not sure we have anything more dignified," I say. I can't suggest Mr. Strett. He's pretty dour even for funerals. He'd look very out of place at a wedding. "Besides, the person you had coming can sing the songs softly. Gary's parents probably wouldn't even recognize the songs then."

I wonder, and not for the first time, what Elaine is doing, thinking she even wants to marry into this family.

"Gary's mother thought maybe I should have someone sing some classical music," Elaine says and it's plain to see she's miserable. "Maybe something in French or Italian."

"Well, where would we get someone like that?" Jerry asks from over by the sound system. "Maybe I could find an old CD or something."

"I can get you an opera singer," my mother says. She's walked halfway down the center aisle and is sitting in one of the pews. "We have one where I work."

"I don't think someone who sings in a casino is suitable for Elaine's wedding," Aunt Ruth says sharply.

My mother shrugs. "The woman is classically trained. She's had solos at Carnegie Hall."

With those credentials, I expect Aunt Ruth to gladly accept the offer, but she doesn't. There's silence until Aunt Inga clears her throat.

"It's such a generous offer." Aunt Inga is walking down the aisle to where Aunt Ruth stands with Elaine and Uncle Howard. "Don't you think we should accept?"

"Gary's parents couldn't object to an opera singer," Elaine says. "It would be one less thing for us to worry about."

Aunt Ruth nods and looks over at my mother. "I guess we have to accept. We'll pay the woman, of course."

My mother lifts one of her eyebrows. "Of course."

I would have thought the offer of the opera singer would soften the feelings Aunt Ruth and my mother have toward each other, but it doesn't. They both spend the next hour or so measuring and remeasuring various parts of the chapel.

"Jerry already measured those," I finally say quietly to Aunt Inga.

Aunt Inga is sitting down on one of the back pews. "I know."

I sit down beside her. "Then why are they still measuring?"

I know I have vowed to be nice about all of this, but it's driving me crazy to see my mother measure something and then Aunt Ruth go and measure the exact same thing. Jerry made the mistake of giving them each a tape measure when they questioned his measurement on the far right aisle.

"They're still working things out with each other," Aunt Inga says. "Neither one of them wants to trust the other."

"You're kidding, right?" I say to Aunt Inga as I sit down beside her. "At this rate, we'll all be dead before they figure out their problem."

Aunt Inga smiles.

I think to myself how silly Aunt Ruth and my

mother are and then I happen to glance over at Elaine who is sitting in the back pew on the other side of the church. I guess I can't criticize Aunt Ruth and my mother for having a problem with each other when I have this thing between Elaine and me.

"It's all because Aunt Ruth never liked my grandmother," I say to Aunt Inga so I won't have to think about Elaine and me. Our problem is different anyway.

Aunt Inga looked at me. "I wouldn't say Ruth never liked your grandmother. She would handle it better if she hadn't."

"Well, she never liked the way my grandmother lived her life, I know that for a fact. She complained that my grandmother didn't work hard enough and liked pretty things and wanted to have some fun."

"It's true she complained," Aunt Inga says. "But that's why she's so hard on your grandmother's memory. She feels disloyal to our mother."

"Why would she feel that?"

Aunt Inga nods. "Watch your mother and Aunt Ruth for a while. You'll see for yourself what their problem is."

By now the afternoon light has turned to dusk. I watch my mother and Aunt Ruth for a few minutes and then Uncle Howard announces he'll take us all out to eat somewhere.

We go to a Mediterranean restaurant that is close by and, all the time, I am watching my mother and Aunt Ruth to see what the secret to their animosity is. I wonder if Aunt Inga is making me figure this one out for myself because she wants me to really think about it. I'm not sure I want a relationship like Aunt Ruth and my mother have, but whether I want it or not, I have one like it with Elaine. I wonder if the coldness between Aunt Ruth and my mother has anything to do with Aunt Ruth calling my mother her half sister instead of just her sister, but I figure it has to be deeper than that.

When we leave the restaurant and I get ready to get into Jerry's pickup, I go over to Elaine and give her a quick hug.

"Don't worry about your wedding," I whisper. "It's in good hands."

Elaine looks at me as if I've taken leave of my senses and maybe I have.

"What was that about?" Jerry says when I climb into his pickup.

"I thought I'd try this new-rules thing with Elaine," I say. "It didn't work."

"Yeah, well, it's Elaine," Jerry says as he backs out of his parking space.

I go to sleep that night counting stained glass sheep while waiting for my mother and Aunt Ruth to finish measuring the chapel. I wonder if the thing Aunt Inga wanted me to notice was that neither one of them can add. And they both were whipping those cloth measuring tapes around like they were ropes. Or long, skinny scarves.

I wake up in the middle of the night with those tape measures on my mind. Isn't it a little unusual that both of them had the same hand movements, as though they'd spent hours and hours flipping long scarves off of their necks for no other reason than that it showed they had style? Just like my grandmother had done?

I wish it wasn't too late to call Aunt Inga.

I do manage to go back to sleep even after I have The Revelation. Before I know it, morning is here and I am wondering if this "ah-ha-I-get-it" feeling is what prophets felt thousands of years ago. I'm sleeping on the air mattress in Cassie's bedroom and the sun is just beginning to rise so it's easy to imagine I'm an Old Testament prophet in a cave somewhere with all of the grayness around me. If I had some of Jerry's old socks in here to bring up the wet, musty smell, it would be totally convincing.

I can't believe it. I would never have wondered how prophets managed to sleep through the night with all the things they had rattling around in their heads until those conversations I've been having with Doug and Jerry and Cassie about things in the Bible. Who knew the Bible people were like, well, real people who couldn't sleep at night?

I wonder if those prophets felt the way I do now. I can't wait to tell Aunt Inga what I've concluded. Of course, Aunt Inga is not too likely to behead me if I'm wrong so maybe this enthusiasm I'm feeling wasn't quite the same for the prophets of old. Especially because they didn't just have to worry about being wrong. They were often in more trouble if they were right.

Oh. That makes me ask myself if I could be in trouble if I'm right about Aunt Ruth and my mother doing the scarf thing as my grandmother used to do. And, even if I'm right, I'm not sure what it means. Were they like little ducks being imprinted on my scarf-waving grandmother? Maybe my aunt Ruth gives my mother such a hard time because she wanted to have my grandmother for her real mother, too.

I debate about waking up Jerry. He would love to get in on this duck and prophet conversation. But then I decide to be kind. Jerry asked Cassie at dinner last night to ask if he could invite everyone over for oatmeal this morning and, in the shock of the moment, she agreed. So, he will be up and wishing he were either a dead prophet or a dead duck soon enough anyway.

I hear a soft knocking on the bedroom door and a whisper. "Julie?"

I don't answer because I don't want to wake up Cassie so I just grab my robe and go into the living area.

Jerry has taken every dish out of the cupboard. Cassie bought that set of white dishes when she moved down to Hollywood from Blythe two years ago.

"We don't have enough bowls," Jerry whispers. "There's only six bowls and there will be eight of us."

I take pity on the poor boy. He'll realize soon enough that he only has three chairs, counting the box he turns upside down for himself. "I can use my coffee cup."

His face brightens. "I can do that, too. So we'll have enough."

I walk over and turn the switch on for the coffee to begin brewing.

"And I can sit on the floor beside the coffee table," I add just to give him a clue.

"Oh, that's right," Jerry says as he looks around as though he's never seen this room before. "We need to have chairs."

Fortunately, it's early and there's a hardware store not too far from here that opens at six every morning. Jerry takes off to buy a couple of folding chairs and I go to take a shower.

By the time Cassie gets up, Jerry is back with the four folding chairs and has even managed to buy a dozen bagels with different kinds of cream cheeses: strawberry, cinnamon, blueberry and onion.

"It'll be a feast," I say. "The aunts will love it."

It turns out I might have a knack for this prophetic stuff. Just as Jerry has a knack for entertaining. Two hours later, we are all sitting in Cassie's place and everyone is looking well-fed and relaxed. Well, except for Elaine, but that's to be expected since she's getting married so soon.

We've been talking about ways to decorate the hallway between the wedding chapel and the courtyard so that the guests will not even see the doors that go into the rooms the Big M uses for their final viewings.

Aunt Inga has asked if there's a church nearby and I think we are all going together to a service. I am just starting to become aware of how much Aunt Inga is the mother of our whole family. I used to feel that she was just my substitute mother, but I sit there realizing she's probably been a fill-in mother to at least two other people. If I'm calculating the dates right, Aunt Ruth was two years old when the aunts' mother died. Aunt Inga was the oldest and she must have stood in as the mother figure for the ten years until my grandmother came along. And, since Aunt Inga was the oldest, she was probably the substitute parent again for my mother when my grandmother died.

I sit and try to puzzle it out. Why aren't Aunt Ruth and my mother imprinted on Aunt Inga instead of my grandmother? I look at Aunt Inga more closely. She's neat in her appearance, but there's no swirling scarf style to her at all. Her hair is cropped in a short no-nonsense style. She wears the same style of basic cotton dress. She must have a half-dozen dresses in the same style. Only the color is different and even that doesn't range too far from the drab colors. There's no fuchsia or turquoise or red in her wardrobe.

All of a sudden it hits me. Aunt Inga is like her mother. And then it hits me again. I wonder how Aunt Inga felt about Aunt Ruth and my mother idolizing my grandmother when she, Aunt Inga, had the hard task of raising them both. Aunt Inga probably did all of the housework, the cooking and the kissing of any bruised knees. Actually, she is still doing Aunt Ruth's house-work. And, all that time, my grandmother was the one who got the glory. If I was Aunt Inga, I would feel jealous and maybe even a little betrayed.

I'm not so sure I like this prophet business anymore. I only have to take things one step further to wonder if Aunt Inga's insistence on us being a family is her way of trying to fix all of those earlier feelings of jealousy, betrayal and discouragement. She's still doing the hard part of trying to make us a family.

Wow. I am still looking at the scene of my family spread out before me, but everything has changed. I stand up from where I am sitting on the sofa and just casually walk over to put my hand on Aunt Inga's shoulder. She's sitting on the folding chair closest to the kitchen area.

"Jerry and I will get the dishes," I say as I give Aunt Inga's shoulder a squeeze. "You guys just sit a minute and rest some more."

For the first time in my life, I really listen in church that morning. I have purposely sat beside Aunt Inga this morning. I want to know what has given Aunt Inga her strength for all of those years. If I had drawn her lot in life, I think I would have been bitter. She gave herself up for her family in some ways.

There was always a little girl in Aunt Inga's life who needed some mothering even though the little girl idolized some other woman. It has, of course, by now occurred to me that it can't have been easy for Aunt Inga to patiently live with my blind adoration of my mother all those years when it was Aunt Inga who clearly gave me the love and care that every child needs. Aunt Inga was my rock; she just wasn't my hero.

I reach forward and put my hand on Aunt Inga's knee. She doesn't think twice before covering my hand with her own. She has never held back any affection from me because I haven't been focused on her.

The minister is talking about planting and harvesting things. It's not the most exciting sermon in the world. But I realize it doesn't need to be. I'm no longer just looking for the things and people in life who have flair. Bright colors and giggles are good, but sometimes the steadfast love of an aunt who sticks with you is even better. I rest my hand on Aunt Inga's knee throughout the sermon. I like the feel of her hand on mine and I think she likes it, too, because she gives me a little squeeze every once in a while.

Chapter Fourteen

The rest of the week I keep thinking of the children's hide-and-seek game that begins with "Ready Or Not, Here We Come." That's what it feels like here. Friday night is coming and, with it, over two hundred wedding guests who have no idea they're coming to a mortuary. Our job is to see that they leave having no idea they've been to one, either.

On Monday, my mother builds a fantastic tunnel out of chicken wire and covers the inside with hundreds of pieces of crepe paper so that the wedding guests will be able to go from the chapel to the outside courtyard and not even see anything that might make them suspicious the Big M is not a wedding chapel. Walking through the tunnel itself will keep them distracted. I've walked through it and it's like being inside a kaleidoscope with all of the shades of crepe paper that my mother used.

The tunnel is one step forward.

On Tuesday, Elaine has a major meltdown when she

hears that Gary's sister, Lynda, has the flu and isn't coming to the wedding. I don't even make Elaine beg me to fill in as her maid of honor. When she asks, I accept. Which surprises her a little, but I decide to wait until after her big event to talk to her about my cease-fire hopes for the two of us. I'm tired of us giving each other The Look when, hello, life is happening out here and we could each use another person on our side.

I didn't just think of this cease-fire on my own, by the way. I've been watching Aunt Ruth and my mother for days and, in my opinion, they are worse than Elaine and I ever thought of being. They don't just have one Look, they have dozens of them. And they compete at everything. They even tried to outdo each other, climbing the ladder higher and higher, to fill tiny gaps in the tunnel cover. By the way they went at it with each other, you would think they were saving lives instead of plugging holes in chicken wire with crepe paper.

I've pretty much figured out that the two of them are still competing for my grandmother's attention, which is bizarre, but not as bizarre as the fact that Elaine and I somehow took on the competition, too. Neither Elaine nor I even *knew* my grandmother. How lame is that?

By the end of the day on Tuesday, I am bursting with my realizations and want to talk to Elaine, but decide it will have to wait. She is a nervous wreck about this wedding and I can't blame her. I've already decided that, if I get married, I'm going to elope. This real wedding business is nothing like the pretend weddings Cassie and I used to have when we were kids.

Speaking of Cassie, she's been working hard. On Wednesday, she went down to the central L.A. Flower Mart and picked up the shipment of roses she had ordered on Monday for Aunt Ruth. I've never seen so many roses—yellow ones, coral ones, and those white roses with reddish-orange stripes coming from their centers.

On Thursday, which is Thanksgiving Day, Cassie, Jerry, Doug and I are at Cassie's shop for hours, making bouquets for the courtyard tables and big floral sprays for the chapel. We even put water tubes on some of the long-stemmed roses so we can insert them into the walls of the tunnel to add fragrance.

It's a wonder neither Aunt Ruth nor my mother thought of the flower idea. That would get them some points with whoever they're trying to impress. Instead, Doug thinks of it. I know. That impresses me, too.

We take the tubed roses over late on Thursday and put them in the walls of the tunnel. The colors of the crepe paper and the smell of those roses made me think of fairy tales. It's all pastels and sweet fragrance. Even Gary's parents will have to agree this wedding is nice.

Speaking of Gary and his parents, I have admitted to myself that I am a little concerned that we hadn't seen Gary around here much. Well, at all, really. Elaine says he's keeping his parents occupied and that's probably true, but the fact that he feels he needs to do that is worrisome, don't you think?

Of course, maybe it's for the best. Uncle Howard had a very nice sign made to slip over that little brass

Hollywood & Vine Mortuary sign that is out front of the Big M, but Gary's parents might still stumble onto something that would tell them this is a funeral home if they came here and wandered around. No one, of course, has told them the real story of the Big M. But that's not surprising. Aunt Ruth still hasn't told them she really doesn't live in Palm Springs.

Before I know it, Friday morning is here and I'm lying on the air mattress in Cassie's bedroom wondering what will go wrong today. I have this feeling that something is going to go wrong, but I don't know what it is. It's how I used to feel about all of my toppling. I would dread not knowing what situation I was going to get myself into. And the dread only made it more likely that, when I toppled, it would be sooner and harder than if I were not so nervous.

Fortunately, it is Elaine's wedding so my toppling nerves shouldn't ruin anything. Besides, we have a lot of professionals on board. Aunt Ruth was in an ordering frenzy earlier in the week so I know that a huge wedding cake will be delivered to the Big M this afternoon and that the caterers will be setting up at five o'clock for the evening reception meal. That should all go well.

We have another professional coming, as well. I asked Miss Billings to help Cassie and me with our makeup around five o'clock and she was delighted. I've told Elaine she's welcome to join us for our makeup session, but she looked too harried to make the decision when I asked so I told her she could just come to the women's lounge if she wanted help with her eyeliner around that time. There's a huge mirror in there and the lighting is good so it'll be perfect.

I roll over and look up at Cassie's alarm clock. It is ten minutes after seven and I decide to lie back down until the alarm goes off at seven-thirty. Today is going to be frantic when it starts. I try to empty my mind of all my worries in sort of a meditation thing, but it doesn't work. I feel I have a wheel of details rolling round and round in my mind and I can't stop it.

Since I can't fight it, I go with it and keep checking things off in my mind.

Aunt Gladys and the rest of the cousins are driving over this morning so they can help set up all of the chairs in the courtyard and move all of the floral arrangements to the chapel. The time of the rehearsal has been changed to four o'clock this afternoon so that Gary will only have to make one trip into Hollywood with his parents. The wedding itself will start at five-thirty and the reception dinner will be served after that.

By eight o'clock we'll be home free. Well, we won't be home actually, but I figure that anything that happens after dinner becomes a colorful anecdote and not a disaster. By then, the knot is tied and people are fed. Everyone will be relaxed. I know by then I intend to be walking around the courtyard with Doug trying to give everyone the impression that we're just friends and neither breakup material nor engagement material. I don't want to announce I was a fraud before, but I would like the record to be accurate.

The alarm goes off and I get up without complaint.

We don't have oatmeal this morning for breakfast. We haven't taken the time to make it all week even though it's the instant kind. We've been reduced to drinking our coffee and eating an energy bar as we ride in the cab of Jerry's pickup to the Big M. It's November and the mornings can be chilly so Jerry usually turns his heater on before we back out of the parking lot. By midmorning the temperature will be fine outside, though.

I get a call on my cell phone when we are halfway to the Big M and I answer it.

"Julie?"

"Hi, Elaine," I say as I listen to the ragged breathing on the line. "Calm down. Whatever it is, we'll figure it out."

Cassie gives me an anxious look and I nod to her. Jerry just keeps driving down Melrose Avenue. He's used to this. I have said those words to Elaine more times than I'd like to count this week, but they always seem to make Elaine take a deep breath so she can at least breathe enough to explain the latest crisis.

"But this one is different," Elaine says with a hiccup and I begin to wonder if this is the ultimate problem.

"Did Gary call? Is something wrong?"

I've been wondering all week if Gary would call the wedding off at the last minute. I don't know if he's off having fun with his parents or if they are giving him such a hard time that they require his full attention. The whole thing doesn't seem right, though, and if he's going to call it off, I'd just as soon he did it before Elaine is standing up there in front of all those people.

"Your dress isn't here." Elaine hiccups again. "Lynda shipped the dress back to Blythe and Aunt Gladys just called to say it didn't come today. Aunt

Gladys checked with the shipping company and the package is still in Atlanta, Georgia."

"Well, we don't need the brown dress," I say. I think of what Aunt Inga would do. I'm doing that a lot lately. "I could always wear one of those orange ones. I think you have one in a size ten, don't you?"

Elaine has cut back on her attendants until it is only going to be me and Gary's best friend walking down the aisle with them so it doesn't make any difference whether I am wearing the maid of honor dress or one of the bridesmaids' dresses.

Elaine's hiccups stop and it's quiet on the line for a minute. "Really? You said you wouldn't wear the orange dress."

"Well, I will," I say. "I'm sure Miss Billings can help me put enough brown streaks in my hair that the orange will look okay with it."

There's more silence. "But you love your hair the way it is. You call it your titian crown. Titian is red, not brown streaks."

I close my eyes. These truly are the kinds of things we've always bickered about. Hair. Clothes. Who could make who do what.

"I'll still have my hair. Those brown streaks will wash out tonight."

"Well, then, thank you," Elaine says a little uncertainly.

"You're welcome," I say with conviction as Jerry turns into the parking lot that's behind the Big M.

Cassie, Jerry and I are silent as we climb out of the pickup and head toward the back door at the Big M. The wedding guests will go in through the courtyard and then take the tunnel to the chapel tonight, but for us, it's easier to just put the key in the lock and walk down the side hallway.

"What was that all about?" Jerry says as I turn on one of the hallway lights.

I look over at him. "Huh?"

"You and Elaine, all buddy-buddy," he says. "Am I missing something? Are you going to get her later?"

I chuckle. "No, it's new rules."

Jerry grunts as if he doesn't believe me.

It's not long before we are working away. Doug gets there about a half hour after we do and he helps Jerry finish stringing some wires in the chapel for the sound system. Then Cassie wants to have a few of the tables set up in the courtyard before we pick up the flower arrangements so we set those up. My mother's singer comes and we show her where she can practice. Fortunately, my mother had the foresight to ask the singer to bring one of the piano players with her.

I go through the tunnel again to make sure all of the crepe paper pieces are securely attached to the chicken-wire frame. Then I check out the kitchen to be sure everything is ready for the cake delivery and the caterers.

It's about eleven-thirty when Aunt Gladys and Jerry's brothers show up and start lifting things around. I see that I've never truly appreciated the value of having all of these male cousins before. The first thing the cousins do is finish setting up all of the tables and chairs in the courtyard. The caterers will put the tablecloths on later so all we do is position the tables. About this time, Elaine and her parents arrive in their car. They tell us Aunt Inga and my mother will be along soon.

It feels good to have us all together. Aunt Gladys probably figured it would feel that way because she sends one of her sons to the car to get the cooler out of the trunk.

"I knew we wouldn't have time to go out to eat," Aunt Gladys says. "So I fixed us a picnic lunch. It won't take long to eat."

"Actually, I think we're in pretty good shape for time," I say as I look up at Aunt Ruth to check my impression.

Aunt Ruth nods. "We certainly have time to eat."

Elaine holds back a little as Aunt Ruth and Uncle Howard walk over and sit in chairs next to Aunt Gladys. Everyone likes to be around Aunt Gladys when she has food. Having all those boys meant she's had lots of practice cooking and she's very good at it.

"You okay?" I ask. Elaine and I are standing in front of the entrance to the courtyard.

Elaine nods, but she looks a little pale. I wonder if that's why brides wear those white veils so no one will see how pale their faces are. Marriage is a big step. I hope Elaine joins Cassie and me later for our makeup session. Miss Billings will make Elaine look alive no matter what her pulse says.

My mother and Aunt Inga arrive just as Aunt Gladys is putting plastic containers on one of the tables. The two of them signal they are going to go inside the chapel and they walk back to the courtyard through the tunnel just to check it.

Of course, Elaine is oblivious to who is doing what. She is just standing there.

"Would you look at that?" I say to cheer Elaine up. "Aunt Gladys made her deviled eggs."

Aunt Gladys always makes these really good deviled eggs for any family picnics. We used to beg her to make them for us when we were kids. We had some peaceful times as kids while eating deviled eggs, which may be why we've all maintained a fondness for them over the years.

I hear the short breaths to my right and I turn to Elaine. "You okay?"

Elaine's hair is perfectly styled and all of her buttons are done up. But something is starting to unravel.

"I'm never going to have deviled eggs again," Elaine says in a soft wail that fortunately doesn't reach the rest of the family.

I'm not used to this comforting thing when it comes to Elaine, but I do my best. I put a hand on her shoulder and give her some pats. "Now, now, that's not true. I'm sure Aunt Gladys will even give you the recipe if you want it."

The short breaths are a little shorter now and, when she looks up, Elaine has a tear running down her cheek. "I can't cook."

Well, she does have a point there. "Maybe Aunt Gladys can make you up a plate and get one of the cousins to hand-deliver them to you. After all, Gary's internship won't be too far away, will it?"

"It'll be in Connecticut," Elaine says. "That's clear across the United States."

I look over at the aunts and cousins all dishing up macaroni salad and deviled eggs. My mother and Aunt Inga have just completed their walk through the tunnel and are heading toward the food line, too. I'm sure Elaine doesn't want everyone to hear what we are saying.

"I know where Connecticut is," I say quietly to Elaine. "I thought the plan was for Gary to get an internship in California."

Elaine has pulled herself together enough to stop sobbing. She looks at me and she's serious. "If I tell you, you have to promise not to say anything."

"I could do that," I say.

"No tricks?"

"No tricks."

Elaine swallows. "His parents want Gary to move back. They want him in Connecticut."

"Well, it's not like they can make him move there," I say. I had never thought that Elaine's wedding would mean she would move clear across the country. "Does your mother know about this?"

I glance over at the food table. Aunt Ruth is just sitting down with a plate of food. Only Aunt Inga is looking at Elaine and me, wondering what is keeping us from the deviled eggs.

Elaine shakes her head. "No, that's why I said you can't tell. Gary just told me this morning. He wasn't going to, but..." Elaine's voice just trails off and she stands here looking over at everyone seated at the tables.

"You mean Gary wasn't going to tell you he wanted to move across the country until after you married him?" Okay, now I'm getting a little steamed up. Not that I don't know that married people move around. Everyone moves. But to have the move already planned and not tell the one you were going to marry? That can't be good.

"He wasn't going to tell me his sister doesn't have the flu either," Elaine says.

This time Elaine looks at me and I look at her. She's grown up in the last month with this wedding business.

"Why isn't his sister here then?" I ask a little cautiously. Out of the corner of my eye, I can see Aunt Inga walking over to us. I make a motion with my head to let Elaine know someone is coming.

"She doesn't think our marriage will last and she said she didn't want any part of it," Elaine says after she looks and sees where Aunt Inga is. "She doesn't like me."

"She's never even met you!"

"She's just listening to her mother," Elaine says with a sigh. "Her mother has met me."

"Well, what's not to like? You're pretty. You're smart." I begin my list.

"I don't have a college degree," Elaine interrupts. "Or a trust fund. And I've never been to Europe. Or met a royal person or even a congressman." Elaine takes a breath. "Gary's mother thinks I'm common."

Elaine is giving me a look now that is nothing like the usual Look. "I don't know what to do."

"All of those things are fixable," I say. "You have two years of college already. You just take some time to finish. And it's not hard to go to Europe. You just need a ticket. You might not have a trust fund, but you're not common—whatever that means!"

Elaine smiles a little. "It means I'm not good enough for her son."

"In her opinion," I say. "Mothers never think the woman their son marries is good enough for him."

"I'm beginning to think I might not be, though," Elaine says. Her voice is quiet and she's serious.

I've never seen Elaine like this. Everything always

turns out the way Elaine wants it. I can't believe Gary's mother has stomped on Elaine's confidence to this point.

"Gary is lucky you're willing to marry him," I say emphatically.

I see that Aunt Inga is beside me and I turn to her. "Isn't Gary lucky to have someone like Elaine want to marry him?"

"Of course," Aunt Inga says as she gives Elaine a hug. "You're a sweetheart."

Aunt Inga's hug does what my words didn't. Elaine smiles.

"I guess it's just nerves," Elaine says as she gives Aunt Inga a hug right back.

"It's not too late to back out, though," I say quietly. "If for some reason you felt you should back out, that is."

Elaine nods. "It will be fine."

Elaine looks as if she's doing better after she has some salad and two deviled eggs. I'm not doing better, though. You see, this is the problem with someone telling you their troubles. I'm beginning to think that Gary's sister may have a point. I don't see how this marriage can last.

Aunt Gladys and Aunt Ruth don't seem too worried and they certainly have had more experience with married life than I have. Aunt Inga keeps watching over Elaine as if she's worried, but Aunt Inga hasn't been married, either. That makes the two married women in the family okay with this wedding and the two unmarried women not so okay.

I look over at my mother. I don't know what category she should fall into. She was married, but it was so long ago, she's probably forgotten all about it. She enjoyed being married, too. I know that from the things she used to say. I wonder why she never married again.

The shock of that thought goes through me. I've never asked myself that question before. My mother was always just my mother. I never thought of her remarrying. That would be worse than her moving to Las Vegas.

My mother is sitting at a table beside the one where the aunts are sitting. She's close enough to hear their conversation and talk with them if she wants. But she's still separate.

I take my plastic plate back to the food table and stick it in the bag Aunt Gladys brought. Then I go sit beside my mother.

My mother's face has changed over the years. She has a few lines around her eyes now and her hair is a shade blonder than it should be so I know she dyes it. She also has started to fidget with her hands. Maybe it's because of all the rings she wears on her fingers. Then again maybe it's because I sat down next to her.

"Your tunnel is beautiful," I say.

"It's just some crepe paper and chicken wire," she says, but it makes her fidget less.

"I'm glad you came down to help."

"Well, Inga asked me and—" my mother looked at me quickly and then looked away "—I owe her so much."

My breath stops. Here is my chance to ask my mother what I have always wanted to know. I'm sure I've had other chances before, but I've never had the courage to find out what she would say. I'm not sure I have any more courage now, but—

"I owe Aunt Inga a lot, too," I say. "I never thought I'd spend most of my childhood with her."

My mother goes very still. "I never thought you would, either."

We are silent for a minute and I wonder if I have the nerve to ask her for more than that.

Finally, my mother begins again. "I always thought, those first few years, that I just needed a little more time to make a good home for you. I was working too much and I didn't have anyone to take care of you when I was working so I thought it was better for you to be with Aunt Inga than a stranger all day."

Okay. "But I went to school most of the time later. I would have only needed day care for another year or so."

I turn away a little so I can blink my eyes a bit. I don't want her to know I carry that hurt from such a long time ago.

"When I finally had enough money," my mother says softly, "I couldn't ask you to come. By then you were more Aunt Inga's than you were mine. I couldn't take you away from her."

"That's not a good enough reason," I say. I even turn back toward her so she can see the hurt in my eyes.

"No, I suppose not," she agrees.

We sit there for a minute until she puts her arm around me. I don't bend toward her, but I let her keep the arm there.

Before long, the cousins have all of the plastic containers put back in the cooler for Aunt Gladys, and are looking around for something else to lift. My mother has gotten up from her chair and gone back into the chapel.

I'm just sitting in the courtyard reliving the past, both the past few minutes and the past many years. I can't believe I actually asked my mother why she hadn't come to take me to live with her. I always thought that if I asked her that the sky would fall down or the earth would start to shake. But I asked my question and nothing happened.

Well, nothing happened on the outside of me. I can feel things inside of me shifting around and they're cosmic. You know, it still feels as though God is looking down at me but, for the first time, I have the courage to look right back at Him to see if He cares about me, after all. And, I think He does. My mother is only my mother; she isn't God.

Okay, this is major. I know part of the reason I'm sitting here thinking I've been wrong about God is because of all those Bible verses that have been rolling around in my head ever since Doug asked me to help him with his homework from that rally. I even rememorized John 3:16 so I could give it to Jerry boom-boom-boom, just like that, the next time he challenged me. At least, I thought that's why I learned the verse.

Now, I'm not so sure. Maybe I learned that verse for me. "For God so loved me, Julie White…" The Sunday school teachers at Aunt Inga's church always had us put in our names. I start again, "For God so loved me, Julie White that…"

Oh, dear, I think I'm going to cry. I blink in panic. Everyone will think I'm upset that Elaine is getting married if I sit here blubbering. Then they'll think I'm jealous, which is so not true. I stand up and walk over to the corner of the courtyard where there's a nice stone wall to lean against. There's a rosebush and, if

I bend down, people will think I'm checking for new buds. That'll give me time to get myself together.

I hear footsteps.

"Julie?"

I look up and there is Doug.

"Are you okay?"

I nod and wipe away a tear from my cheek. "I'm thinking of taking that ice plunge."

"The one in Sweden?"

I shake my head. "The one you took at the rally."

"Oh," Doug says and then he grins. "If you need a friend to take it with you, let me know."

I hold out my hand and he takes it.

"Can I do it now?" I say. "I'm already down here on my knees."

"Sounds good to me," he says as he kneels down beside me. "I said my prayer in front of hundreds of strangers with no one holding my hand."

You know, for such a big decision, you don't really need so many words. I just asked God to make John 3:16 real in my life. Then I asked Doug if I could go to those rally meetings he's been going to every Monday night. He said I would be welcome there.

Then I cried a little more and Doug gave me a packet of tissues he had in his pocket. "They give us those at the meetings."

I dabbed at my eyes and looked over at the rest of the courtyard. The cousins all seemed to be lifting something, except for Jerry who was looking over at us.

"Oh, no," I say as I nod over at Jerry. "He's going to think we're down here on our knees looking for lost pearls."

"Or proposing," Doug adds with another grin.

"Oh, no," I say because he's right. That's just how Jerry's mind would work.

"So, do you want to mess with his mind?" Doug asks.

"What do you mean?"

Doug leans over and kisses me on the forehead. "There, he won't know what to make of that. It's not romantic enough to be a proposal, but it's more than just congratulations for finding some lost pearls."

I smile. "Oh, you're bad."

Doug nods as he stands back up. "Thank you."

Doug lifts out a hand to me and helps me stand up. I look around just in case the aunts are watching. They would have liked to see that. It's not often we see a gentleman in action beside a rosebush.

Chapter Fifteen

❧

I wish Elaine would give me The Look about now. At least, she wouldn't be hunched over and scowling as though she's on the verge of tears. She is standing in her wedding dress and waiting for Gary to show up at the chapel. It is past four o'clock and the rehearsal was supposed to have already started.

"Everyone was right," Elaine says as she twists her shoulder to look behind herself. Her train is partially attached to the waistline of her wedding dress and Elaine has a handful of the material in one hand. "This is too heavy. It's like I'm pulling bricks behind me."

I say nothing about the symbolism of that.

"It just needs to be hooked all the way," I say instead as I walk up to her and quickly do just that. "There."

I stand back. "Your dress is beautiful."

Elaine looks at me as if I'm teasing her and I decide I need to slow it down with the compliments. Neither one of us is used to seeing the other's nice side.

"I liked the sound of having a cathedral train,"

Elaine said softly after a minute or so. "Just the words. I thought it would make the wedding day special. Like we're a prince and princess."

I smile. "I can see that."

"I used to really like Gary, you know," Elaine adds.

I don't think she is even aware of her use of the past tense. Maybe she meant she liked him before she loved him. I am going to ask her what she meant by that, but before I can think of a diplomatic way to do that, I hear Jerry giving a shout telling everyone that Gary is here.

That shout puts everyone in motion. Elaine runs to wrap herself in a huge gray blanket because she doesn't want Gary to see her dress or her veil before the actual ceremony. The soloist moves to her place beside one of the columns at the front of the chapel. I go to the door of the chapel because that's where I make my entrance and I don't want to be late and miss my cue.

The rehearsal is a success. The soloist has a magnificent voice. Of course, the bride looks like a refugee with her blanket wrapped around her head. And, in my opinion, the groom looks glum enough to discourage any bride who could actually see him. If Elaine wasn't so careful to keep all of her dress and veil hidden, she would see who she was standing next to in this rehearsal. But her eyes are in the shadows and she doesn't seem to notice Gary is, well, maybe just a little unhappy.

I look over at Gary's parents. They have been watching the rehearsal from the front row of the chapel and I don't think they could hold themselves any more rigid if they tried. I suppose they don't approve of Elaine's blanket. They do seem to be glaring at it a lot.

At least, I hope it's the blanket they are directing their gaze at and not Elaine herself.

Reverend Banning, the minister from the church in Blythe, dismisses everyone from the rehearsal and I can hear the sigh of relief that goes up from everyone.

"Now everybody just relax a little before the big event," Reverend Banning says in the calming way he has. I'm glad Aunt Ruth asked him to come and do the ceremony. "We'll do fine with the real thing."

I know Reverend Banning has been through this all a hundred times so I am going to trust that he knows what he's talking about.

Jerry and Doug are over making sure everything is the way they want it for the sound system. They look like as though have everything under control so I do the only thing I know I'm supposed to do now. I go to the women's lounge to ask Elaine if she needs anything. After all, I am the combined maid of honor and bridesmaid. I should go see if Elaine needs her hooks done up again.

Oh, and Miss Billings might be here early so she can help us all with our makeup. Reverend Banning is right. Everything will be fine.

Elaine isn't there when I get to the lounge, but Cassie tells me Elaine is in the kitchen talking to Aunt Ruth. I figure they need some time together so I decide to stay here and wait for Miss Billings.

I don't have to wait long. Miss Billings brings her makeup case and it is the size of a small suitcase. She even has a white polyester scarf to tie around a person's neck so no face powder gets on anyone when she does the makeover.

Cassie decided earlier I should go first because I have to go down the aisle, but we'll have time for several people to have their makeup done. I figure, since we're in the lounge at the front of the restroom, we'll have all of the aunts coming by at some point later so we can ask them if they want a makeover, too.

Our only problem when we start is that Miss Billings is too short to do someone's eyes while the person is standing up. Even having the person sit down doesn't work too well. It's not until I lie on the leather sofa in the lounge that Miss Billings starts to work at her best.

I figure we'll do all of the makeovers this way and I hope no one's mind goes in the direction mine is going. You know, Miss Billings working on my face when I'm lying down like the people who she is usually getting ready for their final viewing. Of course, none of the aunts know that is part of Miss Billing's job and I'm not going to tell them.

"I probably need different colors than I usually wear, I mean because of the brown streaks in my hair," I say just so one of us is talking.

"Mmm, hmm," Miss Billings says.

I don't have the nerve to ask Miss Billings if she's using any of her Pearly Pink blush on me. I'm sure my face looks a little yellow because of the orange dress I'm wearing and the brown streaks in my hair, but I do hope I don't look bad enough to be dead.

"Cassie will be here soon," I say.

After that, I keep my eyes closed.

"There," Miss Billings says. "You're done."

Miss Billings stands up and I look in the mirror.

"This looks good," I say and it does. It doesn't necessarily look like me, but I won't scare anyone while I walk down the aisle.

There's not much to do once I finish my makeup. I check on Elaine and Aunt Ruth and they are still talking in the kitchen. I glance in the chapel and see that Gary and his parents are sitting on one of the back pews and talking. I don't want to get in that conversation so I walk out to the courtyard. The caterers have put their white tablecloths on the tables and one of Jerry's brothers has set all of the centerpieces on the tables. Things look very nice.

Aunt Inga and my mother are sitting together at one of the far tables in the courtyard and looking at something. I walk over there and see that Aunt Inga has brought her scrapbook with her.

"I would have won that track meet if I hadn't broken my leg," I say because I can see the newspaper clipping that they're looking at. There was my name, right along with the winners of the race. "Isn't there a picture of me when I had a part in the school play?"

"Of course," Aunt Inga says as she turns a few pages.

My mother and Aunt Inga are beaming at those pictures of me as if I'd won prizes. The truth is, though, that I always felt a little guilty about Aunt Inga's scrapbook since her scrapbook was always skinnier than Aunt Ruth's or Aunt Gladys's.

"Maybe I'll win something yet," I mumble.

"Oh, but dear," Aunt Inga says with her cheeks still pink with the pleasure of showing her pictures. "You don't need to win anything for us to love you."

"Maybe not, but it would help your scrapbook."

I don't know what Aunt Inga would have said to that because we all hear a shriek coming from inside the chapel.

I'm thinking there's a fire or at least a loose bird flying around.

Instead, I see Gary's mom waving her arms around and screeching at her husband and Gary, who have come out of the chapel. One of her cheeks is a bright pink and the other is yellow so I'm wondering if someone had a heart attack. And then I see the white scarf knotted around her neck.

"They've got dead people here," Gary's mom finally says when she stops screeching. She points a bony finger toward the lounge. "I was in there and a woman who works here offered to do a makeover for me." Gary's mom takes an outraged breath. "I thought if she worked in a bridal chapel, she might have some useful suggestions so I let her start. But then she said she works with dead people. Here."

I worry that the Big M will have one more dearly departed to worry about if Gary's mom doesn't wind down a little. By now, everyone has gathered. The aunts. The cousins. Doug and Cassie.

"There's no dead people here right now," I say.

I look over at Miss Billings who has come out of the lounge and is looking horrified.

"I thought she knew," Miss Billings said to me.

"It's all right," I say. Sometimes there's a moment in life when you just have to gather your pride around you. Now is a moment like that. "There's nothing wrong with working with dead people. I'm proud to work here."

I stand victorious.

I stand alone.

Gary points a finger at me and I swear his finger is as bony as his mother's. "You're behind this?"

I nod. I figure he will yell and scream some and, if he's going to do that, he'd better do it now before the guests start to arrive. I wonder if Elaine will let me hide in her blanket with her.

Instead of screaming at me, though, Gary turns to Elaine. She is still huddled in her blanket, but I'm sure she can hear.

"Isn't this the screwup you told me about?" Gary says and his voice is not pleasant and he's still pointing at me. "I don't see how you could let her have anything to do with our wedding."

"She was just trying to help," Elaine says.

I notice out of the corner of my eye that Jerry walks around the circle of people here. I'm hoping it's so he can be closer to me, but then again, he might be heading for the parking lot and his pickup.

"We don't need her kind of help," Gary says. "I still can't believe you'd let your half cousin work on our wedding."

Gary's voice dwindles as he shouts until, at the end, he's almost talking normally.

I look over at Elaine to let her know that I think the worst of this is over when I see that she's let the blanket fall to the floor. She takes a step forward and her head is high and her eyes are flashing. Her cheeks are even rosy and she hasn't had any of Miss Billings's Pearly Pink blush.

"I'll have you know," Elaine says. "My *cousin* did ten times more to make this wedding happen than you did."

Wow. I'm impressed with Elaine and feeling a little warm toward her.

"Now, I know she's not perfect," Elaine continues.

Well, I could have done without that observation.

"But," Elaine spits out. "She's still my *cousin,* and we're going to sit together whenever we want and eat deviled eggs."

Okay, now I think Elaine has succeeded in scaring Gary and his parents, whether because they don't understand the reference to deviled eggs or because they can't believe anyone who would marry into their family would be so lower-class as to actually eat them, I don't know. In any event, there is a full minute of silence in tribute to Elaine's magnificent outburst.

By the way, the train on her dress looks about right on her when Elaine stands there with her shoulders back like a warrior bride.

"I think we should be going," Gary's mother finally says. "Gary, bring the car around."

I look over at Aunt Inga to see if she's praying. She has a very serene look on her face so I try Doug. He doesn't seem to be praying, either. I know God hasn't listened to me in the past, but He and I have new rules, too. I offer up a prayer for help. I'm not sure I think it's a good idea for Elaine to marry Gary, but I don't want to be the reason he decides not to marry her. That wouldn't work in well with my reconciliation plan between the two of us.

"No one will know it's a mortuary," I say to anyone who will listen. "We have a tunnel. And there's no hint in the courtyard."

"Gary!" His mother says a little sharper this time.

I can see Gary is looking at Elaine.

"No, Mother," Gary says. "I'm staying."

Elaine looks as surprised to hear this as I am.

"Well!" Gary's mother says as if she doesn't know what to do now.

I'm starting to hope that this will be one of those funny stories couples tell at their fiftieth anniversary parties. I'm sure we can smooth it all out. Maybe Elaine won't hate me.

"I think you should go, Gary," Elaine finally says into the silence.

I look at Elaine to see if she's okay. I wouldn't want her to make a decision like this based on one wrong step Gary or his mother had taken. But she looks better than I've seen her look for days.

Gary looks at Elaine for another minute, but then he turns around without saying anything and walks out of the chapel with his parents walking behind him.

It's about then that I realize Jerry is standing right behind me. He didn't go to the parking lot after all.

Elaine turns to look at us. "Now what do we do?"

"It's already almost five-fifteen," Aunt Inga says. "It's too late to stop people from coming."

"And the caterers have already started dinner," Aunt Ruth adds.

"Well, then," Elaine says with a grin, "let's have a party."

I'm not the only one who looks at Elaine to make sure she's not just putting a brave face on it, but she looks as though she's fine. Just to be sure, I follow her into the kitchen.

"I'm so sorry," I say.

"Don't be," Elaine says. "The engagement stopped being fun months ago. I don't know why it took me so long to figure out that the marriage would be torture. I couldn't be in a family that didn't like me as much as Gary's didn't like me."

"So you're okay?"

Elaine nods. "I'm tougher than you think."

I grin. "What makes you think I don't know that?"

"Oh, you." Elaine waves me off with a laugh.

"You're a beautiful bride, by the way."

Elaine grins back at me. "Next time though I'm going to elope."

I doubt anyone wants Elaine to elope next time. People said later that this was the best wedding they'd attended in years. The soloist my mother had brought volunteered to do love songs by request while people ate their prime rib dinner. The evening was warm and the roses were fragrant. Even Aunt Ruth and Uncle Howard seemed relaxed and happy.

About halfway through the evening, Doug and I start our rounds. I had suggested that we try to look like casual friends so we could undo those false impressions we created at Elaine's engagement party.

I wasn't quite sure what body language we would use to get our point across, but Doug did. When we get to Aunt Ruth, he takes my hand.

"We're committed friends," Doug announces to Aunt Ruth. "Maybe with a future."

"And maybe not," I add just so we all know. "We're just friends for now."

Aunt Ruth looks at us a moment. "So, you're *committed* friends with no expectations? No plans? No future?"

Doug and I both chuckle.

Aunt Ruth shakes her head and fans herself a little wearily with one of the embossed napkins she'd ordered for Elaine's wedding. "I don't think I'll ever understand the way you kids date these days."

"We're not dating," I say.

"I know," Aunt Ruth says with a sigh.

I'm sure Aunt Ruth will spread the word to the other relatives that Doug and I, while friends, are not on the verge of anything remotely resembling an engagement announcement.

"It feels better to have the truth out there," I say as we go over and sit down at one of the tables.

Doug nods. "It also feels better to make a commitment or two."

I smile at him. He's right about that.

* * * * *

Turn the page for a sneak preview of
SHEPHERDS ABIDING IN DRY CREEK
by Janet Tronstad,
available in November
from Steeple Hill Love Inspired.

Reserve Deputy Sheriff Les Wilkerson had known something was wrong when his phone rang at six o'clock this morning. He'd just come in from doing the chores in the barn and was starting to pull his boots off so he wouldn't get the kitchen floor dirty while he cooked his breakfast. It was the precision of the timing of that call that had him worried. He'd given the townspeople permission to call him after six and it sounded like someone had been waiting until the exact moment to take the call.

Les finished pulling off his boots and walked in his stocking feet to the phone. By that time, enough rings had gone by to discourage any telemarketer.

"We've had a theft," Linda, the young woman who owned the café in Dry Creek, said almost before Les got the phone to his ear. She was out of breath. "Or maybe it's one of those ecology protests. You know, the green people and their protests."

"Someone's protesting in Dry Creek?"

"Well, Charley says that Elmer's been upset about all of the electricity the church is using to light up that outdoor nativity set they got. Charley figures Elmer unplugged the shepherd."

"Unplugging something is not a theft." It wasn't even much of a protest.

"But Elmer came in and he says he didn't unplug anything. He says if we can't see the shepherd, it's because it's not there and somebody stole it."

"The light could be burned out."

"Maybe. Or somebody else could be worried about the electricity and unplugged it. But I told Charley and Elmer not to go over and check. It's still pitch-black outside. They've been looking out the café window for a good fifteen minutes, but it's still too dark to see whether the shepherd is there. And, if it's not there, then it's a crime scene and we need the professionals."

"I see," Les said. And he did. He was responsible for the citizens of Dry Creek and that included their bones. "I'll be right there."

Les usually made a morning trip into Dry Creek anyway before he drove a load of hay out to his cattle in the far pasture. The little town of Dry Creek wasn't much—a hardware store, a church, a café, a dozen or so houses—but the regular sheriff guarded the place like it was Fort Knox and Wilkerson, who was the town's only volunteer reserve deputy, had promised he'd do the same in the sheriff's absence.

Just thinking of the sheriff made Les shake his head. Who would figure that a man as shy as Deputy Sheriff Carl Wall would ever have a wedding, let alone a one-year anniversary to celebrate with a trip to Maui?

It was all Les could do not to be jealous. After all, he was as good-looking as Carl was—or at least, no worse looking. Les even owned his own ranch, as sweet a piece of earth as God ever created and it was all paid for. Not every man could say that. Every time for the past week when he thought of Carl and that wedding anniversary of his, Les started to frown.

If Deputy Sheriff Carl Wall could get married, Les figured he should be married, too. It would be nice to have a woman to do some cooking and cleaning around the place. Of course, he could hire someone to do most of that. But it wouldn't be the same. A woman just naturally made a home around her, like a mother bird making her nest, and he was growing tired of living all alone in his bachelor house. A house just wasn't a home without some nesting going on.

Of course, Les acknowledged as he pulled his pickup to a stop beside the café porch, he would never want to look foolish because of a woman. While they were alive, his parents had given the gossips in Dry Creek enough entertainment to keep them all busy. The two of them had a yo-yo marriage filled with very public partings and dramatic reconciliations. Love was a theatrical cue to them. Les had vowed as a child never to be in that kind of circus. Growing up, he never even made a fuss over his dog because he didn't want anyone to think he shared his parents' temperament.

No, if he was going to get married, Les thought as he stepped up on the café porch, it would be clear to everyone that it was a nice sensible arrangement between two people who were fond of each other. There was no reason for two people to make fools of themselves just because they wanted to get married anyway.

"Oh, good. You're here," Linda's voice greeted Les as he opened the door to the café.

The two older men Linda had called about, Elmer and Charley, were sitting at the table closest to the door and they both looked up from their plates as Les stepped into the café. Their faces were flushed, and excitement shone in their eyes.

"We found this," Elmer said as he thrust a piece of paper toward Les. "Wait until you see this."

Les's heart sank when he saw the sheet of paper. It had a ragged edge where it had been torn from what was probably a school tablet. There must be a dozen school tablets in Dry Creek. The note was written in pencil, and he didn't even want to think about how many pencils were around. Anyone could have written a note like this.

Les bent to read the note.

Dear Church People,
I took your dumb shepherd.
If you want to see him again, put a Suzy Bake Set on the back steps of your church.
It needs to be the deluxe kind—the one with the cupcakes on the box.
P.S. Don't call the cops.
P.S.S. The angel wire is loose.
She's going to fall if somebody doesn't do something.

Well, there was one good thing, Les told himself as he looked up from the paper. There weren't that many people in Dry Creek who would want a Suzy

Bake Set. That narrowed down the field of suspects considerably.

"So the shepherd is really missing?" Les asked, more to give himself time to think than because there seemed to be any question about that fact.

Elmer nodded. "The angel is just standing there with her wings unfurled looking a little lost now that she's proclaiming all that good news to a sheep. You don't see anything where that shepherd should be."

"Who could have done it?" Linda asked.

"There are those two new kids," Elmer stared at his cup. "But what would they want with a shepherd? They've never even been to church."

There was a moment's silence.

Les finally spoke. "Nobody said they wanted a shepherd. It's the bake set that seems to be the goal. If I remember right, there's a little girl in that family." Unfortunately, Les knew as little as everyone else in Dry Creek did about the new family. Elmer and Charley had both wanted him to chat up the widow and learn more about her children.

"Well, it could be the new people then." Les felt a headache coming on. "I'll have to go see."

"You might ask the woman to come eat with you some night here," Charley said as Wilkerson walked to the door. "Just to be sociable. Sort of to show her around town."

"Nobody needs a map. There's only one street."

Ever since Charley and Mrs. Hargrove had managed to match up their two children, they had been itching to try their new matchmaking skills on someone else. Well, it wasn't going to be him. Wilkerson could find his own wife when he wanted one and he would do it when no one was watching. He might have even gotten around to asking the new woman out eventually if people had left him alone.

Now, he couldn't ask her out without looking like he was playing right into the hands of the local match-makers. He would never do that. Not that she was likely to go out with him anyway. Any minute now, he was going to be knocking at her door asking if her daughter was a criminal. It would be kind of hard to ask for a date after that.

DISCUSSION QUESTIONS

1) Have you ever been locked in a competitive struggle with a sibling or someone else as Julie and Elaine were? How did you handle it?

2) The story of Joseph and his brothers in the Bible reflects some of the problems that Julie had with Elaine. Read Genesis 37. What similarities do you see?

3) Did you notice how the roots of Julie's struggle with Elaine began with the jealousy of their respective mothers? Have you carried on any family squabbles like this?

4) Julie particularly resented receiving Elaine's hand-me-down clothes. How would you have felt if you were Julie in that situation? Is there anything the aunts could have done to make the situation better?

5) Why do you think Elaine used to torment Julie? Did someone treat you like that when you were growing up? How do you think a Christian should handle this kind of thing?

6) In the course of the book, Julie makes peace with her cousin, Jerry. Eventually, she sees him with new eyes. Can you think of a similar relationship you have had?

7) Elaine's mother is very determined to climb the social ladder—she even pretends to live in another town. Some people would say this is a white lie and that it doesn't make any difference. What do you think? What were the consequences of lying in the family? What other consequences might there be?

8) Julie learned a lot about life while working at the mortuary. What are some of the lessons she learned?

9) Julie's friend Doug had a difficult time making a commitment because of his childhood. Is there something from your childhood that makes it difficult for you to make commitments? How do you deal with this?

10) Was there, or is there, anything else in your childhood that was or is a problem between you and God? How have you dealt with it?

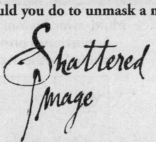

Love Inspired®

*C*elebrate Love Inspired's 10th anniversary with top authors and great stories all year long!

A Tiny Blessings Tale

Loving families and needy children continue to come together to fulfill God's greatest plans!

Look for these six new *Tiny Blessings* stories!

FOR HER SON'S LOVE BY KATHRYN SPRINGER
July 2007

MISSIONARY DADDY BY LINDA GOODNIGHT
August 2007

A MOMMY IN MIND BY ARLENE JAMES
September 2007

LITTLE MISS MATCHMAKER BY DANA CORBIT
October 2007

GIVING THANKS FOR BABY BY TERRI REED
November 2007

A HOLIDAY TO REMEMBER
BY JILLIAN HART
December 2007

Steeple
Hill®

Available wherever you buy books.

REQUEST YOUR FREE BOOKS!

2 FREE INSPIRATIONAL NOVELS
PLUS 2
FREE
MYSTERY GIFTS

Love Inspired®

YES! Please send me 2 FREE Love Inspired® novels and my 2 FREE mystery gifts. After receiving them, if I don't wish to receive any more books, I can return the shipping statement marked "cancel." If I don't cancel, I will receive 4 brand-new novels every month and be billed just $3.99 per book in the U.S., or $4.74 per book in Canada, plus 25¢ shipping and handling per book and applicable taxes, if any*. That's a savings of 20% off the cover price! I understand that accepting the 2 free books and gifts places me under no obligation to buy anything. I can always return a shipment and cancel at any time. Even if I never buy another book from Steeple Hill, the two free books and gifts are mine to keep forever.

113 IDN EF26   313 IDN EF27

Name	(PLEASE PRINT)

Address	Apt. #

City	State/Prov.	Zip/Postal Code

Signature (if under 18, a parent or guardian must sign)

Order online at www.LoveInspiredBooks.com

Or mail to Steeple Hill Reader Service™:

IN U.S.A.: P.O. Box 1867, Buffalo, NY 14240-1867
IN CANADA: P.O. Box 609, Fort Erie, Ontario L2A 5X3

Not valid to current Love Inspired subscribers.

Want to try two free books from another series?
Call 1-800-873-8635 or visit www.morefreebooks.com

* Terms and prices subject to change without notice. NY residents add applicable sales tax. Canadian residents will be charged applicable provincial taxes and GST. This offer is limited to one order per household. All orders subject to approval. Credit or debit balances in a customer's account(s) may be offset by any other outstanding balance owed by or to the customer. Please allow 4 to 6 weeks for delivery.

Your Privacy: Steeple Hill is committed to protecting your privacy. Our Privacy Policy is available online at www.eHarlequin.com or upon request from the Reader Service. From time to time we make our lists of customers available to reputable firms who may have a product or service of interest to you. If you would prefer we not share your name and address, please check here. ☐

LIREG07